"Reveals a promising talent ... Smith can poke fun at feminism even as she celebrates it."

Chicago Sun-Times

"Readers weary of the flood of private eyes and police procedurals should fall upon this with delight."

The San Diego Union

"Joan Smith has turned out a splendid first mystery, and her learned sleuth is a treat indeed. Here's hoping Ms. Smith is back at her typewriter, turning out an equally delightful sequel. Loretta Lawson novels could be a lovely addiction."

The Chattanooga Times

Also by Joan Smith
Published by Fawcett Books:

BABE
AURORA
IMPRUDENT LADY
LACE OF MILADY
VALERIE
THE BLUE DIAMOND
REPRISE
WILES OF A STRANGER
LOVER'S VOWS
RELUCTANT BRIDE
LADY MADELINE'S FOLLY
LOVE BADE ME WELCOME
MIDNIGHT MASQUERADE
ROYAL REVELS
THE DEVIOUS DUCHESS
TRUE LADY
BATH BELLES
STRANGE CAPERS
A COUNTRY WOOING
LOVE'S HARBINGER
LETTERS TO A LADY
COUNTRY FLIRT
LARCENOUS LADY
MEMOIRS OF A HOYDEN
SILKEN SECRETS
DRURY LANE DARLING
THE HERMIT'S DAUGHTER

A MASCULINE ENDING

Joan Smith

FAWCETT CREST • NEW YORK

A Fawcett Crest Book
Published by Ballantine Books
Copyright © 1987 by Joan Smith

All rights reserved under International and Pan-American Copyright Conventions. Published in the United States by Ballantine Books, a division of Random House, Inc., New York.

No part of this book may be reproduced or transmitted in any form or by any means, electronic or mechanical, including photocopying, recording, or by any information storage and retrieval system, without permission in writing from the Publisher.

ISBN 0-449-21688-8

This edition published by arrangement with Charles Scribner's Sons, an imprint of MacMillan Publishing Company.

This is a work of fiction. Names, characters, places, and incidents either are the product of the author's imagination or are used fictitiously. Any resemblance to actual events or persons, living or dead, is entirely coincidental.

Manufactured in the United States of America

First Ballantine Books Edition: August 1989

For Francis Wheen

1

IT WAS JUST BEFORE MIDNIGHT WHEN LO-
retta's train finally pulled into the Gare du Nord. It should
have arrived two hours earlier, allowing time for an unhur-
ried dinner before she set off in search of Andrew's flat,
but the French railway company had compounded the
delay caused by the late running of the ferry by coming to
an unexplained twenty-minute halt just outside Amiens.
The night was hot and sticky, and the broken air-condition-
ing in Loretta's carriage had not improved the tempers of
her fellow passengers, several of them small children
whose patience had worn out long before their feet touched
French soil. The whole journey, far from being the pleasur-
able outing she had hoped for, had been dogged by petty
irritations from the moment she discovered that, contrary
to the information given in the timetable, neither the English nor the French train betrayed any sign of the promised dining-car.

As she walked along the platform of the uncharacteristically quiet station, Loretta hoped she was not too late to
find something to eat before setting off for the Left Bank.
Andrew's directions, although precise, had been accompanied by the warning that the flat was a little tricky to find,
and she did not relish wandering the streets of an unfamiliar part of Paris on an empty stomach at getting on for one

o'clock on Saturday morning. She headed purposefully out of the station.

Accustomed to travelling alone, Loretta automatically adopted the precaution of walking with the air of someone who knows where she is going, a tried and tested method of discouraging unwanted attention from the sort of men who hang around stations. Across the road from the Gare du Nord, lights were blazing at a small brasserie, and she could see waiters deftly weaving in and out between tables; that restaurant, at least, was still bustling with life. She had last eaten there three or four years before, in the course of a weekend which combined business and pleasure; the business being a lecture she had given at a rather stuffy but prestigious institute, the pleasure an English politician with whom she had been conducting an intermittently satisfying affair. They had eaten at the little brasserie before taking the train back to England, she to her peaceful flat in north London, he to his elegant and unsuspecting wife in his Midlands constituency. The memory of previous visits to the city comforted her, investing its dark streets with an air of familiarity, and Loretta edged past the outdoor tables into the *salon*, surprised to feel her muscles relax as the door closed behind her. She realized she had been unusually tense since getting off the train, presumably due to the lateness of the hour.

Loretta caught the eye of the head waiter who, swiftly and without fuss, showed her to a table in the recesses of the restaurant. Grateful that she had been refreshing her French in preparation for the meeting she was due to attend next day, she told him that her train had been late and she was anxious to eat quickly. He summoned a more junior waiter, from whom she ordered steak and a salad, and a glass of red wine. When he returned with the drink, she opened her pink plastic briefcase and took out several sheets of A4 on which was typed the paper she was to present at nine o'clock next morning—a ridiculously early hour, Loretta thought, at which to start a meeting of academics from several countries, including the United States. She could not help but feel that her paper, a feminist discussion on the nature of authorship, would reach more receptive minds a little later in the morning when everyone had had a chance to recover from the travelling they'd done the day before. But the organizers of the symposium, the French members of an international journal of feminist literary criticism, *Fem Sap*—the wit of whose title was rarely reflected in its content—were untroubled by such heretical thoughts. The conference, on recent developments in feminist thought, would not finish until six and even then, as the majority of those attending slipped away for a congenial evening in Paris, Loretta would be expected to attend a meeting of the full editorial collective.

The meeting was ostensibly a routine affair, a discussion of papers to be commissioned and authors whose contributions should be sought, but Loretta was braced for one of those intemperate and robust arguments that occasionally disturbed the collective's deliberations. Schisms arose endlessly among the various alliances formed by European and American feminists, and on this occasion she anticipated a heated exchange on how to deal with the problem of masculine grammatical forms. A group of feminist literature teachers from universities in the United States, backed by a handful of French academics, had come up with a proposal that the editorial policy of *Fem Sap* should challenge the inherent sexism of French and Italian, two of the three languages in which the journal accepted contributions, by refusing to use masculine endings of any sort. Every verb ending and all nouns, they argued, should be treated as feminine. Loretta, who lectured in English literature at one of the colleges that made up London University, conceded that what they were complaining about *was* unfair: the way in which masculine past participles were used for groups that included men and women was a historical anomaly. Nevertheless, she feared the change would bring with it horrible confusion, and there was a whole corpus of

3

literature which would either have to be relegated to the dustbin, or mangled out of recognition, if the proposal was accepted. She took comfort in the thought that the radical position was unlikely to carry the day, and also that the English language did not suffer from anything like the same problem.

Looking up from her paper for any sign that her meal was about to arrive—she had not eaten since breakfast in London that morning—Loretta became aware of the steady and appraising gaze of the man at the next table.

"You are alone, Madame, as I am," he said in slightly accented English.

At once, part of her mind registered two observations: that her French, grammatically correct as it was, betrayed her English origins, and that he had addressed her as Madame rather than Mademoiselle, a courtesy to her age, she presumed, since her wedding ring had been discarded long ago. The analytical part of her brain noted these details, but her predominant reaction was one of irritation, accompanied by a return of the tension she had felt on her arrival at the station.

"I am alone, Monsieur, because that is how it suits me to be," she said firmly. She had learned the hard way that a clear rejection, impolite as it might seem, was the only way to deal with unwelcome advances.

"Pardon me, Madame," he persisted, inclining his head towards her in a gesture intended to be at once apologetic and winning. "It is only that, in Paris, a woman as beautiful as yourself is rarely seen at this hour without a companion. I merely wished to extend to you the hospitality of my country by inviting you to join me."

Loretta regarded the speaker for a moment while she pondered her next move. He looked to be in his forties, but she guessed he was older. His dark hair was slightly touched with grey, his suit well if flashily cut—probably Italian, she thought. He had the air of a man used to giving orders, a company director perhaps, and she recognized

4

that he would not be easily deterred. Her heart sank; she was tired, and depressed by the vicissitudes of her journey from London. She really could not face the fencing match which was bound to follow her civil reiteration that she was perfectly happy on her own.

Then, a thought occurred to her. There was one move that would completely outflank him, if she could summon the courage to make it. She congratulated herself on her choice of travelling clothes; her baggy scarlet trousers and pink T-shirt, selected in deference to the unusually hot September weather, were far more in keeping with what she was about to say than her usual rather formal attire.

"You've made a mistake, Monsieur," she said, looking him straight in the eye. "I prefer the company of women." The statement was not untrue in general terms, though not in the sexual sense in which she challenged him to take it. His eyes betrayed that she had succeeded in startling him and, for a moment, she thought her plan had worked, that he had been embarrassed into retreat by her directness. But then he rose from his seat, towered over her, and spat in her face.

"Whore," he hissed, stalking off towards the door, where he paused to stuff a handful of notes into the pocket of a surprised young waiter. Loretta, frozen into immobility by this unexpected attack, could feel his saliva warm on her cheek as her mind turned over the single word he had uttered. Shocked and exhausted, the only thought in her head was his peculiar choice of insult: it was odd that he had accused her of being willing to sell her sexuality when his real complaint was that it was not for sale—or available on any terms, as far as he was concerned. It would have made more sense for him to have accused her of frigidity. How muddled men were about female sexuality, she thought, for a moment quite detached from her circumstances.

She realized suddenly that she should wipe the spittle from her face and, at the same time, she became aware of a

5

waiter at her elbow. Squirming with embarrassment, he offered her a large white napkin. Would Madame care to visit the bathroom? he was saying, such a thing to happen in our restaurant! Madame will be so kind as to accept our humble apologies, no question of her paying her bill after such an experience. Loretta found herself trembling, her heartbeat audible in her ears.

"No, please, I don't want anything to eat after all," she protested, speaking in English, unable to gather her wits enough to translate the simple phrase into French. The idea of eating made her feel sick. She stood up, wiping her cheek with the back of her hand, scattering the pages of her paper on the floor. Waiters scrambled to retrieve them, creating more confusion. She seized the pages from the hands thrusting towards her, stuffing them back into her briefcase. Then she pushed her way through the small throng of interested onlookers and reached the door, the head waiter scurrying after her with even more apologies.

Loretta remembered there was a taxi rank outside the station. She could not recall when the Métro stopped running but, in any case, a taxi offered the quickest means of escape from her unpleasant situation. She hastened across the road, narrowly avoiding a speeding car whose driver flung an incomprehensible insult at her from the window as he swerved by.

"Rue Monge," she said, throwing herself into the back of the taxi at the front of the rank. The driver set off with such startling speed that Loretta turned to peer anxiously out of the rear window, seized by the fear that she had been followed. Surely her assailant from the restaurant had not lain in wait for her? she asked herself frantically. But there was no sign of pursuit and, recalling other pointlessly hectic taxi rides in foreign cities, she began to calm down. Her nerves, she concluded, were uncharacteristically stretched tonight.

Her thoughts were interrupted by the driver, who

wanted to know the number in rue Monge she was looking for. In halting French—her mind was not yet functioning normally—she explained that it was actually a side-turning off rue Monge that she wanted, a street called rue Roland.

"Rue Roland," repeated the driver in tones of disgust. *"Je peux pas."*

What on earth could be wrong with rue Roland? Loretta wondered. Andrew had not warned her that it was a one-way street, or that there was anything about it that might make access difficult. But she did not feel up to quizzing the taciturn driver. She sat back and looked out of the window in search of familiar landmarks that might render her journey less inhospitable.

The taxi was crossing the river, although she did not know Paris well enough to recognize the bridge they were using. Its stone walls were replete with graffiti: the same phrase had been spray-painted at regular intervals in carefully looped, peculiarly French handwriting. *"Violeurs, nous vous castrerons,"* Loretta read, admiring the attention to detail which had placed a comma after the first word. It was not a bad idea, she thought approvingly, only half aware that the sentiment was quite alien to her usual cast of mind.

They were now travelling down a wide avenue flanked by grey stone buildings with blue slate roofs. Loretta saw the skeleton of a street market, its stalls bare and unwelcoming. Andrew had told her to look out for such a market just before rue Roland turned off the main thoroughfare. She was about to speak to the driver when the car came to a sudden halt next to what she took at first sight to be a lay-by.

"Rue Roland," stated the driver, jerking his thumb out of the window. She peered anxiously from the taxi, and saw why the driver could not turn into rue Roland: the street was at the top of a wide flight of steps, about twenty feet higher than the road she was in. No wonder Andrew had warned her it was difficult to find; if she had been on

7

foot, she probably would not have noticed that the little street was there. She might have searched rue Monge fruitlessly for half an hour. Andrew liked to credit himself with possessing a mischievous sense of humour but, on this occasion, she thought it could more accurately be described as malicious. It was just like him to give her detailed directions but miss out the one thing she really needed to know. But her sense of justice responded. Andrew had no way of guessing that she would arrive in such inauspicious circumstances. Thankful that she had at any rate been spared a hunt for rue Roland, Loretta got out of the taxi and overtipped the driver, receiving from him a non-committal grunt in return.

She climbed the steps and found that rue Roland was wide enough to take a car, although anyone driving into it from the opposite end would find their exit blocked by the iron railings that topped the steps. The small street was not well lit, and the walls, far from being covered in sisterly graffiti, reflected a feud between political parties of the extreme left and right. *"Le Pen—Nazi,"* the Communists had written, while the right had responded with lengthier insults in a French so vernacular that Loretta did not understand half of it. On either side of her, high buildings rose like cliffs; their lack of adornment and crumbling façades revealed the street to be an unexpectedly poor one for the area. A half-remembered classical image of combat to destruction between clashing cliffs struggled out of the recesses of memory; further evidence, she recognized, of her unusually fanciful state of mind. This sense of formless threat, of being under siege, was an unfamiliar one to Loretta and she began to wish she'd booked into a hotel, as she had intended, before she mentioned her trip to Andrew. But it was now much too late to go in search of alternative accommodation. She made out numbers 8 and 10 to her right—her destination, an elderly apartment block whose address was 18 rue Roland, must be on the same side. Now she was passing a high wall with a building set back behind

8

it, presumably the school Andrew had told her to look out for. She could see no numbers on the doors of the next two buildings.

As she stepped back to peer up into the darkness, she heard the sound of running feet and raised voices. Drawing back into the shadow of a doorway, she glimpsed a throng of people running across the opposite end of the street to rue Monge. They were gone as swiftly as they had appeared, but Loretta felt a renewed urgency about reaching the safety of the flat. She walked on, still looking for house numbers. Arriving at 22, she retraced her steps to what must be 18, although nothing about the heavy wooden double doors advertised the fact. She took out the keys loaned her by Andrew and tried the largest of the three which, he had said, belonged to the street door. When it failed to turn, she took it out and pushed the door with her hand out of sheer frustration. It swung open, already unlocked. She stepped into a dark hallway and fumbled for the light switch, discovering one of the push-button sort which turns itself off after thirty seconds.

Loretta took in a curving, almost spiral staircase made of worn wood before she was plunged into darkness again. Pushing the button a second time, she set off up the stairs for the fourth floor, the last part of the climb lit only by moonlight from the open window on each landing. She noticed that the layout of each floor was identical, three doors opening off the landings into flats. It was a steep climb, and she regretted the lack of a usable lift—Andrew had warned her that the block possessed only an old and creaky service lift, once the pride and joy of the long-vanished concierge but now used only by a few elderly residents who still depended on coal fires. On the fourth floor, she located another light switch and the illumination lasted long enough for her to spot the door bearing the name Gardner, as Andrew had instructed. She had no idea of Gardner's identity, except that he or she was one of the people with whom Andrew shared the lease on the flat, but

9

the name at least confirmed that she was in the right place. Her journey was nearly over.

She had been told that there were two locks, both quite stiff: undo the top mortice lock before attempting the Yale, those were her instructions. She inserted a key into the top lock and tried to turn it, only to discover that it was already unlocked. The last visitor to the flat must have forgotten to double-lock the door, she presumed. The Yale key worked after a bit of jiggling in the lock, and Loretta stepped into the flat with a huge sigh of relief.

She was in a long narrow room, the door she had come through set into the end of one of the longer walls. At the far side, moonlight streamed in from an uncurtained window. The room served as both living-room and kitchen, and she was standing in the cooking area; an old stone sink faced her, a very ancient waterheater presiding over it. Above the tap of the heater she could see a yellowing notice, written in large and emphatic letters. Putting her bags down, Loretta approached and read by moonlight the warning left by previous occupants. "This machine is unreliable. It sometimes goes out. Sometimes there is a small explosion when the hot tap is turned on, so always stand back when doing this." It was not a promising start to her stay, and Loretta decided to put off a proper wash until the morning, when help would be at hand if the water heater chose to stage a large rather than a small explosion.

The lavatory she had already been warned about—indeed, she had not been able to avoid noticing its odour on the way up. Andrew had described it colourfully enough to give her a vivid impression of what she would find inside, but he had not warned her about the smell. It stood on the landing, consisted of a hole in the floor, and was shared with the occupants of the other flats. There was a bucket under the sink, Andrew had promised, but it was for use in emergencies only. Loretta concluded that her present circumstances fitted the bill, and rummaged accordingly. The bucket proved clean, and would get her through until morning.

The flat had two bedrooms, she had been told, on either side of a small corridor which ran from one of the long sides of the living-room. She entered the corridor, and was just able to discern the door at the end—she had been warned that, confusingly, this door concealed not a bedroom but a cupboard. She opened the door to her right, and found herself in a small, square room with very little furniture, lit by light from an uncurtained window. The bare mattress of the single bed looked lumpy; Andrew and his friends had spared every possible expense in maintaining the flat, it seemed. She wondered if the other room might prove more inviting, and stepped quietly back into the dark corridor to open the door of the second bedroom. This room was darker, the window covered by a tacked-up piece of light-coloured cloth, but there was just enough light to distinguish its contents. Loretta's gaze took in a double bed, and on it something that rooted her to the spot with shock.

A man was lying on the bed, his back turned to her, apparently fast asleep. For a moment, Loretta's brain seemed to stop working and she felt nothing but fear. She had no idea who the stranger was, how he came to be there, nor what she should do.

Her faculties returning, Loretta realized that the man, most of whose body was covered by bedding, was sleeping so deeply that her quiet entry into the room had not awakened him. She had time to think. She withdrew into the corridor, closing the door gently behind her.

She collected her bags from the living-room and went again into the first bedroom. An old kitchen chair stood next to the narrow bed. It looked about the same height as the door handle, and she jammed it in position so that she would at least have warning if her unexpected fellow guest chose, for any reason, to take a look into the room. Unlacing her black canvas boots, Loretta sat down on the bed fully clothed and began to think. She was already feeling calmer. There was no evidence at all that the unknown man had a sinister motive for being at the flat. She had seen no sign of a forced entry, which suggested he had keys. He might even be Gardner, paying a visit to the flat unexpectedly, and without bothering to warn Andrew. Although the co-tenants were supposed to confer on the dates that each of them intended to use the flat to avoid just this situation, it was possible that there had not been time to stick to the system, or that dates had got mixed up. There was every reason to think the present situation an innocent accident, rather than anything alarming. At any other time, it probably would not have occurred to her to find the situation frightening. She was simply overwrought. Nevertheless, it would be as well to wait until morning to announce her presence, she decided. The stranger might not be too pleased to be woken unexpectedly at such an hour. Loretta stretched out on the bed and waited for sleep. It was unexpectedly quick in coming.

In the morning, Loretta woke from a troubled dream in which she had started to give her paper on authorship only to find she had brought with her the menu from the brasserie at the Gare du Nord. Instead of opening her contribution with a refutation of Flaubert's view on the relationship between art and experience, she had offered her audience a choice between *soupe à l'oignon* and *pâté de campagne*. She woke with a start, hungry and confused. Her watch, which was still on her wrist, showed her that it was twenty-five minutes to nine—no time for the wash she badly needed, or the breakfast of tea and fresh croissants in a café that she had promised herself the night before. It was just as well she had slept in her clothes and need not waste time dressing. Gathering her belongings together, she slipped out into the corridor.

There was no sign of life from the other bedroom. The stranger was clearly enjoying a more leisurely visit to Paris

12

than her own. She opened the front door and, bucket in hand, braved the primitive toilet facilities on the landing. Returning to the kitchen-cum-living-room, she cleaned and put away the bucket, washed her face, and prepared to leave the flat. Since she had no idea who the man was, it seemed prudent to take her bags with her. Hesitating on the landing, she decided to leave the top lock undone. There was no need to puzzle the stranger by leaving the flat in any way different from how she had found it.

In daylight, she noticed, the apartment building looked much more attractive than it had the night before. The wooden staircase was quaintly charming, and the peeling paint gave the block the aspect of an old and trusted friend. Loretta wished she had time to explore, but she was already in danger of arriving late for the conference. As she closed the heavy front door behind her, she noticed that a faded piece of paper next to the doorbell bore the word "concierge," with a line scored through it; it was a pity that there was no present incumbent to find a taxi for her. She decided to make her way down to rue Monge, which was clearly an important route through the city, and look for a cab.

As she walked along rue Roland, she felt slightly ashamed of the nervousness she had felt in the street the night before. By the light of day, rue Roland was entirely unremarkable. Running lightly down the steps, overnight bag swinging from her shoulder, she peered northwards along rue Monge in the direction of the river. Her luck appeared to have changed: a noisy American couple were removing an impressive collection of luggage from a taxi parked outside a hotel fifty yards away. The proceedings took so long that Loretta had plenty of time to get to the spot and commandeer the cab. She arrived at the conference centre, sighing with relief, on the dot of nine.

Her paper, a discussion of the sources from which writers draw their material, was well received. Loretta was gratified; the practice of feminist literary criticism tended to be

13

a tightrope walk among opposing factions who might separately detect either excessive conservatism or extreme radicalism in one and the same piece of work. Today's talk, a scholarly rebuttal of the masculine notion of "pure intellect," seemed to please almost everyone.

It was just as well that the morning provided an easy ride, for the evening meeting of the *Fem Sap* collective proved even more exhausting and dispiriting than she had anticipated. The Franco-American alliance, which wanted to abolish masculine nouns and verb endings, had carried out some effective lobbying within the collective, and support for their proposal was stronger than expected. But since opposition to it was equally vocal, a stalemate was soon reached from which the meeting degenerated into little more than an exchange of insults; anyone who opposed the proposal was accused of not being a "real" feminist. No vote could be taken, since it turned out that the radicals had not followed the proper procedure for giving notice of their motion, and the wrangle looked set to go on all night.

Just after nine o'clock, Loretta decided there was little point in staying. She made her apologies and left the conference building. Her plans had been frustrated for the second night running: she had hoped to get away from the meeting in time for dinner with an American lecturer with whom she had struck up a friendship a couple of years before while on an exchange visit to the US. But the woman, who was not a member of the editorial collective, had promised to wait at her hotel for Loretta only until eight, and would be long gone. Climbing into a taxi, Loretta asked the driver to take her back to rue Roland. She had spent most of her lunch break stocking up with bread, cheese, and wine, just in case the evening's meeting dragged on. As well as ensuring that she would have some supper, it would serve as a peace-offering if the stranger turned out to be hostile to their enforced flat-sharing arrangement.

At this time of night, rue Roland still showed signs of

life. Although the street itself was deserted, there were lights in windows, and Loretta could hear a radio or television as she walked along the street. It was all comfortingly familiar. As she entered the apartment block, she could hear music and voices which she identified as the "Un dì felice" duet from *La Traviata*. Someone on the ground floor evidently shared her taste for Italian opera. On her way up the stairs, she wondered if her unknown fellow guest would still be at the flat. She rather hoped not, since it would be pleasant to recover from the tiresome events at the *Fem Sap* meeting with a quiet supper and a good book.

Her spirits lifted when she discovered the door was double-locked, unlike the previous evening, suggesting that the stranger might have moved on. Stepping inside, Loretta called out "Hello" several times and received no response. The room looked much as she had left it, with no sign of recent habitation. She put down her bags, and crossed into the corridor. The bedroom she had used the night before was empty. She turned to the door of the second bedroom. Just in case the stranger was inside, she rapped on the door sharply with her knuckles. No response. She knocked again. There was still silence. She turned the handle quietly, and peered in. The first thing she noticed in the gloom was that there was no one there. The second thing was a jumble of sheets lying on the bed, their whiteness marred by large, dark stains which looked like nothing so much as blood.

Loretta moved slowly and silently towards the bed. She bent forward and gingerly touched one of the stains. It was dry, but only recently so. She lifted the sheet from the tangle on the bed, and held it up. It was still damp in one or two places. She wiped her finger across one of the damp patches, and it came away smeared. Even before she held her finger to her nose and recognized the sour aroma, she knew she was right. The stains were of blood, and they had been made very recently indeed. Loretta felt her stomach

15

heave and rushed into the living-room to lean over the kitchen sink.

When she found that she was not actually going to be sick, she turned on the tap and splashed her face with cold water. Her heart was pounding and she was shaking with a mixture of fear and shock. She had no doubt that a murder had taken place at the flat, and realized that she had been moving as silently as possible in case the murderer was still on the premises. The foolishness of it suddenly assailed her—five minutes ago she had been noisily announcing her presence, and the murderer, if he or she was still in the flat, could not help but be aware of her. The thought calmed her slightly. There were few places to hide, and the door had been double-locked. All the evidence suggested she had arrived after the killer's getaway. Before giving herself time to think, she rapidly checked the only possible places of concealment: the cupboard at the end of the corridor, and under both beds. She found no one.

The fact that she was not immediately going to be attacked calmed her. Her first impulse had been to run away from the flat and call the police, but now, deciding that she could afford a few moments to think, Loretta sat down in a rather battered armchair standing near the window in the living-room. What, she asked herself, were the *facts* of the case? Presumably whatever had taken place at the flat involved the man she had seen there last night. She began to tremble again as she contemplated the possibility that she had shared the flat not with a stranger but with a corpse. She tried to visualize what she had seen when she opened the bedroom door the night before. A head on the pillow, facing away from her, the hair cut in such a way that she had been sure the figure was a man. Bed linen covering the rest of the body, which had not at the time struck her as strange, but which now seemed out of place in the current hot weather. Could it really have been a body? She knew that it could.

But she was not *sure*. Perhaps the man had been sleeping, and was attacked after she left the flat that morning. In that case, she had no proof that he was dead. In fact, if he was dead, where was the body? Surely the murderer would not attempt to move it in broad daylight? Could the victim have survived the attack, used the sheets to stem the blood, and managed to get out and get help? The situation was full of imponderables. What could she tell the police? Little more than that she had arrived at the flat and found bloodstains there. And what was her own position? She could not help the police by directing them to the flat's owner—she did not even know the names of all four English people who shared the lease. Nor could she put them in touch with Andrew, through whom she came to be staying at the flat: he was enjoying a late summer idyll on a Greek island with an English artist he had met on holiday the year before. She could remember neither the name of the island nor that of the artist, her knowledge of the latter being limited to the facts that he had lived there for ten years and painted bulls. The French authorities, famous for their orderly minds, might construe her vagueness as highly suspicious. And wasn't there some peculiarity of French law which said you were guilty until proved innocent? It would make things even worse if she admitted she had probably spent the previous night in the flat with the victim.

A new thought occurred to her, causing a sharp intake of breath. Her mother, she was forgetting about her mother. She had to be back in England on Monday to take her mother to hospital. Mrs. Lawson was so terrified by the prospect of her hysterectomy that her daughter doubted whether she would turn up if left to her own devices. But if Loretta reported what she had found at the flat, her chance of getting back in time to stick to this schedule seemed remote. The police were hardly likely to allow their sole potential witness—or suspect, she thought with a shudder —to leave the country only hours after raising the alarm. The more she considered it, the less she liked the idea of going to the authorities. Her reluctance was reinforced by her sudden recollection of Andrew's account of the difficulties he had encountered while teaching in Paris during *les événements* of 1968. It had taken days of dogged negotiation to bail out some of his students who had been accidentally caught up in the riots, he had told her, adding that it would take at least a murder to get him within sight of a French police station again. Of course, what had happened in rue Roland might be a murder, but—she always came back to this—she simply did not *know.* Perhaps she could make an anonymous phone call to the police, tipping them off to come and have a look at the flat? On second thoughts, she decided, it might be better to wait until she was at the station next day, when she was well on her way to leaving the country. Even if the call were traced, it would be too late to do anything about finding her. Meanwhile, there was no question of her spending another night at the flat; it was not, she hoped, too late to find a hotel, even if it were not the sort of place in which she would normally choose to stay.

Now that she had decided on a course of action, Loretta felt much calmer. She got up to leave the flat, but suddenly stopped. She had been searching the apartment for a human being; she had not looked for anything that might be a clue as to what had happened. She went back to the door of the bedroom in which she had made her discovery, and paused on the threshold. Taking a deep breath, she opened the door and peered inside. Averting her eyes from the mess on the bed, she glanced quickly round the rest of the room.

A heap of blankets lay on the floor at the foot of the bed; with a shudder, she decided her stomach was not up to examining them for further stains. The rest of the room was curiously devoid of personal objects, and she was relieved to be able to back out and close the door. A search of the room where she had slept the night before proved similarly unproductive. She returned to the living-room, taking in for the first time the evidence of occasional occupation: a large bottle of olive oil on a shelf above the primi-

18

tive cooker bore the date of purchase, two months earlier, on its label. The same date, scribbled in Biro, appeared on several packets and tins further along the same shelf; whoever used the flat in July had evidently stocked up on groceries. But there was nothing of more recent date. Loretta decided to give up the hunt for clues, and bent to pick up her bags.

Her eye fell on a cheap wooden bookcase, half concealed by the chair she had been sitting in earlier, and she automatically moved closer. She could never resist discovering other people's taste in books. The shelves contained an impressive array of green-jacketed Penguins, including *Mischief* and *Green for Danger*. She wondered which of the four co-tenants shared her liking for crime novels. She spotted a much-used guide to Paris, drew it out, and found to her satisfaction that it had been published in 1968. As she put it back, the book next to it caught her attention. Unlike the other volumes in the bookcase, it was shiny and new. Twisting her head to read the title, Loretta gave a little gasp of surprise. The author's name, Toby MacGregor, meant nothing to her, but the title gave away a great deal. *The Resurrection of Little Nell*, it said, and, in smaller letters, *A Challenge to the Authority of Charles Dickens*. What on earth was a deconstructionist text doing in the flat? Deconstruction was the literary fad that had succeeded structuralism, and she considered it even more pretentious and silly than its predecessor. As far as Loretta was concerned, the purpose of the movement was to state the obvious in as convoluted a way as possible, thereby creating a mystique. The trick was to ignore the advice she'd been given at school, and never use a short word when a long one would do. It certainly wasn't the sort of book that Andrew would be interested in: he was a historian, and a traditionalist at that. Nor had he given the impression that the unknown Gardner, or either of the other co-tenants, lectured in English, let alone that any of them had deconstructionist leanings. Sharing Loretta's scorn for

19

the whole business, it was unlikely that he would have forgone such an opportunity for shared mirth.

Loretta was puzzled. She took down the book, and turned to the inside cover. The French critic Roland Barthes, the blurb began, had remarked that "to give the text an Author is to impose a limit on that text."

> The pioneering work of structuralist critics [it went on] has demonstrated the exciting possibilities that flow from this courageous refusal to privilege the text. But it is to the deconstructionists that we must look for the ultimate challenge to the authority of authorship. In this subversive new book, Toby MacGregor, Professor of Nineteenth-Century Texts at the University of Arkansas, commits the final act of insubordination with his challenge to the patriarchal rule of Dickens.

Loretta turned the book over and regarded the photograph of Professor MacGregor on the back cover. So this was the chap who thought he knew better than Dickens, she thought, staring at his angular young features. She'd back Dickens any day.

She was about to return the book to its place when she started in horror, dropping it as she did so. She could hear a scrabbling noise somewhere in the flat. Had the murderer come back? Where could she hide? She looked wildly round the room. A tiny creature scuttled across the floor and disappeared under the sink. It was only a mouse. Loretta fell back into the chair, berating herself for her foolishness. She reached down to retrieve the book, and noticed a piece of paper next to it. Picking it up, she recognized it as a compliments slip from the publisher. The book's publication date was three or four weeks hence, she noted, and the publisher asked to receive a copy of any review written by the recipient.

It took her a moment to realize the significance of what she was holding. This was a brand-new book, so new that it had not yet been published. It must have been sent out very recently—she knew from her own limited experience of reviewing that copies went out about a month ahead—and been brought to the flat in the last few days. Its literary merit might be questionable but it was, without doubt, a clue. Concealing the slip inside the front cover, she put the book into her overnight bag. She opened the front door, glanced round quickly to make sure no one was in sight, and closed it behind her.

2

LORETTA ARRIVED BACK IN LONDON LATE
the following night. She was tired and depressed, convinced now that she had done the wrong thing. Even her
arrival at her flat, an airy maisonette on the top two floors
of a four-storey house in Islington, failed to cheer her.
Once inside, she dumped her bags in the hall, carried her
post into the drawing-room, and dropped into an armchair.
As she looked through the letters, she reflected that her
attempt to give an anonymous tip to the French police had
been a dismal failure. Either they were not used to being
offered information on a Sunday afternoon, or the relevant
department closed down at weekends. Whatever the reason, the switchboard operator had been unhelpful to the
point of obstructiveness, refusing to put her through to anyone of importance unless she supplied her name and business, which Loretta (cravenly, she now admitted) had
refused to do.

After several minutes of fruitless argument, she had
tried to pacify her conscience by telling the man he ought
to send an officer to take a look at the flat marked Gardner
at 18 rue Roland. She doubted very much whether he had
done any such thing. Where did that leave her? she asked
herself, wondering whether there were any aspirins in the
flat. She possessed only one clue to the identity of the man

in the flat, which she had no idea how to interpret, and she had not the least idea what to do next.

This gloomy mood persisted throughout the next day. Stuck in the London traffic on her way to Gillingham, Loretta had little to do other than turn over the weekend's events in her mind. What she needed was someone with a clear head in whom she could confide—and a lot more information. Perhaps she had missed one simple little fact capable of transforming what had seemed like a nightmare into something relatively commonplace. She cursed the fact that Andrew was going to be away, if she remembered rightly, until Friday. Not that he was the ideal confidant. Far from it. If events in Paris turned out to have the innocent explanation she longed for, he would relish the chance to spread the story of her discomfiture at the college where they both taught. She had no difficulty in imagining how he would handle it: "Our poor Loretta seems to have a secret desire to be a Gothic heroine," he would murmur into the telephone. "All those bloodstains and vanishing corpses. Very *Mysteries of Udolpho*, don't you think? Who would have thought it of her?" One of the problems with having a reputation as a feminist was that people were always on the lookout for evidence that you were faint-hearted and feminine underneath it all.

But a conversation with Andrew, handled carefully, might at least give her a clue to the identity of the man she'd seen at the flat. It might be that one of the other tenants had phoned to warn him that a friend intended to use the place, and Andrew had forgotten to pass on the message. He had been so full of his holiday plans that this explanation seemed perfectly possible. Loretta wondered if there was any way of contacting Andrew in Greece. She had an idea that he'd let out his cottage in Oxfordshire— being a part-time lecturer, he was able to indulge the luxury of living outside London—for the weeks he was going to be away. It was just possible that he'd left a phone number for emergencies. She decided to ring his house in Charlbury that evening.

Loretta arrived in Gillingham to find her mother, predictably, in a state of nerves. It was just as well she had arrived early, she reflected, taking over the packing of Mrs. Lawson's small suitcase. It took two cups of tea and half an hour of persuasion to get her mother into the car, and Loretta was guiltily thankful to hand her over to a sympathetic nurse when they arrived at the hospital. After an hour of sitting about, she was allowed to visit Mrs. Lawson in a small gynaecology ward where she had already made friends with a woman who was recovering from the same operation. Loretta guessed the introduction had been effected by one of the nurses, and silently congratulated the hospital on the quality of its staff. She took her leave with a clear conscience, reminding her mother that her father and younger sister were due to visit that evening.

She was relieved that Mrs. Lawson had settled in so well but, as she drove back to London, she gave free rein to feelings of irritation towards her sister. Jenny lived just outside Gillingham, and could perfectly well have taken their mother to hospital; as usual, she had got out of it with a vague reference to her other family responsibilities. Since Jenny's only daughter had a place in a nursery, and Jenny herself obdurately refused to work, Loretta could not imagine what these duties were. What it boiled down to, she thought angrily, was that Jenny considered her role as a wife and mother excused her from anything she didn't feel like doing, and Mrs. Lawson happily went along with her. If her operation had taken place in term-time, even in the middle of examinations, it would still have been Loretta who was expected to accompany her to hospital. It was quite unfair. Loretta braked sharply as the car in front of her made an unexpected stop at a zebra crossing.

* * *

At ten o'clock that evening, after half a dozen fruitless calls to Andrew's cottage in Charlbury, Loretta began to wonder whether she had imagined the existence of his tenants. She decided to look through the *Guardian* for the third time that day, although she had to admit that the possibility of whatever had happened in Paris finding its way into an English newspaper was remote. Glumly, she asked herself whether she shouldn't go to the English police. The idea held no more attraction than the notion of reporting the matter to the French authorities before she left Paris. And now there was the added problem of having to explain why she hadn't done something about it at the time. It occurred to her that she had probably committed an offence, and might even be dragged back to Paris to face questioning there. And all for something that might not be worth the trouble. However she looked at it, she didn't like any of the options open to her. She decided to sleep on it.

Next morning, she tried the Charlbury number again. An American voice answered at the third ring. When Loretta said she was trying to contact Andrew, the woman began to explain that Mr. Walker was away in Greece. Loretta interrupted to ask whether he'd left an address or phone number in case of emergencies, and was told that he hadn't. The friend with whom he was staying wasn't on the phone, and he'd said it wasn't worth leaving an address as a letter would take at least a week to reach him. If anything went wrong at the cottage, he'd told the American woman to speak to the cleaning lady who came in three days a week. She knew all the local people, including a very good plumber. Loretta thanked her, and rang off. It was just as she'd expected, but it was frustrating to come up so quickly against a dead end.

She looked at her watch, and her hand hovered over the phone again. Coming to a decision, she dialled the number of the *Sunday Herald* office in Holborn and asked to speak to John Tracey. She was half relieved and half disappointed when he answered his extension; as often as not when she called the paper he would turn out to be dodging shells in the Lebanon or looking for criminals in Nice.

"John, it's Loretta," she began nervously. She never knew how he was going to react to her.

"My dear Laura, I'm always glad to hear from my lovely wife," he replied cheerfully. "To what do I owe this pleasure?"

Loretta took a deep breath and stifled the reply she wanted to make. Tracey was one of the few people outside her family who knew that she had changed her name from plain Laura to exotic Loretta in the course of the train journey that took her from home to university for the first time. It was a piece of knowledge he used when, as now, he was in an impish mood and wanted to tease her. Although it never ceased to irritate her, she recognized it as a signal that he was feeling well disposed towards her.

"There's something I'd like to talk to you about," she said hesitantly. "If you're not busy, that is." She knew Tracey would not let her get away with telling only half the story, and she was aware of a reluctance to describe events in Paris to someone whose job was asking questions. She recognized that she was afraid of her theories being ridiculed or of their being taken seriously in about equal measure. But she needed Tracey's help, so she ploughed on. "I had an extraordinary experience over the weekend," she said. "Something happened to me in Paris. I can't really talk about it over the phone. Can I buy you lunch and discuss it?"

"It or him?" Tracey teased her. "Don't tell me you're still going to Paris for your dirty weekends? Is it fond memories of me that does it?"

Loretta lost patience. "Look John, I need your help," she said urgently. "Will you meet me or won't you?"

Tracey's tone changed. "All right, I'm at your disposal. I'm supposed to be having lunch with the features editor today, but if it's as serious as it sounds, I'll put him off."

Loretta felt slightly guilty. She might, after all, be placing an unnecessarily sinister interpretation on what had happened. On the other hand...."I'll meet you at the Greek restaurant in Great Titchfield Street," she said. "Will one o'clock do?"

The weather was still stiflingly hot, just as it had been in Paris. Loretta could not remember a September like it. She had suggested meeting in Great Titchfield Street because it was a stone's throw from her office in the English department, and she had not been there to collect messages and post for several days. Not that there was likely to be much correspondence during the long vacation, but it was as well to keep an eye on things. She also needed to pick up some notes she had made for the book she was working on, a critical assessment of Edith Wharton. Work on the project was going well, and she hoped to be able to complete the manuscript by spring next year. If the book was a success, it would considerably strengthen her chances of getting tenure, a slender hope for most academics, particularly women, in these straitened days.

As she emerged from the department into the street, a few large drops of rain fell on to her yellow lawn dress. The sky had darkened dramatically—and unexpectedly— during her half-hour visit to her office. She wished she had brought her umbrella; her bobbed blonde hair tended to curl uncontrollably when it got wet. But the rain didn't get any heavier, and she arrived at the restaurant almost as dry as when she had set out.

Tracey had got there before her, and had stationed himself at one of the three outdoor tables that made the place popular in summer. "Just like Paris," he said, gesturing towards the other tables. Loretta smiled and sat down. Their marriage had been over for five years, time for most of the bitterness to have receded and be replaced by an easy-going friendship. The arrangement was so amicable that, in spite of affairs on both sides, they had not bothered to get divorced. It seemed unlikely, in any case, that either

27

of them would choose to marry again. Tracey's hectic way of life was much better suited to the single state and Loretta had come to the view that, for women, marriage was at best an irrelevance and at worst a shackle. She found it hard to remember that she was, legally, still married to the man sitting opposite her. And yet Tracey had really changed very little over the years since they had met at university. Then he had been a mature student, his appearance unexpectedly youthful in spite of his prematurely grey hair. Regarding him now, in his crumpled denim suit, she would have been hard put to guess his age—actually forty —if she had not already known it.

Tracey had been reading that day's *Times* while he waited for her. "I'm thinking of going to Manchester to follow this up," he said, pointing to a brief news item on the back page about an investigation into alleged brutality at an old people's home. "Damn good story."

Loretta marvelled at his undimmed enthusiasm for his job. He had started on a provincial newspaper straight from school, and returned to journalism as soon as he left university. "Don't you ever get tired of it?" she asked. "Isn't one crook much the same as any other?"

"That's not the point," he answered earnestly. "If it wasn't for a few journalists who are willing to take risks, there'd be twenty times the number of villains waiting to take money out of the hands of old-age pensioners. A free press . . ." He stopped, holding up his hand to prevent her speaking. "I know. You've heard this speech before, and it didn't impress you much last time, either. Have you decided what you want to eat?"

As the waiter took their order, the threatened rain arrived with a vengeance. The diners at the other outdoor tables hurriedly took themselves indoors but, when they were offered a table inside the restaurant, Loretta and Tracey refused. The canopy over the tables on the pavement protected them, just, from the downpour; they felt like observers on a film set as they watched tourists, shoppers, and lunchtime drinkers scuttle for shelter. An old lady hurried into the video rental shop opposite, peering round in surprise when she found herself confronting a collection of soft porn films, and a young man in jeans dived for cover in the doorway next to the kebab house.

Loretta had decided to forgo a starter to give herself plenty of time to recount what had happened in Paris, and as Tracey tucked into broad beans and artichoke hearts she gave him a bald account of everything she remembered about the weekend. Apart from a rather feeble joke about the *Fem Sap* conference—Tracey found any manifestation of organized feminism positively terrifying—he heard her out in silence. When she finished, he pushed away his empty plate and thought for a moment. Above their heads, the rain still drummed on the canvas of the canopy and splashed off on to the pavement.

"There really was a lot of blood?" he enquired at last. "Too much for the sheets to have been used to clean up after an accident? More than if someone had been having, er, a period?" He shifted uncomfortably in his seat.

Loretta suppressed an urge to smile. "Much more," she said.

Tracey took out a cigarette, and lit it. He inhaled deeply. "The trouble is, Loretta," he said at last, "that the alternative explanations are so far-fetched. I know what you're afraid of. You think you spent the night with a dead body, a murder victim in fact, and narrowly escaped being done in yourself." Loretta felt her stomach muscles contract. Tracey certainly wasted no time in getting to the heart of things. "But, assuming you're right, what happened to the body after you left the flat on Saturday morning? Did the murderer come back for it? And why did he, or she," he added, catching her expression, "why did he or she leave it there in the first place?"

"All right, I don't have answers to any of those questions," Loretta admitted. "I've thought and thought, and I haven't come up with more than wild guesses. But I am certain of two things. There *was* a man in bed at the flat on Friday night when I arrived, and the next evening the sheets on that bed were saturated with blood. That's what I can't get away from."

"Well, Loretta, I have to say that if I'd heard this story from anybody else, I'd take it with a large pinch of salt," Tracey admitted. "I'd assume you were exaggerating the amount of blood, or even that you'd had too much to drink on the first evening and had imagined the chap in the bed. But, whatever I think about your feminism, I do trust your powers of observation. So let's consider other explanations first to make sure we haven't missed anything. My idea about an accident, for instance. This water heater you told me about, isn't it possible that it exploded and wounded the man who was staying there on Friday night? After you left on Saturday morning, I mean. He could have used the sheets to stem the blood while he went for help."

"There was no sign of any accident," Loretta insisted. "Remember, I did have a look round before I left. The water heater couldn't explode without leaving *some* trace that it had happened. Anyway, an explosion would be more likely to produce burns than wounds."

"Fair enough," Tracey said, but persisted, "How about this? Your stranger, call him X, is at the flat for a rendezvous with a woman. She visits him while you're at the conference, and they take part in some sort of sado-masochistic ritual. It goes wrong, and he carts her off to hospital."

Loretta shook her head in disbelief. "You've missed your vocation," she said scornfully. "I thought you worked for a quality paper, not the *News of the World*."

"It is possible," Tracey insisted defensively. "You'd be surprised what people get up to." He seemed relieved that the waiter chose this moment to bring their kebabs to the table.

The rain was easing off, and people started to appear on the street again. Loretta was just refilling their glasses with retsina when she heard shouts and the sound of a scuffle in the doorway next to the restaurant. As she turned to look, several waiters rushed out of the kebab house and dived into the doorway, apparently joining in whatever was going on. Seconds later, a struggling mass of people erupted into the road. The man at the centre of the fracas broke free and hurled himself towards Loretta, falling to the ground in his attempt to reach her.

"Help!" he shouted, "They're trying to kill me! I wasn't doing no harm!"

Aghast, Loretta looked round wildly. Spotting an older man in a cook's hat and apron, she appealed to him. "What's going on?" she demanded.

"He is thief," the cook replied phlegmatically. "He get into my flat, my wife see him in bedroom. She scream, and call my son. He chase him, she ring me and I send waiters after him."

The man at whom this charge was directed struggled violently but failed to escape the hands of his captors a second time. "It's not true, lady," he wailed. "You saw me go in there. I was just getting out of the rain."

Loretta suddenly realized that this was the man in jeans who had made for the doorway when the shower began. She was about to speak when Tracey intervened.

"She doesn't know anything about it," he said firmly. "We saw you go in there, but we've no idea what you did when you got inside. Has anyone called the police?"

"Yes, yes, police coming," said the cook, and at that moment they heard the wail of an approaching siren. The alleged thief gave a violent heave and escaped again for a matter of seconds, only to be brought down with a rugby tackle by the largest of the waiters. Within minutes he was sitting in the back of a police Rover while a woman constable made the rounds of the restaurant looking for witnesses.

Loretta and Tracey turned back to their meal. "You seem fated to get a floor-show along with your meals these days," Tracey observed. "First you get assaulted in a restaurant in Paris, and then the local burglar throws himself on your mercy."

"There you are," Loretta said triumphantly. "It just goes to prove that bizarre things do happen quite unexpectedly. If you hadn't seen it yourself, you'd think it highly unlikely that anyone could get involved in that sort of scene while having lunch off Oxford Street."

"Point taken," Tracey conceded. "But I'm not sure how I can help you, even if I accept your theory about a murder at the flat."

"I thought you might have some ideas about what I should do next," Loretta said. "I can't face going to the police—it's not their case, and they'd think I was a complete fool for coming back to London before reporting it. And, as we both agree, it's not clear what there is to report."

"I should think the first thing to do is to contact Andrew," Tracey suggested. "Surely he'll have left a forwarding address with someone."

"I'm not a complete dimwit," Loretta said impatiently. "I've already tried that." She explained that Andrew was currently beyond reach, and opened her briefcase. "There is this," she said, producing a book. "It's the one I found in the bookcase." She handed it to Tracey.

"Good God," he exclaimed. "*The Resurrection of Little Nell: A Challenge to the Authority of Charles Dickens*. Is it a misprint? Surely he means authorship, not authority? But I had no idea there was any doubt about who wrote *The Old Curiosity Shop*."

"There isn't," Loretta laughed. "Haven't you heard of deconstruction? Post-structuralism? It's very fashionable in some English departments these days."

"Don't forget I'm just a humble journalist," Tracey said. "It's a long time since I left university." He began to read the introduction. "There are four words I don't understand in the first sentence," he complained. "What's semiology when it's at home? Sounds like the science of doing things by halves. You don't teach this stuff, do you?"

Loretta admitted, with a private feeling of satisfaction, that she didn't. "But I'm considered very old-fashioned," she confessed. "Anyway, that's not the point. I didn't invite you here to discuss trends in English literature." Leaning across, she retrieved the book, took out the compliments slip and handed it to Tracey. "It hasn't been published yet," she said. "What I want to know is, how many copies would be sent out before the publication date?"

Tracey considered the piece of paper. "It depends," he said. "If the author was a best-selling novelist, presumably dozens. Hundreds even. But that wouldn't apply in this case. Have you ever heard of Toby MacGregor?"

Loretta shook her head. "I haven't even heard of the publisher," she said. "It's certainly not one of the big ones like OUP."

"In that case, it's probably a small company publishing academic texts that they've picked up for a song," Tracey said. "Which means they're probably rather mean, and send out as few review copies as possible. The *TLS*, perhaps *The Literary Review*, and a few specialists in the field who might review it in academic journals. I don't suppose they'd bother with newspapers, and it's hardly going to interest the readers of *Woman's Own*. Maybe only half a dozen copies."

"How can I get a list of the people it was sent to?" Loretta asked urgently. "Whoever took it to the flat is almost bound to be on it."

"Simple," said Tracey. "Ring them up and ask."

Loretta looked doubtful. "Why should they tell me?" she objected. "It's not as if I can tell them why I want to know. I can hardly say I think one of the people who received it has been murdered."

"Or is a murderer," Tracey interrupted. "It could just as

easily belong to the person who did it as the victim. Or do you think a taste for this semiology business is incompatible with the lust to kill?"

"Be serious," Loretta rebuked him. "You're supposed to be helping me. I can't see why the publisher should hand over a list of people who got review copies just because I ring up and ask for it. I don't even know who to speak to."

"You'd be surprised at what people will tell you," Tracey assured her. "It's easier than you think."

"It is for you," Loretta objected. "You've been doing this sort of thing for years, and you sound plausible. Even if I could think of a cover story, I'd give myself away by sounding nervous. But you could do it."

Tracey was taken aback. "Hang on a minute, Loretta, I'm not sure I want to get mixed up in this," he said.

"You're not getting mixed up in anything," Loretta said angrily. "It's not as if I were asking a huge favour. You said yourself it was simple."

Tracey thought for a moment. "Oh, all right," he said with ill grace. "I'll ring and say I'm doing a piece about how small publishing houses make a living these days. I can say I'd like to take this book as an example—how much they pay the author, size of the print run, how many copies get sent out for review. But don't get any ideas—after this you're on your own." Loretta thanked him, and paid the bill.

"Where will you be this afternoon?" Tracey asked as they parted. "I'll let you know how I get on."

In matters like this, Tracey could be relied on to keep his word. When the phone rang in her flat just after five o'clock, she picked it up and recognized his voice.

"I've got it," he said, "for what it's worth. Nine copies —I was almost right. Have you got a pen?" The book had gone to the journals he had mentioned at lunch, plus three upmarket Sunday newspapers. Loretta wondered whether this was a wildly optimistic gesture on the part of the publisher, or a reflection of structuralism's fashionable status in the media. She suspected it was the former. The list was completed by the names of four individuals, all lecturers in English, whom Loretta knew by reputation.

When Tracey rang off, she sat and pondered her next step. She could, with a bit of thought, invent excuses for ringing up the lecturers on the list to make sure they were alive and well. Of course, that would establish only that none of them was the victim. It would not rule out any of them as the murderer. The newspapers and journals were a much greater problem. Because she had visited Tracey's office occasionally during the years of her marriage, she knew that books were often left lying around where anyone could pick them up. If the papers had decided against reviewing MacGregor's book—a strong possibility, she thought—any member of staff could have taken a fancy to it. Even if she got through to the right person in the literary section of each journal, there was no guarantee that he or she would be able to tell her its exact whereabouts.

She decided to start with the academics on her list. It was a good time of day to ring a university department if you didn't really want to speak to the person you were asking for, she thought—there was a good chance that they would have gone home, but the department secretary would be able to tell her whether they'd put in an appearance in the last few days. She looked at the first name, and was aware of an irrational feeling that because Hermione Dangerfield was a woman, she had nothing to do with the case. If the man she had seen at the flat was the killer, there was no reason to suppose his victim was not a woman. Loretta rang Directory Enquiries and got the number of Kent University.

She started to dial and stopped when she remembered that it was still the long vacation. Dr. Dangerfield might well be away on holiday. Well, she thought, it couldn't be helped. She had no other leads to follow up. A minute later she was through to the English department. The story she

35

had prepared—that she was carrying out a survey on whether female lecturers were commissioned to write reviews less frequently than their male colleagues—seemed uncomfortably thin. It was with immense relief, then, that she heard the department secretary say that she had missed Dr. Dangerfield.

"She's just popped out to the dentist," the woman explained. "Can I get her to call you tomorrow morning?"

Loretta quickly demurred; she would ring back, she said untruthfully. Putting the phone down, she drew a faint line through Hermione Dangerfield's name at the top of her list. The next name was that of Bernard Romilly, whom Loretta knew to be a pompous Reader in English at Durham. She found it hard to imagine his wanting to review a post-structuralist tome: perhaps the publisher had been hoping to provoke a literary controversy by encouraging a hostile review.

She rang Durham and, to her horror, was put straight through. Romilly responded explosively to her explanation about an imaginary survey; the problem was not the exclusion of women from academic journals, he snapped, but the favouritism shown towards anyone who happened to teach at an Oxbridge college. Although the view was one with which she had some sympathy, it was expressed in such a way that, by the time she got off the phone, she was feeling a hearty dislike for Bernard Romilly. If an inflated ego was sufficient excuse for murder, he would have been bumped off years ago. What was clear was that—deserve it though he might—Romilly had not fallen victim to an enraged epistemologist in Andrew's flat in Paris.

There were two names left. It was now after six but, since both taught at Oxford colleges, there was a reasonable chance that someone would be able to tell her whether they'd been seen since the weekend. She decided to start with Martin Smith, a well-known authority on the Brontë sisters.

The switchboard operator at the college was helpful; Dr.

36

Smith was away on holiday, she said, and due back in the next few days. Loretta's heart leapt: had he stopped off in Paris on his way back to England? She pressed the woman for a more exact estimate of when Dr. Smith was due back, but the result was inconclusive. He had been very vague, the switchboard operator said, confiding that Dr. Smith was not, at the best of times, a very reliable timekeeper. All she could suggest was that Loretta give it a few days and try again. Frustrated, Loretta rang off. How was she to find out whether anyone on her list was missing if they were as imprecise as this about their plans? Her enthusiasm waning, she turned to the last name on the list.

Hugh Puddephat was, she knew, one of the leading lights in the post-structuralist movement. Had he too gone off on holiday for an unspecified period of time? She got through to the college, and learned that Dr. Puddephat was at this very moment attending a conference in Italy. He was due back in England later in the week. Loretta expressed her thanks for this information, and rang off.

Another potential victim off the list, she thought. If Dr. Puddephat was even now discussing trends in deconstructionist theory in some charming little town in Italy, he could not have been the object of foul play three or four days ago in Paris. As far as corpses were concerned, the only candidate remaining to her was the maddening Dr. Smith. Loretta supposed she would have to ring his college again at the end of the week. She did not feel she had achieved very much for a whole afternoon of detective work.

Later that evening, unable to think of any more avenues to explore, she tried Tracey's home number. The phone rang only once before she heard the click that told her she was about to get his answering-machine. She put the phone down, resolving to try him at work next morning. But her luck was definitely out. There was no answer from his extension and when she succeeded in getting transferred to the news desk, a secretary told her that Tracey had gone to Manchester for the rest of the week. Declining the woman's invitation to leave a message, Loretta once again rang off. He was following up the story about the old people's home, she guessed, and nothing annoyed him more than interruptions when his sights were set on exposing some sort of villainy. She would just have to wait. In any case, she had other things to think about: her mother's operation was due to take place next morning. She had done what she could for the time being, and Andrew would be back on Friday. Making a note to ring Charlbury and Martin Smith's college at the end of the week, Loretta did her best to contain her impatience for the next couple of days.

On Wednesday evening, her father rang with the news that her mother's operation had been a success; Loretta drove down to Gillingham the following afternoon, and spent half an hour at Mrs. Lawson's bedside. Her mother was weak, but a houseman assured her that this was the effect of the anaesthetic. There was nothing to worry about. Loretta spent the night at her parents' house, and returned to London first thing on Friday morning.

As soon as she arrived at her flat, she made her second call to Dr. Smith's college. She tapped her fingers impatiently on the arm of her chair while she waited for the college to answer. Now that her mother's operation was out of the way, her need to know what had happened in Paris had returned with renewed force. As a result, her request to speak to Dr. Smith came out in an indecent rush, and she had to repeat herself before getting an answer. When she did get a reply, it did nothing to diminish her excitement. No, the woman said, Dr. Smith wasn't back, nor had there been any message from him. Loretta was far from being the only person who wanted to get hold of him, she added, making little attempt to conceal her irritation with the absent don.

Loretta thanked her and rang off, wondering what to do next. Clearly, the attitude of the college staff towards Smith's non-appearance was simply one of annoyance, but then the college authorities didn't know what she knew. At this point, Loretta pulled herself up short. She was allowing her imagination to run away with her. There might yet be a straightforward explanation for Smith's absence and, apart from the book by Toby MacGregor, she had no evidence to connect him with the flat. Feeling sorely in need of Tracey's thoughts on the matter, she tried the *Sunday Herald* news desk again. He was still in Manchester. With a cluck of impatience, she tried Andrew's cottage in Charlbury. The phone rang for ages with no reply.

Loretta's sense of frustration grew in leaps and bounds over the course of the weekend. Andrew's phone continued to ring unanswered every time she tried it and, by Sunday afternoon, she was kicking herself for not checking the time of his return with the American woman she had spoken to at the cottage at the beginning of the week. Nor did she have any luck with Tracey. Instead of returning to London on Saturday, as she had expected, he left a message with the news desk to the effect that he was spending the weekend with friends in Chester and would not be back in town until Monday. Loretta had no idea that Tracey knew anyone in Chester, and he hadn't given their number to the news desk. She could only hope that it would occur to him to ring and ask how she had got on with the list.

When the phone rang on Sunday evening, she confidently expected to hear Tracey's voice on picking it up. She didn't.

"I phoned to thank you," said Andrew Walker. "I've never seen the flat so tidy. You must have spent the entire weekend cleaning the place up. How did you find time to go to your conference?"

"The flat?" Loretta gasped, completely thrown off balance. "You've been to the flat? But I thought . . . you said . . . what about Greece?"

"Oh, yes, that," Andrew said dismissively. "Well, it's a nice enough place for the first three or four days but then it does become rather boring. One can have enough sea and sand, you know. To cut a long story short, I decided I'd had my fill after a week and got a boat to Italy. I've been wending my way back to England through Switzerland and France, which is why I'm a couple of days late. I had a much better time than I would have done on that wretched island."

"But the flat," Loretta protested weakly. "When did you stay at the flat?" What about the blood? Surely he'd seen the blood?

"I took the sleeper from Stresa to Paris on Tuesday night," he replied. "I took myself off to rue Roland and slept most of the day. I needed it after a night on that train, I can tell you. Take my advice, if you're going on a long train journey, do it by day."

"So you arrived on Wednesday," Loretta prompted. Why was he keeping her in suspense?

"Yes, and as I said, the place has never been so spick and span. It's the first time anyone's polished the floors since we rented it, and that's . . . well, quite a number of years."

Polished the floors? Loretta thought wildly, trying to picture the flat in her mind. If she remembered what the floors were like at all, her impression was that they were of dull wood with occasional threadbare rugs. If Andrew was telling the truth, it could only mean that someone had been back to rue Roland and done a very thorough cleaning job, which would also explain why Andrew hadn't mentioned the bloodstained sheets—presumably they'd gone as well. But who? It could only have been the murderer. Loretta felt a chill pass through her body. It was quickly followed by another sinister thought. *Was* Andrew telling the truth? Or was he testing her? Had he been involved in whatever had happened in the flat, might he even now be trying to trick her into revealing what she knew?

The unlikeliness of this suspicion did not take long to dawn on her. No one would commit a murder in a flat which they had loaned to a friend for the weekend. She was very nearly convinced by this thought. She was steeling herself to come clean with Andrew when another idea struck her. The evidence of the crime had been removed from the flat. Andrew had actually been there, and found nothing amiss. How would her story sound if she told it now? How could she explain that she had found bloodstained sheets in the bedroom but failed to go to the police, and that now the crucial evidence had disappeared? Even Tracey, who knew her much better than Andrew, had been initially sceptical about her story.

She realized that Andrew was in the midst of describing the interior of a church he'd visited in Paris. She hoped she had been making the right noises at intervals. While he rhapsodized about the workmanship of the roodscreen, she gathered her thoughts. She would not, at this point, take him into her confidence, but she might be able to extract some information from him. "I'm afraid I can't take credit for the state of the flat," she said when he paused for breath. "I hardly spent any time there, and I certainly didn't get down on my hands and knees to do any scrubbing or polishing. One of your co-tenants must have been there recently."

"That's odd," said Andrew. "I happen to know none of them has stayed there since, let's see, July it must have been. I remember Alex phoned up to say he was going then, but he hasn't been since. He's a television producer, you know, and he does a live programme on Friday evenings. He wanted a weekend there before he got really tied up with the show. It's his name on the door by the way, he's Alex Gardner." The other two tenants, he explained, were also out of the running: Jim was working in the States, and Colin had been laid up for several weeks with a broken leg. "I suppose it must have been Alex," Andrew said finally. "He never used to be tidy—perhaps he's turned over a leaf in middle age."

Loretta thanked him for the loan of the flat, and asked how she should return the keys.

"Hang on to them for the time being," Andrew said. "I've got a spare set, as you'll have gathered."

Offering to buy him dinner next time he had a free evening in town—a promise he would hold her to, she knew —Loretta rang off. It looked as though the man she'd shared the flat with on her first night in Paris had been there unofficially. So how had he got hold of the keys? Perhaps the stranger was someone who had once used them legitimately, as she had, but had hung on to them. Or had them copied? That seemed the most likely explanation. It also opened up a dauntingly wide field of candidates for the deception—anyone who had stayed there since Andrew and his friends rented the flat in 1968, in fact. It didn't bear thinking about. She was settling down into a state of unrelieved gloom when a new thought struck her. Andrew *had* been holding something back, she realized triumphantly. It wasn't Greece he had got tired of, she was willing to bet, but his friend the painter.

Next morning, as she leafed through the *Guardian* while eating a croissant, she spotted a headline which made her sit bolt upright in her chair. "Police Appeal Over Missing Don," she read. So Martin Smith *had* disappeared! She put down the uneaten half of her croissant, and read on. Thames Valley Police, said the paper, were appealing for information on the whereabouts of an Oxford don who had failed to turn up at a conference in Italy the previous week. Loretta blinked. Italy? The college authorities had called in the police, she read, when the conference organizers got in touch to ask whether Dr. Hugh Puddephat had been taken ill. Loretta skimmed through to the end of the story. Not Martin Smith, but Hugh Puddephat. That would teach her

42

to take things at face value. Of course, the woman she had spoken to at the college had simply assumed that Puddephat was safely at the conference. She didn't have proof that he was there. Loretta went back to the beginning, and re-read the item more closely. It appeared that Puddephat had last been seen in Oxford on the Wednesday before the conference, and police were anxious to trace anyone who had seen him since. It couldn't be a coincidence, Loretta thought. But did it mean that Puddephat was the victim of what had happened at the flat? Or was he the guilty perpetrator, fleeing across Europe from the consequences of what he had done? At that moment, the phone rang. Loretta grabbed it, and heard Tracey's voice.

"Hugh Puddephat's missing!" they exclaimed in unison.

3

IT WAS HARD TO TELL, LORETTA THOUGHT, which of them was the more disappointed by the other's prior knowledge of the news. Tracey regained his wits first. "What are you going to do about it?" he asked bluntly.

Loretta was irritated; she had not had time to think that far ahead. "I'll go to Oxford, of course," she said, hoping her tone was convincing enough to conceal that she had no idea what to do once she got there.

"Wait a minute," said Tracey, in a friendlier tone of voice. "What about going to the police? Shouldn't you consider that?"

Loretta remembered that Tracey knew nothing of her conversation with Andrew. "So you see," she said, as she finished explaining that the sheets must have disappeared from the flat, "I haven't got anything at all to back up my story."

"I see what you mean," Tracey said thoughtfully. "And the link between this chap Puddephat and the flat is a pretty tenuous one at the moment. Maybe you're right. But shouldn't you try and find out some more about him before you go rushing off? And, unless you're intending to announce to the world what you're up to, you're going to need some sort of cover story."

44

"Oh, I'll look up the books he's written at the college library and take a couple out," said Loretta airily. "I can leaf through them on the train, and they might give me something to go on."

"I may be able to do better than that," said Tracey. "Let's see, it's nearly ten o'clock. Let me make a very quick phone call and come back to you."

Five minutes later, the phone rang again. "If you've got time to go into the *Herald* office this afternoon, I've arranged for you to have a look at his file in our library," he told her. "They've just checked, and there are several cuttings in it. Seems he was involved in some sort of scandal three or four years ago. I shan't be in today as it's Monday, but I've given your name to Bill, the head librarian, and he's expecting you. Oh, one more thing. Have a look in *Who's Who* while you're there. They'll have an up-to-date copy if you ask for it. The library's on the second floor, by the way. You can't miss it."

She ought to be grateful for this lesson in investigative technique, Loretta thought as Tracey rang off. But she couldn't help wishing he had offered to take a more active role in the affair. The prospect of inquiring into a murder single-handed was not one that she relished. But, looking on the bright side, she might have more idea of how to proceed after her visit to the cuttings library that afternoon. And, although she had come up with the idea of a visit to Oxford very much on the spur of the moment, it wasn't a bad one. She would need somewhere to stay for at least a night, and her closest friend in the town was herself an academic. There was a good chance that Bridget would be in touch with all the gossip about Puddephat's disappearance.

Picking up the phone, she dialled the number of the college at which Bridget Bennett taught English. She smiled as she waited to be connected to Bridget's college rooms; Tracey would strongly disapprove if he knew whom she was calling. Loretta and Bridget had belonged to the same women's group several years before, a group which Tracey had nicknamed "the coven." He held its members, incorrectly, responsible for the break-up of his marriage. She had few friends to whom he objected as strongly as Bridget. But, if he wasn't going to give her more concrete help himself, she would have to find other allies. Not that she had made up her mind about taking Bridget into her confidence—she would leave that decision until later. But, if the time did come when she needed another confidante, Bridget was the person she would choose. Bridget's voice came on the line and, within minutes, the whole thing was arranged. Loretta would arrive at her friend's house in Woodstock Road in time for supper, and the whole evening would be free for a chat. Feeling much more cheerful than she had after her conversation with Tracey, Loretta put the phone down.

Early that afternoon, as soon as she could get away from a lunch with colleagues from her department, Loretta set off for the *Sunday Herald* building. She was glad to escape; it had been a working lunch, set up to discuss a new second-year course on the influence of gender on literary style, and the syllabus had provoked considerable opposition from two of her older male colleagues. She felt her contribution to the discussion had been negligible; it had taken her all her patience just to keep her temper. A walk was exactly what she needed, although the continuing hot weather made it less pleasant than it might have been. She arrived at the *Herald* building at half past three, and walked past the uniformed commissionaire to the lift. As she got out, she spotted a sign to the library, and set off in the direction in which it pointed.

In spite of Tracey's assurance, the library was not easy to find; after the initial good start, it was signposted only intermittently, and at the end of one corridor she was left to guess. Choosing a left turn, she soon found herself facing a blank door which might, for all she knew, lead to the cuttings library. Opening it, she found herself in a large room in which row upon row of men sat behind video screens. The walls and doors, every available space in fact, were covered with pictures of large-breasted women from popular newspapers. Loretta shuddered, and began to back out. One of the men spotted her and emitted a stagy wolf-whistle. Loretta felt herself blush and her fury rose: she was equally angry with the man, who had done it to discomfit her, and herself, for reacting. She hastened back into the corridor and slammed the door. Retracing her steps, she encountered one of the paper's rare female employees, who offered to show her the way to the library. No wonder she couldn't find it, Loretta thought, as she followed the woman down a maze of identical mushroom-painted corridors. When they reached the right room, Loretta thanked her guide and went inside.

The library was a big room with banks of filing cabinets to each side. Down the middle there was a row of desks, all empty except one. Monday was evidently a slack day for the paper. The library's sole occupant, an elderly man whom she took to be Bill, looked up interrogatively from the newspaper he was reading. "Yes, miss?" he asked. When Loretta gave her name, he thought for a moment, then his brow cleared. "Ah yes, miss, you'll be wanting the cuttings on that don chappie. I got them out this morning when Mr. Tracey rang. Come with me." He led her to the last desk in the line, on which she could see a sheaf of pink sheets of paper. As she got closer, she could see that each had one or two articles from various newspapers stuck to it. "'Fraid there's nothing very recent," the librarian said. "What's 'e done this time, committed a murder?" The man chuckled at his own joke.

Loretta forced a smile, and judged it better not to answer. "Is it all right for me to sit here?" she asked.

"Help yourself," said Bill, ambling back to his own desk and a waiting copy of the *Morning Star*. "By the way, try and keep 'em in order, miss," he added, over his shoulder. "Newest on top."

Loretta sat down and examined the pile. She had never been in a cuttings library before. How useful it must be, she thought, to have all this information on tap. But surely the library staff didn't go through each and every national paper every day? Flicking through Puddephat's file, she saw that they did. The top cutting was from the *Sunday Times*; underneath, she spotted items from both the *Guardian* and the *Sun*. It was an impressive collection.

Returning to the top of the pile, she began to read the *Sunday Times* story. It came from the paper's Atticus column, and was a couple of years old—it looked as if Bill hadn't yet got round to filing the latest news on Puddephat. "Hotheads At High Table," the headline said, and a faint bell began to ring. She went rapidly through the story, and remembered that she'd read it at the time. Puddephat had refused to take his place at a formal dinner to welcome the new master of his college because he had been placed opposite Dr. Theodore Sykes, a fellow member of the English faculty. Indeed, Puddephat had scandalized other dons by storming out after claiming the place-setting was a deliberate insult. Puddephat's anger, the paper said, could be traced to a most unflattering review of his new book, written by Sykes, in the *TLS*. The cutting went on to quote from the review, which had certainly been unusually savage: "puerile nonsense" and "unmitigated twaddle" were two of the phrases Sykes had used.

> When I rang Dr. Sykes [the paper's diarist had written] he agreed that the review was "a little harsh," but insisted the whole affair was nothing more than "a storm in a port glass." When I got through to Dr. Puddephat, on the other hand, his language was refreshingly unacademic, and cannot, I regret, be repeated in a family newspaper. The ivory towers of Oxford look set to shake to the sounds of battle for some time to come.

The missing don certainly seemed to inspire strong passions, Loretta reflected. She turned to the next sheet of cuttings, and began to read an article from the *Sun*. Loretta would have guessed its origin even if the paper's name had not been stamped on the cutting. "Warning For Death-case Egghead," said the headline mysteriously.

Oxford don Hugh Puddephat has been given an official warning by college bigwigs—go easy with the girls [Loretta read].

The warning occurred after Puddephat's name came up at the inquest into the death of an attractive flame-haired student, Melanie Gandell.

Puddephat, 37, has been told to watch his step after the girl, a 19-year-old first-year student at the college where he teaches, committed suicide. She mentioned the dashing don in a note found in the room where she took an overdose of pain-killers.

A tight-lipped college spokesman yesterday denied there was evidence of an improper relationship between the two. But he admitted that the college's boss, Professor James Lorimer, had spoken to Puddephat "to reiterate the need for constant vigilance on the part of teaching staff when dealing with impressionable adolescents."

Puddephat, who is separated from his glamorous blonde wife Veronica, was not available for comment yesterday. Reporters were turned away from the college, where he has lived since the break-up of his marriage, by the porter, Mr. Des Koogan, a former army boxing champion.

Loretta's interest was caught. She turned to the next cutting in the hope of finding a less lurid account of the case. The article was not a news report, however, but one of those background features that appear on the women's pages of quality newspapers after some well-publicized court case. It bore the name of a celebrated woman journalist and was headlined "A Don's Dilemma." On further examination, it turned out to be a sympathetic discussion of the pitfalls facing university teachers when their students become too

49

attached to them. Puddephat and Melanie Gandell were mentioned in the first paragraph, but did not appear in the rest of the piece. It was composed, in fact, of quotes from lecturers identified only by their first names, who recalled difficult situations they had—quite innocently—got into. And what about female teachers? Loretta thought indignantly, noting that all the interviewees were male. Doesn't it happen to us?

She passed on to the next sheet. It turned out to be a cutting from the *Guardian*, and contained much that she wanted to know. The inquest had taken place three years ago in Oxford, which explained why Loretta didn't remember the case: she had been in the middle of a six-week working holiday in Italy when it happened, writing a lengthy paper on women's fiction from 1900 to 1930. She had seen English newspapers only on odd occasions when friends, or her then lover, came out to visit her. The facts of the case were simple. The girl, who was reading English at Puddephat's college—one of the first women students there, in fact—had been found dead in her room just before the end of the summer term. The suicide note was mentioned, but not quoted; Loretta wondered if it had not been read out at the inquest. It did not seem likely that the *Sun*, at any rate, would have felt any qualms about printing it in full. Puddephat had given evidence, saying Melanie Gandell had been one of his brightest students, and he had gone out of his way to encourage her academically as a result. He blamed himself for crediting her with a maturity she did not possess, and regretted that his attempts to assist her studies had been so tragically misinterpreted by her. He had never thought of trying to foster an attachment which he would have considered quite improper. The coroner passed a few remarks in his summing-up on the heavy responsibility shouldered by those placed *in loco parentis*, but accepted that the girl's affections had been aroused unintentionally. The verdict, inevitably, was one of suicide.

The *Herald* file on Hugh Puddephat contained only two

more cuttings, both considerably older than those connected with the inquest. The first, Loretta was surprised to find, was from a society magazine. How diligent the library staff were, she marvelled. It was a picture, rather than a story, and showed two people at a race-course. "Dr. and Mrs. Hugh Puddephat share a joke between the showers at Ascot," the caption stated. Although the man was smiling, he looked ill at ease in morning dress, while the woman's face was all but invisible under a large hat.

The final story had been cut from a newspaper gossip column in 1973. "An English Romance For Peer's Daughter," Loretta read. The headline was, it transpired, a ponderous attempt at humour. The gist of the story was that the Hon. Veronica Grahame, second daughter of Lord Stonybrook, had met and fallen in love with Puddephat while attending his lectures on Lawrence at Oxford. Love had blossomed, the journalist had written without much originality, among the dreaming spires. So he made a habit of it, Loretta thought to herself. The knowledge that Puddephat had married one of his own students in the first place certainly threw a new light on his protestations of innocence at the inquest into the dead student. Could this womanizing be the reason why his marriage had not lasted? Loretta pulled herself up sharp. Two episodes in, what was it, nine years, hardly amounted to womanizing. Her brief encounter with the *Sun* had evidently had a bad influence on her. And, in spite of the fact that she now knew a great deal more about the missing man, she still had no answer to the essential question: had she been examining the life of a victim of violent crime, or that of a murderer?

Checking that the cuttings were still in order, Loretta got up. The one thing she hadn't done was look up Puddephat in *Who's Who*. She left the pile on the desk where she had found it, and made her way to where Bill was sitting. He had put away the *Morning Star*, and was contentedly butchering a copy of that morning's *Guardian* with a pair of scissors.

"See your mate's in trouble again," he said, gesturing to the story which had sparked off her investigation. "Funny bugger, if you ask me. They ain't like other people, though, these dons. A day's work wouldn't do none of 'em any 'arm." Reflecting that the librarian's opinion of academics was about as low as hers of journalists, Loretta asked politely for the current *Who's Who*. "Nicked," said Bill succinctly. "Last year's do yer?" Loretta said it would. Bill ambled off, momentarily disappearing from view, and returned with a heavy volume in a red jacket. "There y'are," he said, opening the page at Puddephat's entry. "That's what yer wanted, innit?" Taken aback by his affability, Loretta nodded her agreement. Bill put down the book, and went back to his scissors.

Loretta peered at the bare facts of Puddephat's life. William Hugh Puddephat was born in 1945 in London, and attended a direct grant school. He was awarded his first degree by the college where he was now a fellow, spent a year in the United States, and came back to the same college to complete his PhD. His marriage, she noted, had been childless. The only detail that gave any clue to his character, his description of his hobbies as "the pleasures of Lawrence's prose and vintage port," did little to endear him to her. It also, she noted in passing, gave an added edge to Theodore Sykes's gibe about "a storm in a port glass." Puddephat's pompous *Who's Who* entry had not gone unnoticed among his enemies. If she could think of a good reason to ask questions about the missing don among his colleagues, she might well come up with some interesting answers.

With this thought in mind, Loretta set off for Paddington. She arrived with twenty minutes to spare before her train was due to leave but, after she had queued for a ticket, was only just in time to catch it. She had to walk nearly its full length before finding a seat in a non-smoking carriage. It was only when she sat down that she realized why there were several spaces: her section of the carriage contained a group of unruly Italian teenagers who were obviously well beyond the control of the two middle-aged nuns accompanying them. She sighed, but decided that unless she wanted to stand all the way to Oxford, she had no other choice. Unzipping her overnight bag, she took out a copy of one of Puddephat's books. By a stroke of luck, she had spotted it on a colleague's bookshelf before lunch. "Take it," the woman had replied when Loretta asked if she could borrow it. "I can't make head or tail of it." Stowing her bag by her feet, Loretta settled down for an hour's read.

Hugh Puddephat, she discovered, had certainly moved with the times. The book was stuffed with interminable quotations from obscure American academics who seemed to be in the vanguard of the deconstruction movement. Unlike the names of the French theorists who had laid the groundwork for structuralism—Barthes, Foucault, Derrida, for instance—most of these names were unknown to her. In spite of Puddephat's enthusiasm for them, she was not inspired to find out more about them. The very name of the movement offended her. She imagined the English departments of various American universities converted into huge breakers' yards in which was being dismantled the edifice of world literature . . .

Crunch . . . "There goes Milton," cried an associate professor, wispy hair covered by a hard hat, in the recesses of her imagination.

"I hear the bulldozers are moving in on George Eliot Thursday," mouthed one of his colleagues in a satisfied Southern drawl.

She was roused from this disturbing fantasy by the arrival on the table in front of her of an Italian youth who was trying to escape the clutches of two boisterous female companions. Loretta put down her book, grasped him by the shoulders, and heaved him back into the arms of his tormentors. She peered round for the nuns, but they were nowhere to be seen. Loretta guessed they had sought refuge in the buffet car. The struggling teenagers, cheered on by their friends, were lurching in her direction again. She stood up, clapping her hands to gain their attention. Several surprised faces looked blankly at her, including those of the chief trouble-makers. Loretta pointed in a deliberate fashion at the teenage boy in the excited trio.

"*Cazzo!*" she said scornfully. This unexpected obscenity drew gasps of astonishment from the teenagers, and Loretta pressed home her advantage by threatening dire penalties in colloquial Italian if a single one of them misbehaved during the remainder of the journey. Chastened, they settled back in their seats and talked in hushed voices until the train pulled into Reading, where they all got off.

Loretta was a third of the way through Puddephat's book when she arrived in Oxford. She took a bus into the shopping centre, stopped to buy Bridget some flowers, and got another bus to Woodstock Road. Although Bridget was a fellow of a very respectable college, she had sensibly chosen to live in a 1930s semi within easy reach of the centre of town rather than in college rooms. Loretta had stayed there before, although it was more usual for her to see Bridget when the latter made one of her frequent visits to London. The bus stopped only yards from Bridget's house and, as she alighted, Loretta saw her friend's 2CV turning into the drive. Bridget had only just beaten her to it. As Loretta drew abreast of the house, Bridget was locking the car door.

"Loretta!" she exclaimed. "I was afraid you'd be waiting on the doorstep. I'm sorry I'm so late."

"Not at all," said Loretta, leaning forward to kiss her cheek. "You couldn't have timed it better."

Bridget opened the front door and led the way into the hall. "Put your things in here for the time being," she said, pushing open the door to the living-room. "Oh God, I'd forgotten about the mess," she added, taking in the empty coffee mugs and sheets of paper strewn around the room.

"We've just started a support group for women in the English faculty, and we had a meeting here last night. Never mind, it'll have to wait. Come into the kitchen." Loretta dumped her overnight case on the floor and shut the door. In the kitchen, she found Bridget on her knees rummaging in the fridge.

"Nothing much in here," she said. "What on earth's this? Yuk, that should have gone out ages ago." She leaned across and dropped a paper bag into the kitchen bin. "I meant to get some food on my way home, but I got held up at college," she explained, examining various other articles in the fridge with distaste. She looked at her watch. "I tell you what, why don't we have supper at Brown's?" she suggested, rising to her feet.

"Sounds fine," Loretta said uneasily. Now that she was face to face with Bridget, her mind was fully engaged in a debate as to how much she should tell her friend about events in Paris. With Tracey apparently intent on limiting his own involvement, she longed to talk things over with someone who might offer more active help; at the same time, she felt an almost superstitious reluctance to go through the story again in the kind of detail a confidante would need. As a consequence, the question of where to eat was one that made little impression on her.

"That's settled then," said Bridget. "I'm sorry to rush you out, but we ought to leave straight away if we're going to get a table. It gets very crowded in the evenings."

Brown's was already more than half full, but Bridget and Loretta were able to find a table in a relatively uncrowded corner where an old-fashioned ceiling fan was doing an effective job in keeping stuffiness at bay.

"I can recommend the salads," said Bridget, studying the menu. Loretta took her friend's advice and then listened in surprise as, in spite of the hot weather, Bridget ordered a casserole. "I didn't have any lunch," she explained, registering Loretta's surprised expression. "And the temperature doesn't seem to have any effect on my appetite." It was a mystery to Loretta that Bridget remained so slim. Since her own thirtieth birthday, she had noticed an unwelcome tendency to put on inches if she didn't keep an eye on what she ate. Bridget seemed untouched by such problems. The waiter arrived with the red wine they had ordered, and Loretta took a decision. She was about to plunge into her story when Bridget spoke first.

"Before you tell me what you're doing in Oxford, I must tell you my news," she said. "Have I ever mentioned a man called Hugh Puddephat to you?" Loretta stared at her, amazed. "You've probably come across his work," Bridget went on, "though I'm sure you'd think it was pretentious rubbish. Anyway, he's disappeared off the face of the earth. And I seem to be the last person to have seen him." Catching sight of herself in a wall mirror, Loretta closed her mouth and waited for Bridget to go on. It had not occurred to her that her friend might be personally involved in the business. "That's why I was late," Bridget continued. "Two policemen simply turned up at my rooms as I was leaving, without any appointment or anything, and insisted on interviewing me. It was absolutely infuriating. They made me go through the whole thing three times, though I had hardly anything to tell them. And they kept calling me 'love.' Even when they left, that didn't seem to be the end of it. They said I might have to go down to the police station and be interviewed there later in their inquiries. They behaved as if I'd got something to do with the wretched man's disappearance. You know why, don't you?" she added suddenly. Loretta looked blank. She was still trying to take in the fact that Bridget might be a witness. "That time at Greenham," Bridget went on. "I told you about it. I sat in the road during a demonstration and got hauled off to the police station in Newbury. They didn't charge me, but I'm on police files. It's the same force, you know."

It sounded plausible. Loretta's occasional visits to the

Cruise missile base had never involved her in getting arrested, but she was well aware that some police took a dim view of peace protesters. "But what did you tell them?" she asked, recalling herself to the matter in hand.

"Nothing spectacular," Bridget said. "Just that I saw him on a train to London a couple of weeks ago. On the Thursday to be exact. That's why they were so interested. Apparently their last previous sighting was at his college the night before. Anyway, I'd already found a seat when he jumped on as the train was about to leave. He didn't look too pleased to see me, but then he knows what I think of his work. There weren't many people sitting near us, so I tried to make polite conversation, but he wasn't having any. He had a bag with him, a small suitcase really, so I asked if he was off on a late holiday. He seemed taken aback, and muttered something about having business in Germany. Which is odd, because he was expected in Italy on Monday, apparently."

The point had already occurred to Loretta, who was doing some rapid calculations. Where on earth did Germany fit into it? Bridget had seen the missing man on a Thursday. If Puddephat had been at the flat in Paris on Friday evening, he could hardly have squeezed a trip to Germany in between. Or was Germany, rather than Italy, his real destination after whatever was due to happen in Paris? She supposed it was equally possible that, for reasons known only to himself, Puddephat had been lying to Bridget. Regretfully, she acknowledged that his behaviour on the train threw no light at all on what had happened at the flat. If anything, it made matters worse. She realized that Bridget was eyeing her curiously, and swallowed a mouthful of wine. "I had no idea you'd turn out to be mixed up in all this," she blurted out, "I don't know what to do." She paused, and then rushed on. "That's why I came to Oxford, you see—about Puddephat's disappearance."

At that moment, an extremely thin waiter arrived bearing their food. While he was putting down the plates, Loretta made up her mind. It was as well she had ordered something that wouldn't go cold. "Start eating," she told Bridget, "and I'll try to explain."

Halfway through Loretta's description of her weekend in Paris, Bridget lost interest in her food. When Loretta finished, Bridget put her hand sympathetically on her friend's arm and said: "How terrible for you. And you think . . . ?"

"I don't know what to think," interrupted Loretta. "I've no real proof that Puddephat was at the flat, and I'm only guessing at what went on there. I should have gone to the French police at the time, but I didn't, and now the evidence has gone. If Andrew's telling the truth, that is. I'm beginning to suspect everybody."

"I think you're right to be wary of Andrew," Bridget said thoughtfully. "It doesn't sound as though he's involved in it, but it's as well to be careful. And I can see the problem about going to the police. I wonder if there's any way we can find out more without drawing attention to ourselves?"

Loretta was grateful for Bridget's assumption that she would have a part in whatever action they decided upon; she was a more reliable friend than Tracey, she thought to herself. "How much do you know about Puddephat?" she asked eagerly. "I've read all the cuttings on him in the *Herald* library but I haven't yet got much sense of what he's like."

"Not very nice," Bridget said briefly. "An odd character, really. Very arrogant academically, and one of the people most opposed to the women's support group in the English faculty."

"Wasn't he involved in some sort of scandal a few years ago?" Loretta prompted. "Something to do with a girl who killed herself?" She was keen to hear Bridget's version of the story.

"That's right," her friend replied. "A nasty business,

and the real story never came out. The poor girl was absolutely infatuated with him, not knowing that his tastes lie in quite a different direction. He's rumoured to be gay," she added, seeing Loretta's surprised expression. "Funnily enough, that's why the whole episode did him less harm than it might have done. When he split up with his wife, a while before, she spread some damaging stories about him, and I think the college was secretly quite relieved to have some evidence that he was het after all. Not that he's the only gay don at Oxford, far from it, but in his case the rumours were about boys. That sort of thing worries the college authorities no end, as you can imagine. But the inquest put a stop to all that. There was no evidence of actual impropriety, you see, but Puddephat admitted he'd been friendly with the girl and given her extra coaching. He came out of it as someone who might have committed a slight indiscretion, no more, and a heterosexual one at that. They were so relieved at the college that they let him keep his job."

"How does he get on with the other fellows?" Loretta asked, rapidly adjusting her idea that the business of the girl's suicide had damaged Puddephat's career.

"He's very thick with the new master, Humphrey Morris, which counts for quite a lot," Bridget said thoughtfully. "And that's odd, too. He got into the most terrible row with one of the other fellows during the election for master a couple of years ago. He and this other chap, a rather nice English fellow called Theo Sykes, each had their own candidate for the job when the previous master, Lorimer, retired. They both did a lot of lobbying, which you're not supposed to do, but the college turns a blind eye to it. There are ways and means, you see—discreet supper parties and so on. And Sykes's man won, Morris, that is. Puddephat was incandescent with rage, apparently. But the strange thing is that, since then, Sykes and Morris have fallen out. No one seems to know why. In fact, Sykes's fellowship comes up for renewal at

Christmas, and the word is he won't get it. He claims Pud-dephat is behind it."

Loretta's head reeled. The picture that was emerging was quite different from the one she had gleaned from the cuttings. It confirmed her view of the fallibility of newspaper reports. "I seem to have got entirely the wrong end of the stick this afternoon," she said sadly. "Perhaps I should start again from scratch. I had a vague idea of trying to talk to people who knew Puddephat, but I don't know how to go about it."

"That's one thing I can help with," Bridget said triumphantly. "You should talk to a friend of mine who's a history don at the same college as Puddephat. All you need is a cover story—confiding in Geoffrey is like taking an advert in the *Oxford Mail*." Loretta laughed, and both women were silent for a moment.

"How about this?" Loretta said at last. "Suppose I say I sent Puddephat something—an outline for a book, or some notes for it—and now I'm worried about getting them back. Yes, that's it. I'm going to write a book on, um, the influence of structuralism on feminist literary criticism, and I'd asked his advice." It was brilliant, she congratulated herself. On hearing of the don's disappearance, she'd naturally rushed up to Oxford in the hope of tracking down her precious notes.

"Why didn't you keep copies?" Bridget objected.

Loretta considered. "It's the long vacation, and the photocopier had broken down," she said. "All right, I know it's weak. Perhaps no one will ask. After all, we're trying to pick holes in it. Other people may accept it at face value. People often do silly things."

"You may be right," Bridget conceded. "Just be prepared for the odd lecture on what a foolish girl you've been. Can you spend some time in Oxford tomorrow? I'll ring Geoffrey first thing to see if he's free for a chat."

The next day was Tuesday, Loretta thought, and the autumn term didn't start until Friday. She could just about manage a day away from London. "That's marvellous," she said sincerely. "And thanks."

"It's nothing," said Bridget airily. "I saw you through your first marriage, so the least I can do is see you through your first murder investigation."

Loretta winced. Once they had got over the first shock, neither Bridget nor Tracey seemed able to take her story entirely seriously. But then they hadn't seen the blood, she reminded herself.

"You'd better eat your salad," Bridget pointed out. "You haven't touched it yet."

An hour later, having paid the bill, the two women got up to go. At that very moment, a waiter turned abruptly from clearing the next table and crashed into Loretta. As the red wine from a half-empty glass dribbled down her yellow dress, Loretta reflected that bad luck is supposed to come in threes. Eating out should now be safe for some time to come.

4

THE FOLLOWING DAY'S PAPERS CONTAINED surprisingly little about Puddephat's disappearance. Studying *The Times* in Bridget's kitchen, Loretta found only two paragraphs about the affair. The master of the college, Professor Morris, had issued a tetchy statement to the effect that, while it had been considered advisable to seek police assistance, there was at present no cause for alarm. A police spokesman had been equally unforthcoming: inquiries were continuing, he said, and several leads were being followed up. The *Guardian* carried much the same information. "Nothing new here," sighed Loretta.

Bridget, in the middle of making fresh coffee for herself and Earl Grey tea for Loretta, was unperturbed. "Give it time," she said, making space on the table for two large white breakfast cups and saucers.

"I still feel we could do with another clue," Loretta persisted. "Even a small one."

Bridget laughed. "What have you got in mind?" she asked. "An anonymous note revealing the whereabouts of the body, postmarked from a small town in Germany? A bloodstained dagger, buried to its hilt in the door of Puddephat's rooms? I doubt if life is like that. Now, just give me five minutes to drink some coffee and I'll ring Geoffrey."

Loretta was rinsing the cups when Bridget came back

from the phone. "It's all fixed," she said gleefully. "I told him your cover story and he swallowed it quite happily. He even asked if you'd like to stay for lunch. The place is buzzing with gossip, so it's an ideal opportunity. He said to come to his rooms just after twelve."

"I hope I can carry it off," Loretta said anxiously. Turning up at Puddephat's college to make her own inquiries was a much more daunting prospect than her leisurely visit to the *Herald* library. "My story really is a bit thin."

Bridget sighed impatiently. "As you said yourself last night, people often do silly things. And the only person who can disprove it is Puddephat himself. If you're right about him being involved in nefarious activities in Paris, he's not likely to turn up and expose you. Anyway, most of what I told Geoffrey is true—that you and I are old friends, and that you lecture in London. Don't worry, I'm sure it'll be all right." She opened her briefcase, and started looking through the papers in it. "Hang on a minute," she said suddenly. "We haven't considered suicide. Perhaps the answer is that Puddephat killed himself at the flat?"

"Why bother going all the way to Paris to do it?" Loretta pointed out. "And you're not suggesting he managed to remove his own body from the bedroom."

"Silly me," said Bridget sheepishly. "I'm getting carried away."

Loretta was very nearly convinced by Bridget's confidence in her. All the same, she could feel butterflies in her stomach when she arrived at the imposing entrance to Puddephat's college at twelve. She soothed herself with the thought that the small deception she was about to practise was not the only reason for her attack of nerves: her own college in London, housed in a nondescript modern block, had nothing at all in common with the medieval gateway in front of her. Although the college had been admitting female students in recent years, its outward appearance still succeeded in impressing the visitor with its austere and indefinably masculine grandeur. The college coat of arms, consisting of two unlikely beasts locked in grim combat for possession of a narrow scroll, reposed at the centre of a stone arch surmounting heavy wooden doors. It was intended, she supposed, to represent the struggle between good and evil over knowledge; she was heartened to observe that the effect was, in fact, faintly comic.

The college doors were firmly closed, affording entry only through a smaller aperture, barely the size of a human being, cut into one of them. Lowering her head, Loretta stepped through the narrow gap, and found herself looking from the shadow of the gateway across a carefully tended lawn to the far side of the college. Tall windows stared bleakly down at her from what she guessed to be the great hall.

Before she could take in any more of the scene, a short, red-faced man bustled out from an office to her left and planted himself squarely in front of her. "Yes, miss?" he demanded pugnaciously, reminding her of a sentry at a besieged garrison. "What were you wanting?" His grey moustache bristled; he was so close that Loretta could make out the individual hairs. A bell rang in her mind, and she almost laughed aloud.

"Mr. Koogan?" she began, remembering the "former army boxing champion" who had shooed away the *Sun* reporter during one of Puddephat's previous sallies into the public print. "I have an appointment with Dr. Simmons. Could you direct me to his rooms?" she asked. Firmness, she thought, was the only way to deal with the officious little man.

Koogan was not impressed. "I'll just check with Dr. Simmons," he said. "Master's orders. You might be from the newspapers, for all I know. What name is it?"

Loretta hoped Mr. Koogan's experience of journalists was not limited to representatives of the *Sun*. She was not too pleased at the thought of being mistaken for a reporter from the tabloid press. "It's Ms. Lawson," she said, with careful emphasis on the Ms. Loretta was perfectly entitled to call herself Dr. Lawson and usually did so. But she wanted to impress upon the porter the existence of an appropriate form of address that did not reveal a woman's marital status. She was wasting her time.

"*Miss* Lawson," the man repeated. "Just wait there a moment." He disappeared into his cabin and, with the air of someone with all the time in the world, set about checking Loretta's bona fides.

It was just as well she had arrived early, she thought. The college had been one of the last to open its doors to women students, and she could see why.

It was a good three minutes before Koogan reappeared. "Dr. Simmons has confirmed your appointment, miss." His voice was tinged with regret. "Second floor, Erasmus wing." He turned his back on her and retired to his cabin. Loretta was about to knock on the window and ask for further directions, when she shrugged and gave up. Geoffrey's rooms couldn't be that difficult to find.

Turning to the right as though she knew where she was going, she approached the wing of the building which made up the right-hand side of the square. A door was set in the wall half-way down and, as she got closer to it, she spotted a brass plate bearing the single word "Erasmus." Pushing open the heavy door, she began to climb the stairs to the second floor, admiring the way in which the stained-glass windows on each half-landing cast triangles of coloured light on to the worn stone steps.

Simmons's rooms were next to the staircase, not, as she had hoped, overlooking the quadrangle, but facing away from the main college building. Her knock was answered by a loud "Come in!" and the door flew open. Geoffrey Simmons stood in the doorway. Small, dark, dressed in baggy corduroy trousers and check shirt, cigarette in hand, he was not at all what Loretta had expected. Apart from anything else, he looked to be only just in his twenties.

"Loretta!" he exclaimed, greeting her as if she were a friend of many years' standing. "Come in! Take a seat! Well, you must be feeling sick!" Loretta sank into an armchair with one of its arms missing, and tried to make sense of this reception. Sick? Why should she feel sick? "God, I bet you wish you'd kept copies of your notes," he rushed on. "You must be feeling a right berk."

Light dawned on Loretta, and she launched herself into her part. "Absolutely," she said with feeling, dispelling a pang of guilt with the observation that she was certainly not presenting herself in a flattering light. "I feel a complete idiot. But, then, you live and learn." She hesitated. Perhaps her last remark was a bit sententious?

Simmons hadn't noticed. "Sherry?" he asked abruptly. He was already taking glasses and a bottle from a cupboard. "Awful stuff, this, I hardly ever drink it." Without waiting for a reply, he handed a generous glassful to Loretta. Tasting it, she discovered it was actually quite pleasant. "Why on earth did you want old Puddephat's opinion in the first place?" he asked. "Quite frankly, I wouldn't even ask his advice on how to build a hamster cage. Since he got obsessed with this American nonsense—what d'you call it, demolition?—he's gone right off his head. Never uses a word of less than five syllables. He only survives here because old Humphrey's keen on him. That's the master, by the way, Humphrey Morris. He's an engineer, doesn't know the first thing about literature, but Puddephat makes it all sound scientific by using these very long words. A lot of the arts fellows think Humphrey's a bit of a twit and tend to talk down to him. But Puddephat goes on about hermeneutics and ontology, and the master pretends he understands. Nauseating sight. Mind you, if Puddephat has sunk beneath the waves after a heavy lunch in some little trattoria, we won't have to put up with it any more. Look on the bright side, that's what I say."

"What d'you think has happened to him?" Loretta asked, keen to keep Geoffrey's mind off his original question of why she had sought Puddephat's advice. "God knows," Simmons replied cheerfully. "Something pretty serious. Term starts next week. You can get away with a lot of things at Oxford, but disappearing off the face of the earth just before term starts is not one of them. " 'Course, if it's foul play we're talking about, Theo Sykes would be my chief suspect. He thought he'd got a job for life when he got his old mate Humphrey in as master—they were at school together, you know—but all that's backfired pretty badly. I don't know what they fell out over, but it must have been serious. There's been a distinct *froideur* between them for months. And Hugh saw his chance. He's very well connected, Hugh—brother-in-law's a Tory MP and all that. He got Humphrey on to some Royal Commission on the training of engineers, or something of the sort. Anyway, Theo's fellowship is up for renewal any day now, and he ain't going to get it. If I was the chief rozzer on this case, I'd have some questions to put to Theo, I can tell you!" Simmons paused, and Loretta took her chance.

"Is Theo...Dr. Sykes...here at the moment?" she asked. It was still possible, as far as she knew, that Sykes was Puddephat's victim and not the other way round.

"Saw him at breakfast," Simmons said helpfully. "But the main question is, how can I help you get back your notes?"

"I thought he might have left them with somebody else at the college," Loretta suggested weakly. "To get another opinion on them, I mean." Her heart sank as she realized what she had laid herself open to. Would Geoffrey insist on taking her on a tour of every English don in the college? But she was in luck.

"Not a chance," Simmons said. "He wouldn't think anybody else's opinion worth having."

"Oh, dear," said Loretta, trying to sound contrite in spite of her secret relief. "It looks as if I've wasted your time."

"Not at all," protested Geoffrey. "I always enjoy having

guests at lunch. The food's pretty dismal, by the way. I only eat here 'cause it's free. One of the perks of being a fellow. How long have you known Bridget?"

Loretta was beginning to get used to Simmons's abrupt changes of subject. "A long time," she replied. "About six years, I should say. Maybe seven. She was doing her PhD. in London when I met her. In fact it was a rather odd coincidence," she said, warming to her theme, "I was introduced to her at a party, and we got on quite well. Then I saw an advert for a new consciousness-raising group in *Spare Rib*, and went along to the first meeting. Bridget was already there when I arrived. So we were in the same group together for a couple of years."

Simmons looked aghast. "Bloody hell," he said, "Women's groups scare me stiff. Not that I'm against them. Not in principle. But if any girlfriend of mine joined one, I'd have a fit. I suppose you talk about men's willies and all that sort of thing? No, don't tell me. Gives me the shivers. Let's go to lunch."

Loretta couldn't help smiling. At least Simmons was frank. Tracey had at first pretended not to mind her joining the group; it was only later that his real bitterness about it emerged.

Simmons was struggling into a black gown. "Sorry about this," he said. "Rules. They insist on us wearing them to every meal except breakfast. Bloody nuisance." He leaned across his desk and switched on an answering-machine. Catching Loretta's eye, he looked abashed. "It's just for social things, really," he said. She laughed, dispelling a fantasy in which other historians were leaving urgent messages on the machine about the foreign policy of Pitt the Younger, and, still smiling, followed Geoffrey out of the room.

Lunch was served in the great hall whose exterior Loretta had observed from the gate. Her impression of a bleak, high-ceilinged room was confirmed when she entered: the

68

hall took up the top two storeys of the three-storey building. At the far end of the room, marooned on a dais in splendid isolation, sat those fellows of the college who were in for lunch that day. Their black gowns flowed to the floor where they were frequently trampled underfoot by passing waiters. Loretta noticed that, today at least, there were no women at the table. As they approached the dais, she became aware that an animated discussion was taking place among a group of half a dozen dons at one end of the long table. Her heart quickened—perhaps they were discussing Puddephat's mysterious disappearance? Simmons signalled her to an empty chair on the fringe of the disputatious group, and walked round the back of the table to take a chair opposite. Leaning across to the fellows closest to him, he attracted their attention long enough to introduce Loretta. Several heads nodded in her direction, then returned to the matter in hand. A man with unfashionably long hair—it had probably been that way since his own undergraduate days, Loretta guessed—was stabbing the air with his fork. "No, no, *no*, Griffith," he insisted. "I can't let you get away with that. Statistics, man, you're ignoring the statistics!" Loretta began to wonder if she had been mistaken. It didn't sound as if they were discussing Hugh Puddephat. But, then, why was the conversation so heated?

"Come along, Daly," replied a languid, fair-haired don further down the table. "Griffith's right. It's only because you're a Yorkshireman yourself that you're taking that position. Boycott probably wouldn't get into the team, never mind open the batting. The choice is between Grace, Fry and Jack Hobbs. Boycott simply isn't England material, old man."

"Aren't you forgetting Ranji?" piped up an elderly voice from the very end of the table. "Sixty-two—and 154 not out in his first test against Australia in 1896."

Loretta was disgusted. They were arguing about cricket. One of their colleagues had vanished in mysterious circumstances and all they could do was make up imaginary England cricket teams. She leaned forward to address Simmons, intending to remind him of the reason for her visit to the college, but he began to speak.

"Ranji wasn't an opener," he said scornfully. "And I have to say I'm with Griffith on this Boycott business. Now, what about Botham?"

Appearances were deceptive, Loretta concluded sadly: in spite of his youth and casual dress, Geoffrey Simmons was still very much one of the fellows. She turned her attention to the bowl of soup which had just been placed in front of her. It was tomato, and definitely out of a packet. She could tell from the small lumps of matter floating on its vermilion surface. She stirred it with her spoon without much enthusiasm.

Simmons suddenly recollected his duties as host, and broke off in the middle of a discussion about whether Botham's personality was right for the England team. "What's the latest on old Puddephat?" he asked the man sitting to his left, away from the sporting dons.

"The master's furious," the man replied with obvious pleasure. "Local paper sent a man round this morning even though Humphrey said he wouldn't see him. Got into the secretary's office, and refused to leave. Humphrey threatened him with the police. He's in a right old stew. Says there'll be television cameras next." The thought did not seem to disturb him unduly.

Another don joined in. "I hear the English faculty has been on to Humphrey already," he volunteered. "They're in a flap over who's going to take Hugh's lectures if he doesn't show up. Prof. Wylie told Humphrey he'd have to renew Theo's fellowship—can't lose two senior lecturers at once, you know—and Humphrey just about blew a gasket. That's why Humphrey's not at lunch. He's sulking in his rooms."

So Theo Sykes was already on the verge of benefiting from Puddephat's disappearance, Loretta thought excitedly.

She drew a red circle round his name on her mental list. But surely Sykes couldn't have predicted this outcome? she objected silently. Not if he arranged it at the most awkward time of the year? a little voice rejoined. The coincidence was certainly suggestive. She wondered what excuse she might use as a pretext for calling on Sykes.

"You're a friend of Dr. Puddephat?" she heard someone ask.

"I was just explaining to Michael here about your notes," Simmons interjected, to her relief. Lost in her own thoughts, she had missed the beginning of the conversation.

"Not a friend," she said hastily. "I've never met him. It's just that I'm planning to write a book which is rather in his field, and I wanted his advice. Unfortunately, I wrote to him in rather a hurry, and didn't take copies of the notes I sent him. The photocopier had broken down, you see," she added, remembering her discussion with Bridget the night before.

"They always do," said the man to her right, nodding in sympathy.

It was going rather well, she thought. "But it can't be helped," she added brightly. She'd already found out much more about Puddephat than she'd hoped—she'd even got a promising suspect in the shape of Theo Sykes—and there was no point in banging on about her non-existent book outline.

But the don sitting next to her was determined to help. "Have you tried Koogan?" he asked Simmons. "He's got keys to everyone's rooms. You might be lucky," he said, turning to Loretta. "Your notes might be sitting on top of Hugh's desk."

"Oh, I don't want to put Dr. Simmons to any more trouble," Loretta began, anxious to avoid taking the deception any further. But the matter was out of her hands.

"Idiot," cried Simmons, striking his forehead with the palm of his hand. "Why didn't I think of that? Tell you

71

what, Loretta, we'll go and see him as soon as lunch is over. No, I won't listen to any objections. It really isn't any trouble."

"Doubt if you'll get much change out of Koogan," the don called Michael observed, and Loretta brightened up. It didn't seem likely that the porter would turn out to be co-operative.

"But it's worth a try," Geoffrey insisted. "After all, what's Loretta going to do if she can't get her notes back?"

"Happened to me once," said the man sitting next to her, the one who had been so understanding about the malfunctioning photocopier. "Not just notes, either. I asked my cleaner to post four chapters of my book on Roman agriculture and she left the envelope on a bus. Mind you, she had the decency to come and confess, and I got it back from the bus company. But I had a very nasty moment when she first told me." This cautionary tale produced a moment's silence, as all those present contemplated the awful prospect of having to rewrite a large chunk of a book from memory. Loretta's mind went off at a tangent. Would there really be any harm in having a look around Puddephat's rooms? She might find another clue, even if it wasn't the bloodstained dagger Bridget thought she was hoping for. Something, for instance to connect Puddephat more definitely with the rue Roland flat. By the time the main course arrived—an unappetizing leg of chicken in breadcrumbs accompanied by boiled sprouts—Loretta had done a complete U-turn and was fervently hoping that Koogan would consent to lend them a key.

As soon as lunch was over, Simmons led Loretta out into the quadrangle. Immediately, they heard raised voices and saw that the porter was engaged in an altercation with two men in trench coats. It looked as though the men had got no further than Loretta before encountering the college's human watchdog. As she drew closer, she heard Koogan shout: "You 'eard what I said. Out! Out! The master won't

72

see you, and that's final. I've got my instructions, and none of you newspaper people are getting into this college while I'm here to stop you. We don't want none of you bloody vultures 'ere. Out!" He moved a step nearing the smaller of the two men, who happened to have two cameras slung around his neck. "If you don't get off these premises forthwith," he added menacingly, eyeing the Japanese hardware, "I'll smash your effing cameras for you."

The men exchanged glances and, apparently concluding that Koogan meant every word he said, stepped back into the street. The porter planted himself firmly in the aperture, presumably in case they changed their minds. Loretta turned to Simmons, feeling it was not an auspicious moment to trouble the porter with a sensitive request. But before she could restrain him, Simmons had reached the gateway.

"Mr. Koogan," he began blithely, only faltering when the man turned and bestowed a look of simmering fury upon them. It was at this point, Simmons said later, that he realized their request was bound to fail. But he plunged on: "This is Dr. Lawson," he said, gesturing towards Loretta. "She came to pick up some papers she sent to Dr. Puddephat, and she needs them at once. Could you just let us into his rooms so she can get them? They are very important," he added plaintively. It was no use.

"You must be bloody joking!" snapped the porter. With that, he turned on his heel and strode into his cabin, slamming the door behind him.

Simmons turned to Loretta and shrugged his shoulders. "Well, I made a right balls of that," he admitted frankly.

"Don't worry," Loretta assured him, disappointed though she was. "It was very kind of you to try. I was afraid he was going to hit you."

"Oh, he wouldn't do that," Simmons said dismissively. "Hitting a fellow counts as damaging college property." Loretta smiled, and put out her hand to take leave of Simmons. Instead of shaking it, however, he grabbed it and pulled her out into the street. Spotting the two journalists huddled together in conspiratorial conversation a few yards away, he hauled her off in the opposite direction. "Listen," he said releasing her hand, "I've got an idea. Puddephat's rooms are on the opposite side of the quad from mine. They're on the ground floor, and they look out on to college land. There's a garden going down to a stream. They're supposed to be a smaller version of Christ Church meadows. The windows are sash ones, dead easy to open. No one uses the garden much after dark. If you come back tonight, I'm sure we can open one of the windows and get in."

"But what if we're caught?" Loretta asked nervously.

"The master would hush it up," Simmons assured her. "The college is getting enough unwelcome publicity already, without charging one of the fellows with burglary. Anyway, we won't get caught. What d'you say?"

Loretta wavered. She had intended to return to London that afternoon, but one more night wouldn't make a great deal of difference.

Simmons saw her uncertainty, and pressed home his advantage. "Ring Bridget and ask what she thinks," he suggested. "I bet she'll tell you to go ahead. There's a phone box across the road."

All right, thought Loretta, casting caution to the winds. She'd put herself in Bridget's hands. Opening her purse to look for change, she crossed the road to the phone box. "What shall I do?" she asked, after explaining Simmons's proposal.

"I think you should do what he says," said Bridget recklessly. "In fact, I'll come with you. You never know what we might find."

"I don't like deceiving Geoffrey," Loretta said, feeling a twinge of conscience.

"That's the least of our worries," said Bridget. "He'd be even keener if he knew what we're really up to. Tell him we'll arrive at his rooms at eleven o'clock this evening.

There shouldn't be anyone in the garden by that time."

Loretta stepped from the phone box, and passed on Bridget's message.

"Good old Bridget!" exclaimed Simmons. "I knew I could count on her."

Loretta wasn't so sure. Her trip to Paris had already involved her in an unsolved crime, very possibly a murder, not to mention withholding evidence from the police. Was it really wise to risk adding burglary to the list?

5

THE TWO WOMEN WERE SLIGHTLY LATE IN arriving at Geoffrey's college that evening. There was no single incident that Loretta could pinpoint as the cause, merely a series of minor hold-ups; and Bridget had mislaid her car keys, causing them to set off a few minutes after the time they had agreed. Loretta speculated to herself that Bridget's nerve was becoming a little less steady now that her own involvement in the affair was taking on a more practical aspect. During the course of the evening, while Loretta cooked couscous for her friend, they had somehow avoided any reference to what was to happen later. Their conversation had been unusually impersonal, in fact, and largely to do with work. Loretta was aware that she had consumed rather more Rioja than she had intended, certainly enough to make her glad that Bridget was driving.

When they arrived at the college, it seemed even more forbidding than it had in daylight, and as she walked from the car towards the entrance, Loretta felt as though she were about to cross a threshold in time as well as space. She could imagine dark-robed figures moving silently along the stone corridors in place of the healthy young men and women she knew to be living inside. It was a scene straight out of *The Monk*, she told herself impatiently. She was too well acquainted with Gothic literature for her own good. Turning to Bridget, she sensed the other woman's hesitation to be as great as her own. Firmly, she pressed the bell set into the wall beside the heavy doors. The incongruous sound of an electric doorbell brought her back to the present. The small door opened a fraction and a jovial face, decidedly not that of Mr. Des Koogan, peered out.

"Yes, miss?" he greeted her cheerfully, his words wafting to her through a distinctive cloud of port.

"Loretta Lawson and Bridget Bennett for Dr. Simmons," she replied, her spirits lifted by the welcome contrast between the night porter and the irascible Koogan. The door opened to its full extent, and the two women stepped through.

Loretta drew in her breath: at night, the courtyard was eerily beautiful. Drained of its colour, the central square of grass might have been a stretch of water were it not for the absence of reflected buildings on its calm surface. The stone buildings surrounding it seemed less solid in the moonlight, as if they might at any moment shimmer and disappear. Bridget's hand in the small of her back reminded her gently that she was obstructing the entrance.

"Enchanting, isn't it?" Bridget murmured as they set off in the direction of Geoffrey's rooms. "It had the same effect on me the first time I saw it at night."

Geoffrey Simmons, Loretta quickly discovered, was quite unperturbed by the prospect of the night's adventure. When they entered his rooms, in answer to his hearty "Come in!" they found him sitting in the broken armchair, surrounded by books, his feet comfortably supported by a small wooden stool. "You here already?" he demanded. "You must be early."

"We're late, as a matter of fact," Loretta began, but Geoffrey was already in full flow.

"Bloody second-year essays," he remarked, gesturing at the pile of papers in his lap. "Supposed to have marked them weeks ago, but never got round to it. Dreadful bunch. Haven't got two original ideas to rub together between the whole lot of them. God, I hate teaching. Mind you, I expect much the same could be said about *my* second-year essays if I'm absolutely honest. I remember writing most of them with the assistance of liberal quantities of dope. Just as well I didn't keep them." Loretta marvelled at Geoffrey's composure. She wondered what it would take to make him even slightly nervous. He seemed to be expecting her to say something.

"Sorry?" she replied nervously to his unheard question. "I didn't quite catch . . ." Her words were interrupted by a triumphant shout of amusement from Geoffrey.

"I knew it! You've got cold feet! Here—have some whisky. That'll warm up the old bones."

Common sense and terror battled within her. Terror won, and she downed the proffered double Scotch in one go. At this rate, she thought, she was in danger of being found snoozing gently the next morning at the scene of the crime. Not that it *was* a crime, she told herself hastily. They would be on college property, and that was somehow different—not like breaking into a stranger's house in the outside world. She was feeling better, if a little unsteady, already. "Tools of the trade," she heard Geoffrey saying, reaching into the top drawer of his desk. He took out a thin plastic ruler. "For the window-catch," he explained patiently as Loretta and Bridget stared at him. "How were you proposing to open it?"

The two women exchanged guilty looks. They had not given the details of the break-in a moment's thought, so keen had they been to avoid the subject in the course of the evening.

"Bloody good burglars you'd make," Geoffrey said scornfully. "I just hope neither of you ever has to turn to a life of crime. I don't suppose you've brought gloves with you, either? Gloves, fingerprints . . . get it? Well, I suppose the police have been through the place already. Let's hope they've got all the prints they need by now."

Loretta frowned to herself, aware that Geoffrey was

taking great pleasure in showing off his superior knowledge. Before she could think of a suitable reply, Bridget did it for her. "Not all of us have the time to watch videos of *Minder* every weekend," she said crushingly. "I'm afraid Geoffrey has other addictions on top of his predilection for cricket," she added, turning to Loretta.

Geoffrey rolled his eyes dramatically and headed for the door. "Cheap, Bridget," he muttered over his shoulder, and strode off down the corridor, leaving Loretta and Bridget exchanging amused glances with each other. Bridget pulled the door shut and they set off after him.

He led the way across the quadrangle to the wing of the college opposite his own. Once inside, they found themselves facing a glass door, which gave on to the college garden. Geoffrey turned the Yale lock and opened it. "It's kept locked at night," he explained in a low voice. Loretta and Bridget stepped on to the grass; Geoffrey followed and shut the door behind him.

"How do we get back in?" asked Loretta, alarmed.

"We'll let ourselves into the corridor from Puddephat's rooms," Geoffrey replied. He was pretty confident about his ability to get into the rooms in the first place, Loretta noted.

He set off along the side of the building. The grass sloped gently away from the college towards what must be the bank of the stream he had mentioned earlier. Loretta could not see the water, but its course was clearly marked by the graceful trees, mostly weeping willows, through which a light breeze was whispering. For the second time that evening, Loretta felt a sense of unreality quite at odds with the purpose of her visit. It was the setting for an assignation with a lover, she thought, picturing a cloaked figure slipping across the grass for a brief and forbidden meeting. Not so much *The Monk* as Barbara Cartland. She told herself sternly that she must shake off this tendency towards romantic fantasy. It was a sure, if embarrassing, sign that she was feeling in need of a new lover. But now was not the time to worry about it.

Geoffrey had stopped outside the fourth ground-floor window from the garden door—Loretta was relieved to observe a lack of lights in the rooms adjoining it—and was already slipping his ruler into the gap between the two parts of the sash window. He turned and grinned at his companions. "Hope it's the right room," he said cheerfully.

Loretta gasped.

"Take no notice," Bridget whispered. "He knows what he's doing."

After a few seconds of manoeuvring, Geoffrey gave a small cry of triumph. "Got it!" he exclaimed. He pushed the bottom half of the window upwards and swung one leg over the sill. Bridget swiftly followed. Sweeping a nervous glance around the dark garden, Loretta joined them in Puddephat's sitting-room.

Bridget closed the window and drew the curtains together. "Best take no chances," she said. "Do you think it's safe to switch on a light?"

"Don't see why not," replied Geoffrey, moving through the gloom to a desk on which Loretta could just make out the shape of a lamp. "We can only be seen from the river, and no one's likely to be down there at this time of night." The low light of the lamp made them blink. Loretta looked around curiously, taking in the shelves of books, the beautiful—and obviously valuable—antique furniture, and the magnificent kneehole desk on which Geoffrey had found the lamp. It stood against one of the walls of the room. Loretta wondered why Puddephat had resisted placing it next to the window with its enchanting view.

Geoffrey was speaking again. "You take the desk, Loretta," he instructed her. "It's the most obvious place to find your notes, and you know exactly what you're looking for. I'll have a root in the bedroom." Bridget winked at Loretta and followed Geoffrey into the other room.

It was by far the most sensible arrangement, since

Geoffrey did not know the real purpose of their visit, but Loretta was seized with apprehension as soon as she was alone. What on earth was she doing in this stranger's sitting-room? she asked herself. What could possibly give her a clue about what had happened at the flat in rue Roland? She had no idea what she was looking for. She forced herself to take deep breaths. Now I'm here, she told herself, I might as well have a look round. Approaching the desk, she was struck by the painting hanging above it. It was, she thought, a disconcerting choice for an object that you would have to look at every day. She would not be able to work with such a scene constantly before her eyes. It looked very much like a Francis Bacon, and an original at that. Everything about the room suggested money. Loretta wondered whether Puddephat's fellowship provided an unusually large salary, or whether the objects were a relic of his marriage. She examined the desk, its surface entirely barren. Was Puddephat exceptionally tidy, or had he known he would not be coming back to these rooms after his trip to Paris? Tentatively, she opened a drawer on the right-hand side of the desk. At once, the illusion of order was shattered. Inside was a jumble of pieces of paper, the top one being a red demand for payment of a large telephone bill. Rummaging through, Loretta found receipts from restaurants, postcards from friends, the stubs of several used cheque books. She guessed that the contents of the drawer represented several months of the missing man's life.

At the very bottom, her fingers touched what felt like a photograph. Drawing it out, she found herself looking at a face which was striking both for its good looks and its expression of surprise. The boy in the photograph, whose age could have been anywhere between fifteen and twenty, was staring at the camera with startled eyes. The photo had been taken indoors and in poor light: the boy was sitting at a table, his head resting on one hand, a candle flickering nearby. From the objects visible on the table, Loretta guessed the occasion was some sort of supper party. Perhaps he had been caught unawares by a flashgun? She wondered who the boy was. One of Puddephat's students? It really was hard to tell his age from a black and white photograph. Whoever he was, his looks were almost, but not quite, pretty. His fair hair was parted on one side, and a lock of it fell across his forehead. His large eyes might have been girlish had it not been for his unusually heavy eyebrows. There was certainly a homoerotic quality about him, and Loretta remembered what Bridget had said about Puddephat's interest in young men. At the same time, she recognized that the photograph was exerting a considerable pull on her own imagination. Where, she wondered, did the boy's own inclinations lie? She shook her head and returned the picture to the bottom of the drawer. She had no evidence to connect the boy with Puddephat's disappearance, and she was wasting time. In any case, she would know the face again if she came across it. The next drawer was full of scribbled notes on A4 paper, lecture notes by the look of them. She tried the third.

Suddenly Bridget erupted into the room, calling Loretta's name in a terrifying loud whisper. "Look at this!" she hissed. "I found it among his socks. Sickly yellow ones, by the way." Loretta looked at her in bewilderment. Bridget was holding a sheet of writing paper. It dawned on Loretta that the latter half of Bridget's remark had been to do with Puddephat's taste in footwear, not the object she was holding.

Loretta took the single sheet of paper from her. The thick creamy vellum was covered in a large black scrawl. The writer appeared to have been so anxious to commit the message to paper that the conventional opening had been dispensed with.

I am so angry I can hardly write [it began, and there was ample evidence in the shaping of the letters that this was indeed so]. Your suggestion last night was just about the most obscene thing I have ever heard. How could you do this to me? Since your skin is clearly thicker than even I had supposed, I am writing to make sure there is no misunderstanding between us. The answer is *no*, *no no*. Not now, not ever. I never believed I could wish anyone dead, but last night changed all that. Stay away from me, do you understand. I want *nothing* to do with you. If hell existed, it would be too good for you.

The letter was signed, with an abruptness that matched its content, simply "R." Loretta's mind went straight back to the boy in the photograph. Had her surmise been correct? Had Puddephat provoked this storm by propositioning the boy? She found it hard to believe, in this day and age, that anyone would react with such loathing to a homosexual advance. On the other hand, if it came unexpectedly, and from an admired authority figure, the boy's tutor perhaps, might it not seem like a betrayal of trust?

"Well!" she heard Bridget exclaim impatiently. "Say something! It must be a clue. Somebody hated Puddephat enough to kill him!"

"I wonder," Loretta said hesitantly. She did not want to show Bridget the photograph, and was angry with herself for this uncharacteristic piece of selfishness. After all, it was Bridget's doing that she was here at all. Her sense of fair play won. "I think it might be connected with this," she said, reaching into the top drawer for the picture and handing it to Bridget.

Her friend's reaction was less intense than Loretta's had been. "Nice-looking kid," she said. "But what's he got to do with the letter?"

"He could be R," Loretta pointed out unwillingly.

Bridget held the picture at arm's length and studied it. "I suppose it's possible," she said. "But does he look the sort of person who'd sign with just an initial?" Loretta shrugged, took the photograph from Bridget, and put it back in the drawer. As she closed it, Geoffrey appeared in the doorway.

"Any luck?" he asked Loretta. "Apart from the hate mail in his sock drawer," he added, casting a disapproving glance at Bridget.

Loretta recalled why she was supposed to be in Puddephat's rooms. "Afraid not," she said. "No sign of my notes at all. It looks like I'm going to have to have a go at doing the outline again from memory." As she finished speaking, a very loud bell began to ring. "A burglar alarm!" she gasped, frozen to the spot. Her mind filled with images of police cars, interrogations, court scenes.

Geoffrey shook his head. "Stop panicking," he commanded. "It's only the fire alarm. I bet some silly bugger has set if off by accident. Usually happens at least twice a term. It doesn't tend to happen in the vacation, though. Perhaps it's a real fire at long last. Bloody rotten luck for us."

Already, above the din of the bell, Loretta could hear doors opening and closing, feet on the move above her head. "What do we do?" she asked in a loud whipser. "Stay put?"

"Too risky," Geoffrey answered, frowning. "They check all the rooms to make sure no one's slept through it. And we can't risk being seen in this wing. It's not as if we're near my rooms. We couldn't be further from them."

Loretta could see the only course of action open to them. She switched off the lamp and moved to the window. "I take it they don't search the grounds as well?" she asked, parting the curtains and throwing up the window. She climbed out into the garden and crouched close to the wall, waiting for the others to follow.

Geoffrey came next, grumbling in a low voice. "I hope you two like fresh air," he muttered, joining her next to the wall. Bridget was last, gently closing the window behind her. "We'd better go down to the stream and hide in the bushes," said Geoffrey. "At least I'll be able to have a cigarette down there." He made a sudden dash for the undergrowth. Loretta followed, becoming aware that the grass was damp beneath her feet. Her cream shoes were far from waterproof, and already she could feel an unpleasant sensation around her toes. When she reached the bushes, Geoffrey was spreading his jacket on the grass between the stream and a weeping willow. He settled himself comfortably on it and lit a cigarette. She heard the sound of twigs cracking as Bridget came up behind her. "Come on, you don't expect me to give up my jacket," Geoffrey exclaimed, in response to a disapproving look from Bridget. "I'm not Sir Walter Raleigh, you know."

"At times like this," Bridget said sharply, "I can see why I gave you the push after six weeks. You've got the manners of a pig. Now move over." Protesting, Geoffrey moved to one side as Bridget lowered herself to the ground. Loretta crouched on the grass, looking at her friend in surprise. She had no idea that Bridget and Geoffrey had ever had an affair. "There's room for you as well, Loretta, if Geoffrey is sensible about this," Bridget insisted.

Loretta perched herself uncomfortably on the very edge of the jacket. The sudden intimacy of the situation was rather unwelcome. She needed time to digest the idea of Bridget and Geoffrey having been lovers, even for a short period. Wasn't he much younger than Bridget? She didn't know Geoffrey's exact age, but the gap couldn't be less than five or six years. It might well be more. Suddenly the idiocy of these thoughts struck her. What on earth was wrong with a woman having a younger lover? Her reaction was a relic of her schooldays, when convention insisted that any potential boyfriend should have a head start of at least two years on the object of his affections. She blushed at being caught out in such unthinking prejudice.

"Well, you can't complain I'm not honest," Geoffrey was saying, his good humour restored by the cigarette which was now polluting the night air.

"Far from it," Bridget conceded. "But you can take these things too far." They exchanged complicit smiles, and Loretta reflected that the end of the affair did not seem to have soured their friendship. She wondered if that was one of the benefits of a younger man. Her own affairs, always with men considerably older than herself, had not ended so amicably. She was not even on speaking terms with Anthony Swan, the Labour MP who had accompanied her to Paris three or four years before. And Tracey's attitude to her tended to consist of affection heavily tempered with caution. She felt a sudden pang for John Tracey. He might have some ideas about what she should do next. And she would enjoy impressing him with what she had managed to find out about Hugh Puddephat so far. Which was, she congratulated herself, a not inconsiderable amount of information. There was his background: his marriage, his concealed homosexuality, his involvement, whatever it was, with the Gandell girl. Then, most significant of all, there was the letter from "R." At the time of writing that message, its author had certainly been in the right frame to oust Theo Sykes from the role of chief suspect. *If*, of course, a crime had been committed. Loretta felt deeply frustrated. In spite of what she had discovered, she still felt nowhere near the heart of the mystery. Once again, she found herself thinking about the boy in the picture. Was he the author of the letter? She hoped not. He could be anyone—a friend's son, or a nephew. He might even be Puddephat's own son, she thought, her imagination suddenly taking flight. Not by his marriage, of course, but as a result of a teenage affair. It was possible, she thought, but not very likely. No, she could not picture Hugh Puddephat as the adolescent father of an illegitimate son. In any case, if there was an innocent explanation of the existence of the photograph, why had it been hidden at the bottom of the drawer? Her sense of its deliberate concealment was overwhelmingly strong—it had been placed out of sight, but in a place where its owner could easily put his hand on it. Why?

During these deliberations, Loretta was aware that Bridget and Geoffrey were talking in low voices. Now Bridget broke off in mid-sentence and put her finger to her lips, nodding her head in the direction of the college buildings. A light had gone on in one of the downstairs rooms in Puddephat's wing. A figure was briefly visible against the window, then the light went out. This performance was repeated in the next room along. "Checking everyone's out," whispered Geoffrey. In silence, they watched the man's progress along the length of the corridor.

When the light went out in the last room, Bridget began to get up. "Thank God for that," she said.

Geoffrey pulled her down again. "Not yet, idiot," he hissed. "He's got two more floors to do. If we go back now, he's bound to hear us." Sure enough, a light came on in the middle floor of the wing. At the same time, the first spots of rain began to fall.

"Oh, no," moaned Bridget. "I can't bear it."

Loretta watched sadly as damp patches began to appear on her cream linen suit. She could not have packed a more unsuitable set of garments for tonight's escapade, but then no such prospect had even crossed her mind when she was leaving London. She shifted uncomfortably on the ground. Geoffrey chose this moment to propose a game of I Spy, an idea which met with so marked a degree of hostility from Bridget that he lapsed into silence.

The rain cast a decided dampener on their spirits and, as it became heavier, Geoffrey was moved to make a mild complaint. "Lot of trouble these notes of yours have caused," he remarked idly to Loretta. Consumed with guilt, she looked questioningly at Bridget, wondering whether she shouldn't tell Geoffrey the truth. But Bridget's response was a slight shake of the head, and Loretta remained silent. If Bridget, who knew Geoffrey much better than she had realized, judged it better to conceal the real reason for their visit to Puddephat's rooms, she would have to go along with her. It was another five minutes before her thoughts were interrupted again by Geoffrey's voice.

"Pleasant though this is, I think it's time to call it a night," he announced, getting to his feet.

"Are you sure it's safe?" enquired Bridget.

"No," he replied evenly, "but my clothes are so wet my skin is beginning to take in water. If I don't get into dry clothes soon, I'll die of double pneumonia." Loretta and Bridget stood up to join him, bending and stretching their cramped legs to restore them to life. Then, for the second time that evening, all three of them made their way to Puddephat's window and let themselves into his rooms. Geoffrey went straight to the door, and pressed his ear to it. "Seems to be clear," he said, opening it. "Most people should be back in their rooms by now. Come on." Bridget was in the corridor as soon as he stopped speaking. Loretta followed, and Geoffrey closed the door softly behind her. He led the way swiftly and quietly to the exit which gave on to the quadrangle. "Now to see if it was a real fire," he said with a grin, opening it a fraction. Loretta blinked; the possibility of a real emergency, rather than a false alarm, had simply not occurred to her. "No, we're OK," he said, after a hasty glance outside.

"How d'you know?" asked Bridget.

Geoffrey flung open the door. "No fire without smoke," he announced, gesturing towards the peaceful courtyard. "Probably a fault in the alarm system." He looked at his two damp companions. "Brandy," he said firmly, "that's what you need. Let's go and drink to a life of crime." They squelched off in the direction of Geoffrey's rooms and a bottle of Rémy Martin.

6

THE PILE OF MESSAGES THAT GREETED LO-
retta when she arrived at her college just after twelve next
day was a sure sign that the beginning of term was only
two days away. Hanging her coat on the back of the door in
her office, she observed the utilitarian nature of her sur-
roundings with even more dissatisfaction than usual. She
disliked the stark brick walls, and the aluminium window
frame, never an object of beauty, had recently acquired the
additional disadvantage of being jammed shut. She thought
longingly of Hugh Puddephat's rooms in Oxford. The
Francis Bacon would have to go, of course, but it would be
easy to find something more to her taste. A simple black
and white photograph perhaps? She realized she was staring into space. The Puddephat business was exerting far
too great a hold on her; she must put her mind to all the
business connected with the new academic year. Her most
urgent task was to arrange interviews with all the students
to whom she was tutor. The first-years would be a mixed
bunch, some bursting with confidence, others in need of a
great deal of encouragement. The second- and third-years,
who were already familiar faces, would make fewer de-
mands on her; it was too early in the year for anxieties
about exams. Looking at the messages which had accumu-
lated in her absence she saw the folly of rushing off to

Oxford so close to the start of term and felt faintly annoyed with herself. She usually enjoyed this part of the year immensely, but for once she was feeling quite unprepared for it. She would just have to forget about Paris and Oxford for the rest of the day and get on with some work.

She started flicking through the messages, most of them in the handwriting of Mrs. Whittaker, the secretary of the English department. There was to be a staff meeting the following afternoon, Loretta read, at which the new course on gender would be discussed again. She was outraged, guessing that the objectors had carried on their fight after her departure from lunch on Monday. It really was a bit much, she thought, to leave it until now to make trouble about the course. The first lecture was due to take place next week. And if the head of the English department wasn't so ineffectual, he'd have told them so on Monday. She took out her diary and made a note of the time of the meeting. She was determined that the new course would not bite the dust because of a rearguard action by a couple of old fogies like Maurice Webb and Henry Hedger. She snapped shut the diary and looked at the next piece of paper. It was a request from a colleague: he'd be grateful if she could cast her eye over an article he'd written for a quarterly journal, by Friday if possible. Why couldn't he have asked her earlier? Loretta wondered. Friday was, after all, the first day of term. She supposed she could fit it in, if it really was urgent. The next missive was a postcard from the college library, which had acquired a book for her on inter-library loan. Could she pick it up within forty-eight hours? Another piece of paper simply recorded that Tracey had called the day before. He hadn't explained what he wanted, or asked her to call back, but Loretta's resolution wavered momentarily. It was just possible that he'd discovered something about Puddephat. Anyway, whatever he wanted, she was keen to ask his advice on what to do next. Her hand went out to the telephone, then drew back. She'd been neglecting her work for the past day and a half.

Tracey could wait until the evening. She put the note to one side, and looked at the final message.

Her heartbeat quickened when she saw that Andrew Walker had telephoned twice that morning, and would like her to return his call as soon as possible. Had Andrew found out what had happened at the flat? Calming down, she decided that this was very unlikely. Unless Andrew was lying, she knew from his own lips that the evidence had vanished by the time he arrived at rue Roland. That being the case, what did he want? It was only three days since they had spoken, and they were not particularly close friends.

The answer suddenly came to her, and she smiled. The most likely explanation was her offer to buy him dinner in return for the loan of the flat. With term approaching fast, it was quite likely that Andrew was coming to London on department business, and had seen his opportunity to call in the debt. Well, she thought, nothing would suit her better. With Puddephat's disappearance in the news, it would not seem odd if she made a casual reference to it over dinner. It was an ideal opportunity for her to find out whether Andrew knew the missing don, and whether Puddephat had ever had any connection with rue Roland. And all in the course of a social event that had been set up not by her but by Andrew. It couldn't be better. She looked up Andrew's number in her address book, hoping he was not already on his way to London.

The phone rang half a dozen times before he answered it. "You've just caught me," he said, recognizing her voice. "I was shutting the front door when I heard the phone ring. I'm on my way up to town. There's been a cock-up in the first-year timetable, and Prof. Day's summoned me to a meeting to sort it out. Bloody nuisance, but I can't get out of it. That's why I called, as a matter of fact. I suppose you wouldn't be free for dinner this evening?"

Loretta's smile widened. "What a good idea," she replied. "Where would you like to eat?"

Andrew hesitated for a second, apparently taken aback by the ease with which he had gained his free dinner. "Well," he said slowly, judging how far his luck could be pushed, "I always think L'Escargot is very reliable . . ."

"I'll book a table for eight thirty," said Loretta cheerfully. Hang the expense, she thought rashly—her salary cheque was about to go into her account, and she hoped it would be a productive evening. She was thrilled to be back on the trail again.

She rang the *Sunday Herald* number, placating her conscience with the thought that she might not have time to ring Tracey that evening after all; but when she got through to the news desk, she discovered that he had taken the shuttle to Glasgow the morning before. It was too early to say when he might return. With a shrug of impatience, Loretta rang off. She dialled his home number and left a short message on his answering-machine.

Loretta was the first to arrive at the restaurant. A waiter led her to the table she'd booked downstairs, and left her to study the menu. It did not take her long to work out that the meal was going to cost her considerably more than she'd saved by spending a rather miserable night in rue Roland. Nevertheless, she was looking forward to the food. A salad of sun-dried tomatoes to start, she thought, and then perhaps the salmon?

At that moment, Andrew hurried in, slightly out of breath. He kissed Loretta's cheek, and sat down opposite her. "Let's have some wine while we think about food," he said, picking up the wine list. After a quick glance, he ordered something which sounded horribly expensive. "You've been working too hard," he said, turning his attention to Loretta. "You look quite tired, and term hasn't even started. What have you been up to?"

Loretta suppressed her irritation. Up to that moment, she had been feeling perfectly well. The black velvet dress she was wearing—the weather had changed at last—set off her pale skin and blonde hair, and she was looking forward to a new academic year. Some people seemed to have a talent for saying the wrong thing, she thought to herself. Or had her efforts to get to the bottom of the rue Roland mystery taken an unexpected toll on her? She doubted it.

"You don't look all that well yourself," she told Andrew with uncharacteristic malice. "And you've just had a holiday."

"No amount of holiday can compensate for the beginning of the autumn term," Andrew answered gloomily. "A new academic year, a new set of faces to memorize. The trouble is, Loretta, that I've discovered I don't like students. One year they've got long hair and spend their spare time reading Marx, the next they're shorn like sheep and as conservative as hell. And whichever sort they happen to be, they always think they're the first of their kind. What I need is a nice little research job where I can write my books and keep well away from them."

Loretta smiled. Any minute now, Andrew would start talking in disparaging tones about the habits of "young people," a favourite topic of his since reaching the age of forty. She suspected that his distaste for students was stimulated not so much by their ideas as by their youth. Perhaps she would feel the same when she reached his age. It was not a pleasant thought, and she decided to change the subject. "I'm going to have the salmon," she announced, handing the menu to Andrew.

After a short discussion on the merits of the duck, he decided to join her; and while they waited for the first course to arrive, he regaled her with a colourful account of that afternoon's meeting in the history department to sort out the timetable. Inexplicably, two compulsory first-year lectures had been scheduled for the same day and time, and the error had only just been noticed. Neither of the lecturers concerned was willing to agree to a change at this late date; when one of them finally gave in, the alternative proposed by the unpopular head of department was a slot already occupied by one of Andrew's lectures. He was an excellent storyteller and in normal circumstances Loretta would have enjoyed his acerbic comments on his colleagues' conduct at the meeting. Tonight, however, she was keen to steer the conversation round to the subject of Hugh Puddephat. As soon as Andrew paused for breath, she took her chance. "I was up in Oxford at the beginning of this week," she said, as casually as she could. "I stayed a couple of nights with a friend who lives in Woodstock Road. She teaches English, and she was telling me about this don who's disappeared. Hugh something, I think his name is." She paused, then added, "Hugh Puddephat, that's it." Was she overdoing it? She crossed her fingers and plunged on. "You know lots of people at Oxford. Have you ever come across him?"

"Oh, yes, I know Hugh," Andrew said unsuspectingly. "We were at college together, as a matter of fact. There was a time when I knew him quite well. He and I and a few other people used to hang around together when we were students. We were all gay but scared stiff to do anything about it. This was after Wolfenden, of course, but before the change in the law. Mind you, Hugh was always a bit different from the rest of us. I was profoundly relieved when the law was relaxed in 1967, but I think it just added to Hugh's problems. It took away one of the reasons he used to justify trying to suppress his homosexuality, you see. In the end, he married one of his own students. Partly in the hope of keeping himself on the straight and narrow —you'd be surprised how many gay men do that—and partly because he thought it would do his career a bit of good. Veronica's an Honourable, you see. I rather liked her, though I couldn't see how the thing would work. She had absolutely no idea, and Hugh went out of his way to keep it from her. That's why I began to see less of him. After he was married, he even started making jokes at dinner parties about limp wrists and fairies. So I gradually stopped visiting them. They spent their honeymoon at rue Roland, by the way—Hugh was the classic brilliant but penniless academic at the time and, to do him credit, he didn't want to take Veronica's money. Or Veronica's father's money, to be more accurate."

So there *was* a connection between the flat and Hugh Puddephat, thought Loretta, her heart beating fast. "I suppose most of your friends must have stayed there at one time or another," she said casually. "Has Hugh ever stayed there since?"

"Once or twice, but a very long time ago," Andrew said. "Certainly not in recent years. Veronica used it occasionally. In fact, now you come to mention it, I'm a little bit peeved with her. She got in touch months ago, at the end of the summer term, in fact, to ask if she could borrow the flat. It was a little bit awkward, because she wanted to spend a long weekend there in July, and I had to sort out the dates with Alex to make sure they didn't clash. She came and collected the keys, and that was the last I heard from her. The keys came back through the post, without even a thank-you note. I don't even know whether she used the flat, or whether she changed her mind and didn't go for one reason or another." He paused, and then shrugged. "I'd completely forgotten about that. Perhaps it was Veronica who spring-cleaned the flat? Though it's no more in character for her to do it than it is for Alex. After a year or two of keeping house for Hugh, she put her foot down and said it was ridiculous not to use her money. Ever since then, she's had a cleaning lady and a gardener. I can't quite picture Veronica down on her knees with a scrubbing brush. Don't get me wrong, Loretta," he added, "It's not that I don't like her. But I have always felt rather uncomfortable in her presence. And that's Hugh's fault, not hers. When he introduced me to her, just before the wedding, he sort of . . . well, he didn't come out and say it, but he got the message over that he didn't want her to know I was gay. So I've always felt in a false position where Veronica's concerned."

Loretta was only half listening. Had Veronica's visit to the flat in July—if she had indeed made one—anything to do with what had happened there in September? She felt sure there must be a connection, but at the moment she couldn't see what it was. Perhaps she should engineer a meeting with Veronica? She decided to try a different tack. "What d'you think has happened to Hugh?" she asked.

"I've no idea," Andrew admitted. "I suppose he'll turn up sooner or later. I think the most likely thing is that he's had some sort of accident. He may be sitting in a hospital bed somewhere in Italy at this very moment, wondering who he is and why he knows all these long words like hermeneutics." He paused, a puzzled look on his face. Fearing that he was going to ask why she was so interested in Puddephat's disappearance, Loretta rapidly changed the subject. In any case, she'd probably got as much out of Andrew as she was going to.

The subject of rue Roland did not come up again in the course of the evening until Loretta was stepping into a taxi for Islington outside the restaurant. "Oh," she cried, pausing by the door of the cab, "I've forgotten to bring your keys."

"Never mind," said Andrew. "They're only the spare set. Wait till the next time I see you." Loretta climbed into the taxi, and headed for home.

First thing next morning, her telephone rang. It was Tracey. "Did I wake you up?" he enquired innocently. "There was a message from you on the tape when I got back last night. I thought it might be urgent."

"Not this urgent," said Loretta, looking at the clock on her bedside table. It was seven thirty. "I was only returning your call, as a matter of fact." She was mildly irritated, well aware of what Tracey was up to. Her reticence about certain areas of her private life irked him, and he occasionally found an excuse to ring early in the hope of catching her unawares. Resisting the temptation to call his bluff by pretending someone was with her, she asked how he had got on in Glasgow.

"Wild goose chase," he said grumpily. It appeared she had touched a raw nerve. "All the fault of the news desk. They insisted on me going up there to see this chap who was supposed to have proof of a fiddle being carried out by a bunch of telephone operators at one particular exchange. It would have been quite a sexy story if it was true—lots of money involved. But the crucial thing he hadn't told us was that his girlfriend was one of the operators involved in the ring, and he'd just had a big row with her. That's why the story sounded plausible in the first place—he knew enough about the operation to string us along. He'd even been inside the building, and could describe who sat where. I only began to smell a rat when he couldn't come up with the documents he claimed to have. He said he'd put them at a friend's house for safe keeping, and the friend just happened to have gone away on holiday. I took him out for a boozy lunch, and in the end he admitted he'd made the whole thing up. By then, of course, I'd wasted two whole days in Glasgow. And it's too late to put together the story I really wanted to do this week. I told the news desk they should send someone else, one of the junior reporters. They've got to learn that this business is plagued with fantasists and people with grudges. It's an occupational hazard of investigative journalism. How's your investigation coming along, by the way?"

Loretta swallowed her distaste at Tracey's cold-bloodedness. She disliked the casual way in which he made decisions profoundly affecting other people's lives—choosing whose tale of woe should be front page news, and whose story deserved nothing more than the wastepaper bin. But she needed his help. "I've found out a lot," she said, "and I'm very keen to talk it over with you. The trouble is that term starts tomorrow, and I'm rather tied up with work. Are you free at the weekend?"

Tracey suggested meeting for a drink when he finished work on Saturday evening. "What about going to a movie?" he added, asking if she'd seen a French film which had opened in London a couple of weeks ago. She hadn't, and they agreed to meet at seven.

Loretta put down the phone with a sense of unease, wondering if she'd done the right thing. It meant a delay of two more days before deciding what to do next, and she was reluctant to wait so long. But it couldn't be helped. The beginning of the autumn term was, apart from exams, her busiest time of year. Her discovery in Paris couldn't have happened at a worse time from that point of view, and she would just have to accept it. Frustrated, she picked up that day's *Guardian* and looked to see whether there were any stories about the search for Puddephat. She found nothing, although she didn't know whether to put this down to a lack of success on the part of the police or the massive coverage afforded to the hijacking of a wide-bodied jet over Italy. The presence of a minor American film star among the hostages had prompted more than usually exhaustive coverage of the event, and several columns were devoted to a blow-by-blow account of the aircraft's comings and goings. Putting the paper to one side, Loretta told herself that she would have to put Hugh Puddephat out of her mind until Saturday.

Loretta arrived punctually at her office next day at ten o'clock. The pattern of the first day of the autumn term was fixed; the first-years, who had arrived at their halls of residence the day before, came to the department in the morning to sign up for various optional courses. At eleven, they split up into small groups and assembled in the rooms of the lecturers whose courses they had chosen. Just after eleven, Loretta was handing out reading lists to the dozen students who wanted to attend her seminars on Virginia Woolf when there was a knock at the door. It must be a latecomer, Loretta thought to herself, calling, "Come in."

The door opened, and Mrs. Whittaker put her head into the room. "A Mr. Tracey is on the phone," he said. "He wants to speak to you urgently. I've explained that you're tied up until twelve, but he wouldn't take no for an answer." The secretary's features clearly showed her disapproval of Tracey's behaviour. It was an unwritten rule in the department that teaching sessions were not to be interrupted by phone calls, especially not private ones.

Loretta stared at the woman for a moment, thoughts racing through her head. Tracey was well aware of the rule; something must have happened. Realizing that not only Mrs. Whittaker, but twelve newly arrived first-year students, were waiting for her in expectant silence, she pulled herself together. "Please tell him I'll ring him on the dot of twelve," she told the secretary. "And I'm sorry you've been troubled." She didn't know how she was going to contain her impatience, but it would not do to make an enemy of Mrs. Whittaker. And she did have a responsibility to her students. But what on earth could have happened?

As soon as the last student had filed out of her office, Loretta picked up the phone. It was still switched through to the secretary's office, and it took an infuriatingly long time to get a line. She was holding her breath when she finally got through to Tracey's extension. "What's happened?" she demanded, without preamble.

"They've found the body," he told her, equally blunt.

"Body?" she gasped, a wave of nausea passing through her. In her mind, she was back at the flat in rue Roland, a jumble of bloodstained sheets confronting her.

"Puddephat," Tracey added, dispelling all doubt. "It came up on the PA tapes an hour ago. You know, the Press Association teleprinter. You've seen it in the corner of the office. The police announced it this morning."

More images whirled through Loretta's head—the figure she had seen in the bed, a body being dragged to the door, herself in handcuffs waiting to board the ferry. Or would they fly her back to Paris? She had been right, and she had done nothing about it! But I didn't *know*, she argued back, picturing all too clearly the disbelief on the policemen's faces. And there was my mother to think about, she pleaded. You couldn't expect . . . She pulled herself together, and asked a question. "Where did they find him?" she asked weakly.

"They haven't said officially," Tracey said, "but I called a mate of mine at the Yard as soon as I heard. He's making some inquiries, and he's going to ring me back." At that moment, Loretta heard the sound of another phone ringing. "That's probably him," Tracey said. "I gave him another extension number in case we were talking when he rang. Look, can you meet me at lunchtime? The pub opposite the office in half an hour?" Loretta agreed, and put the phone down.

The sour taste in her mouth made her retch a couple of times, and after a moment, she got up and walked out of her office to the coffee machine. She fumbled for change and pressed the button for black coffee. Hating it, she drank half and left the rest standing in its cup on a window sill. She went back to her office, put on her coat, and went to find a taxi.

Tracey was waiting for her in the pub. "Read that while I get you a drink," he said, handing her a piece of paper which she recognized as PA copy. "Are you all right?" he asked, putting his hand on her arm. "You look absolutely green. I think you need a brandy." Loretta didn't argue.

As Tracey made his way to the bar, she put the story on the table in front of her.

A police investigation is under way in two countries after the identification of a body in Paris as that of Dr. Hugh Puddephat, the missing Oxford don [she read].

The body, which was discovered in the city yesterday

morning, was identified through fingerprints. No papers or personal items are believed to have been found with it.

Details of how Dr. Puddephat died have not yet been released, but police say foul play is suspected. They have no idea what Dr. Puddephat was doing in France at the time of his death. He was last seen in England a few days before he was due to attend an important conference in Italy.

A spokesman for Thames Valley police, who have been investigating the don's disappearance, said that two detectives would be flying to Paris today to continue their inquiries.

The story ended with a quote from Professor Morris, master of Puddephat's college, who said he was "devastated" by the news. Des Koogan would have his work cut out to keep at bay all the reporters and photographers heading for the college, Loretta thought with the ghost of a smile. Tracey returned with her brandy. She drank it at one gulp. "Good God, that was a double," he said. "You are in a bad way. Are you sure you want to hear any more?"

"Yes," Loretta said flatly. "I can't just pretend it hasn't happened." The warm feeling induced by the spirit made her aware of how cold she had been since hearing the news. "Tell me everything."

"All right," said Tracey. "On your head be it. It's not very nice." He sipped his own drink, which looked like another double brandy. Perhaps he was as shocked as she, but more skilled at concealing the fact.

"Because they knew Puddephat was supposed to be going abroad," Tracey began, "the cops put out a message through Interpol. To be on the safe side, they sent it to several countries. There was some confusion about what his real destination was, apparently. Nothing happened until yesterday, when an unidentified body turned up in Paris. The French police ran a check on fingerprints, and found they'd got Puddephat. The Yard released the news this morning."

"Why is Scotland Yard involved?" Loretta interrupted. "I thought it was being investigated by Thames Valley police."

"It is," Tracey said patiently. "But the Interpol office is at the Yard. Anyway, as I was saying, that's all they're admitting publicly. But I've got the inside story from my mate. Off the record, of course."

A thought occurred to Loretta, and a look of alarm passed across her face. "Does he know about me?" she asked anxiously.

"No, don't worry," Tracey said. "I told him we were thinking of putting someone on to the story, and needed to know if it was worth following up. I didn't mention you at all. Now, about where the body was found. D'you remember a church in rue Roland?"

Loretta considered the question. "I can't picture it," she said, "but it could be at the far end from the flat."

"That must be it," Tracey agreed. "And they've been having some restoration work done on it. Some local worthy died and left some money, apparently. They closed it while the really major stuff was going on, and it opened again last Sunday. So the builders have gone, and all the old biddies turn up in their Sunday best to say their Hail Marys, or whatever it is they do. And there's this smell. At first they think the builders have messed up the drains. So they swing a bit of incense about, and wait for the workmen to come back and investigate. But by yesterday, it was pretty bad. So they search the church, and there it is. Puddephat's body hidden in the altar."

Loretta stared at him, appalled. The picture he had painted was so vivid that once again she felt as if she were about to be sick. Tracey, on the other hand, seemed to have cheered up considerably. He even appeared to be enjoying himself. Loretta reminded herself that telling stories was part of his job, and he had probably heard much worse than this in his time.

"One of the odd things about it is that he was wearing

brand-new clothes," he added. "You know, those blue things that French workmen always wear. Whoever killed him got rid of his own clothes and put them on the body afterwards."

"So he was murdered?" Loretta asked miserably.

"Oh, yes," said Tracey. "No doubt about that. A frenzied attack, my mate said."

Pushing this thought aside, Loretta asked another question. "But how did he get from the flat to the church?"

"Well, assuming he didn't put himself there, which is unlikely since we know what you found at the flat, someone must have carried him there," Tracey replied. "That's one thing the police have no idea about. And they know nothing about the flat, of course." "But how can I go to them now?" Loretta cried, sensing the implied criticism in his tone. "They'll never understand why I didn't go to them in the first place. God knows how many offences I've committed! D'you want to see me in prison?"

"All right, don't jump down my throat," Tracey protested. "I'm trying to help you. I can see your problem perfectly well. I've got one myself, if it comes to that." Loretta looked blank. "Here am I," he explained, "with inside information about a very good story, and I can't use it because of where it comes from. It's not a very happy situation for either of us."

"Selfish pig!" Loretta snapped. "Has it occurred to you that I nearly disturbed the murderer—that I might have been killed as well? And you just think about your wretched paper!" They glared at each other across the table.

"All right, I'm sorry," Tracey said. "Why don't you tell me what you found out in Oxford?"

Calming down, Loretta outlined what she had discovered about the dead man.

"I'm astonished, Loretta," Tracey said when she described the raid on Puddephat's rooms. "You should be a journalist yourself. In all my years on newspapers, I've never gone as far as breaking and entering. But it sounds as if it's paid off. He certainly made a few enemies. There's the Sykes chap, and R, whoever that is. And they're only the ones we know about. The question is, was either of them in Paris that weekend, or was it somebody else we don't know about? That's equally likely, you know, when you think about it. And what about his wife? She doesn't sound too keen on him, though I don't know if she counts as an enemy for our purposes. If you want my advice, I think I'd wait a day or two before doing anything. See what turns up. My contact at the Yard may know more by the end of the day. What d'you think of that?"

To Loretta the suggestion was a reprieve. She turned down Tracey's offer of another drink, and agreed to speak to him again that evening. Then she excused herself and went in search of a strong cup of tea.

When she left college at a quarter to five, Loretta was still feeling tense and restless. For once, she was reluctant to go straight home to Islington. On the way to the tube station, she passed a cinema where an American comedy was about to start. On impulse, she turned into the foyer and bought a ticket. Her mind was not on the film, however, and she left after an hour. When she arrived home, the phone was ringing. She picked it up, expecting to hear Tracey's voice. Instead, she found herself talking to Bridget. She sounded excited.

"Geoffrey just got hold of me," she said. "The police have taken away Theo Sykes! They came for him this afternoon, Geoffrey says. There was the most tremendous row—Sykes refused to go with them at first, and the master was brought in to persuade him. Geoffrey thinks he's going to be charged with the murder. You do know about the body, don't you?" Bridget asked anxiously as Loretta remained silent.

"Oh, yes, I know about the body," Loretta said, still

trying to take in this new twist of events. "But why have they arrested Sykes?"

"It turns out he was in France at the time of the murder," replied Bridget. "So it looks like it's all solved already. Aren't you relieved? This means you won't have to go to the police after all."

"Oh, yes," said Loretta, realizing that her reaction was proving a disappointment to Bridget. "I suppose I'm a bit shocked by it, that's all." Arranging to call Bridget the next day, she rang off. At once, the phone sounded again. This time it was Tracey.

"Looks like you're off the hook, Loretta," he began. "They've got him."

"I know," said Loretta. "I've just heard."

"Who told you?" Tracey asked indignantly. "I've only just found out myself."

"Bridget rang," Loretta explained. "But do tell me what you know. I'm sure you've got far more details. How did they get on to him, for a start?"

"Ferry tickets," Tracey told her, pacified. "As soon as the ID was confirmed yesterday, the Thames Valley boys started going through their files. They had a rough idea of when the murder took place from the state of the body—not exact, but within a day or two. When they first interviewed Sykes, on Monday this is, he told them he was staying at a cottage in the Lake District entirely on his own for the first two and a half weeks in September. The cottage belonged to friends, he said, but they were diplomats and happened to be in Syria. Just out of curiosity, a bright young DC ran the names of some of the witnesses through the Sealink computer this morning. And guess what? Sykes went to Paris a couple of days before you did, and came back on the Monday. When the cops went to see him again this afternoon, he flatly refused to say why he was there, where he stayed, or anything about the trip. So they pulled him in. They think it's only a matter of time before he breaks. According to my contact at the Yard, the theory is that he met Puddephat by chance, and saw his opportunity. They don't know how Puddephat got there, by the way. He hasn't shown up on any of the ferry company computers, or any of the airline ones, for that matter. They checked right at the start of the inquiry. It looks like he may have travelled under an assumed name, God knows why."

"But why would Sykes kill Puddephat?" Loretta asked. "I know he didn't like him, but surely that's not enough?"

"You're forgetting the business of Sykes's fellowship," Tracey pointed out. "Sykes stood to gain by Puddephat's death. With Puddephat out of the way, the English faculty were on the spot. They were a fellow short, and the start of the autumn term is a terrible time to get a replacement. With Sykes about to go at Christmas as well, they were really up the creek. They've been putting pressure on this chap Morris to renew Sykes's fellowship, and the clincher is he was going to do it on Monday."

"I'm not a hundred per cent convinced," Loretta said thoughtfully. "And why did your friend tell you all this?"

"It's off the record again," Tracey explained. "They're likely to charge him over the weekend, so Gerry was tipping me the wink there's no story for us. And there isn't, not with a charge pending."

Loretta thanked Tracey, and settled down on the sofa with a new book about Jane Austen. She persevered for fifty pages before admitting that she hadn't taken in a word.

7

LORETTA'S BEDROOM WAS A LARGE ROOM on the top floor of her maisonette in Islington. It had stripped floorboards with pastel rugs dotted on them, and white walls. It also contained the piece of furniture in which she took most pride—a Victorian brass bed that she polished lovingly every three months. Loretta regarded the room as a refuge from the outside world and, in spite of her discoveries, she was fast asleep next morning when the buzzer on the entryphone sounded in the hall a floor below. Putting a hand out for the clock, she found it was only a quarter to eight. She was on the verge of ignoring the summons, on the reasonable assumption that the visitor had pressed the wrong buzzer, when it sounded several more times. So insistent was the noise that she padded downstairs in her nightshirt and picked up the handset. "Yes?" she said, yawning audibly. She could not imagine who might want to see her at this time on a Saturday morning.

"Police, miss," said a businesslike male voice at the other end. "Sorry to bother you. Can I come up for a moment?"

Astonished, Loretta pressed a button, which released the door at street level. Listening intently for the sound of feet on their way up the stairs, she could detect the movements of only one person. She stood rigid, fighting down a feeling of panic. How had they got on to her? she asked herself. Surely Tracey hadn't given her away? She wondered again how many offences she had committed since failing to go to the police in Paris. At least they couldn't know about her visit to Puddephat's rooms. Or could they? She was about to find out.

Opening the front door of the flat, she came face to face with an out-of-breath uniformed policeman. There were no stripes on his jacket so presumably he was a constable. She was surprised that they hadn't sent at least a detective. He also looked rather young.

"Miss Lawson?" the visitor began, his eyes sliding away from her face. Loretta hesitated, but decided against getting into the Miss or Ms. argument at this time of day. As she confirmed her identity, she noticed that the policeman was blushing. A flash of intuition told her that he was embarrassed by her attire. His discomfort gave her confidence. If he insisted on turning up when she was almost certain to be in bed, he could hardly complain about her nightshirt.

"Come in," she said, stepping back and waving him into the flat. The constable entered the hall and hesitated, nervously removing his helmet. Loretta led the way into the drawing-room and settled herself in an armchair. If there was going to be trouble, she might as well make herself as comfortable as possible. As the young man perched on the edge of the sofa, she took the bull by the horns. "I can guess why you're here," she began, "I just hadn't expected you so early."

"I'm sorry miss, but the station has been trying to get hold of you for several days," he interrupted. "You never answer your telephone."

"That's because I'm at work," Loretta said shortly. He was as bad as the pair who called on Bridget, she thought impatiently. Didn't he know that millions of women worked? Then the significance of what he had said came home to her. They had been trying to contact her for *sev-*

eral days. That meant they had connected her with Puddephat's disappearance *before* the discovery of the body. But how? Loretta was deeply perplexed. "Well, where do you want to start?" she asked, bracing herself for the questions to come. "Do I have the right to call a lawyer?" Now it was the policeman's turn to look astonished.

"It's not usual in a matter like this, miss," he said. "I don't want to stop you, but if you send off a cheque this weekend, that'll be the end of it." He fished inside his jacket and pulled out an envelope. "All the details are in there," he added, handing it to her. "Miss Loretta Lawson, that is you, isn't it?" he went on, seeing her hesitate.

Light was beginning to dawn on Loretta, and the relief was so great she almost laughed out loud. "That's right," she said. "You must excuse me, Officer, I'm still half asleep." She was opening the envelope as she spoke. Inside was a summons for non-payment of a parking ticket. She had completely forgotten about it until now. "Thanks very much for coming. How rude of me, I should have offered you some tea or coffee." He demurred at once, and she surmised that he was as keen to leave as she was to see the back of him. She promised to get out her cheque book as soon as he left, and saw him out. Closing the front door, she leaned against it, a hand to her throat. She felt faint when she thought how near she had come to disaster. She certainly needed a cup of tea, even if her erstwhile visitor didn't.

When the *Guardian* arrived half an hour later, she plucked it from the letter-box with impatient hands. The discovery of the body had made front-page news, in spite of the continuing saga of the hijack, and one of the features staff had put together a hasty obituary on an inside page. There was nothing about the arrest of Theo Sykes but that might be because the news had broken too late. The front-page story lacked most of the details with which Tracey had supplied her, and amounted to little more than a rewritten version of the PA copy she had seen. Just in time, she remembered to switch on the radio for the eight-thirty news on LBC. The headlines included a row between two Conservative MPs over remarks one of them had made about the weight of the Princess of Wales, an attack on the Prime Minister by a junior bishop in the Church of England, a house fire in Cardiff, and the discovery of a woman's body in South London. The inquiry into Puddephat's murder did not feature at all. She wondered if there had been some procedural delay in charging Theo Sykes. Or perhaps police press officers did not work at weekends? She must check with Tracey. She remembered she had agreed to go and see a movie with him that evening. The original purpose of the meeting—to discuss her discoveries in Oxford, and ask his advice on what to do next—had been overtaken by events, but she had nothing else to do that evening, and Tracey was usually good company. She looked at the clock. Saturday was the one day on which he seemed to arrive early at the *Herald* office, but she doubted whether he would have got there yet. She made a mental note to ring him later. She took a couple of cookery books from a shelf in the kitchen, and sat down at the dining-table to look through them. She had invited several friends to lunch the next day, and she had given no thought to what to cook. She was writing out a shopping-list when the phone rang.

It was Tracey. "About tonight," he said. "I suppose you won't want to see me now your little mystery's been cleared up?" Loretta knew that tone of voice. Tracey was in one of his self-pitying moods, and expected her to do something about it. These depressions were usually connected with his job; she guessed he was still irritated by his wasted trip to Glasgow and consequent lack of a story for the next day's paper. Saturday was the busiest day of the week at the *Herald* office, and Tracey hated having nothing to do while his colleagues got their stories on to copy paper, consulted lawyers and argued with sub-editors. Nevertheless, her heart sank at the thought of spending an evening with him in his present state of mind, and she was tempted to invent a sore throat in order to get out of it. But he had been very helpful over the Puddephat business, she admitted to herself, and his moods were unpredictable—he might be on top of the world by the time he arrived at the cinema.

"I'm still keen if you are," she said brightly, pretending she had not noticed anything was amiss. "By the way, I've just been listening to the news. There was nothing about Sykes being arrested."

"I don't think he has been arrested," Tracey said, diverted from his problems. "As far as I know, he went along voluntarily. After some persuasion, that is. But I expect they'll charge him some time today. My contact at the Yard isn't working over the weekend, so I'm afraid I can't find out much for you. If you keep listening to the radio, you'll probably hear any news as quickly as I do. So where shall we meet tonight? At the cinema?" They agreed on a time, and Tracey rang off.

So Sykes had not actually been arrested, Loretta mused. She must have misunderstood Tracey last night when he rang to say that Sykes had been taken away. Or was it Bridget who had said something about an arrest? She wished she knew more about police procedures. If the police were sufficiently confident of their case against Sykes, surely they would not hesitate to take him into custody? Nevertheless, Tracey still seemed convinced that a charge was imminent. Perhaps the question of whether or not Sykes had been arrested was only a technicality. She made her way upstairs and ran a bath. Lying in the water, she considered the evidence against Sykes again. He had been in Paris at the time of the murder. He had lied to the police as to his whereabouts, even before the body had been discovered. He disliked the dead man, and stood to gain professionally by his death. It still seemed far from conclusive. Loretta wondered if the police had found other evidence about which Tracey had not been told. That

111

seemed the only possible explanation. If they hadn't, she was far from happy. What about the letter from the mysterious "R"? And why had Puddephat's wife suddenly borrowed the keys to the flat in rue Roland only a couple of months before he was murdered there? Then there was the business of the dead girl, Melanie something. Loretta wished she knew more about that. Climbing out of the bath, she dried herself, and dressed in black ski pants and a thick jersey knitted by her mother. The weather had changed abruptly from unseasonably hot to unusually chilly, and most of her shopping needed to be done outdoors in Chapel market. Then she wrote out a cheque in payment of the forgotten parking-ticket, put it in an envelope and went out.

Walking the half-mile to Chapel market, she turned over and over in her mind the many questions about the murder that remained unanswered. The case against Sykes looked weaker by the minute. As she made her way from stall to stall, Loretta remembered her promise to ring Bridget. She would welcome her friend's view on the current state of the case. She hurried her way through her shopping, returned to the flat, and rang Bridget's number. There was no reply. She piled a week's dirty clothes into the washing-machine, and sat down with a book. At regular intervals, she listened to the news on the radio. It was not until three o'clock that there were any developments.

By now, several more MPs were embroiled in the row over whether or not the Princess of Wales was dangerously underweight, and the death toll in the Cardiff fire had risen to four. Puddephat's murder was the last item in the bulletin. "Thames Valley police have confirmed that a man is helping with inquiries into the murder of Dr. Hugh Puddephat, the English lecturer whose body was identified in Paris earlier this week," the newsreader reported. "The man, who has not been named, was taken to police headquarters in Oxford yesterday afternoon. A senior French detective is on his way to question the man, a spokesman said." That was all.

Loretta guessed there were legal reasons for the terse nature of the item. But at least it provided a possible explanation for the delay in charging Sykes. She had quite forgotten that the French police were involved in the inquiry. Even so, she would still like to mull the thing over with Bridget. She dialled her friend's number again.

"I've just seen the local paper," Bridget said when she answered. "It doesn't say much."

Loretta passed on what she had learned from Tracey. "I'm not at all happy about it," she finished.

"I see what you mean," Bridget said. "When Geoffrey rang last night, I assumed they'd got more on him than that. But I don't see what you can do about it. Even if you went to the police now, your story doesn't shed any light on who did it. All you know is *where* it happened."

"That's true," said Loretta. "But I have this feeling I ought to do something. I wish I could find out about R, for instance, but I can't think of a way to do it. I wonder if there's any way of finding out more about the girl who killed herself—Melanie Gandell, that's her name."

"Couldn't Tracey help with that?" Bridget asked. "Or perhaps I could find out something through faculty records. Tell you what, I'll have a stab at that on Monday morning. At least I'll be able to tell you where she came from. Though I'm not sure how that helps you."

"I think it's a matter of stumbling around in the dark until we find a clue," Loretta said gratefully. "The other avenue I could try is a bit of research into Puddephat's wife." She told Bridget about Veronica's odd behaviour over the Paris flat. "But I haven't been able to think of an excuse for getting in touch with her," she admitted. "If you have any bright ideas, do let me know."

Loretta felt more cheerful after her chat with Bridget, slightly less at the mercy of events. Her next call was to Tracey. "Are you busy?" she asked when she got through.

"Quite," he said warily, sensing she was about to make a request of him.

"I just wondered if you could look in the library for me," she explained. "I've seen the articles filed under Puddephat's name, but I didn't look under Melanie Gandell. There might be something in there I've missed."

"What's the point, Loretta?" Tracey asked irritably. "The police have just confirmed they're holding Sykes. It's only a matter of time before they charge him."

"Yes, I heard it on the radio," Loretta agreed. "But I'm still not happy. Come on, John, humour me. It'll only take you five minutes." Reluctantly, Tracey gave in. If he found anything of interest, he said, he would bring photocopies with him to the cinema.

Loretta was paying for the tickets at the cash desk when she felt a hand on her shoulder. She turned, and found Tracey beaming at her.

"Loretta," he said affably. "I hope I haven't kept you waiting." In contrast to the last time she had spoken to him, his mood seemed positively sunny. She soon found out why. "I'm off to Berlin tomorrow," he explained. "Great story. It's so good, I can't even tell you about it. So I mustn't get to bed too late. And by the way, here are your cuttings. I still think you're wasting your time. I should be charging you for all this research."

Loretta held up the tickets. "That's why these are on me," she said. "I'm afraid I can't afford professional rates." Tracey laughed, and put his hand under her elbow to guide her into the cinema. As he turned towards the smokers' seats, Loretta stopped and headed in the opposite direction.

"Come on, Loretta," Tracey complained. "I can't sit through a whole film without a cigarette." Loretta was unmoved. It was an argument they had had before, and one which she invariably won. Grumbling, Tracey followed her to the non-smokers' seats. There was no time to look at the cuttings he had given her, and Loretta put the envelope in her bag. For the next two hours she was absorbed in the film, which turned out to be as good as she had hoped.

Tracey, on the other hand, did not like it; they had an amicable disagreement about its merits on the way to a nearby pub. "I can't stay long," he warned her as she carried their drinks to the table where he was sitting. "But I can give you a lift home. My car's just round the corner."

Loretta was surprised and touched. "There's no need to do that," she protested. "It's still quite early. I can take the underground. It's miles out of your way, and you need an early night."

"I thought you might ask me to stay," Tracey said hopefully, instantly dispelling her feeling of gratitude. "We are still married, after all. And we're both at a loose end. Come on, Laura, for old times' sake." He cast her a look which, she guessed, was calculated to suggest a combination of nostalgia and affection. It didn't work.

"We agreed when we separated that we wouldn't behave like this," Loretta replied in aggrieved tones. It was just like Tracey to take unfair advantage of her attempts to remain on friendly terms with him. She dashed off her orange juice, and stood up. "The best thing you can do is go home and tuck yourself up with a hot-water bottle," she advised, pulling on her coat.

"I suppose your feminist friends would be proud of you," Tracey said sarcastically. "How to get rid of your unwanted husband in one easy lesson. And after all the running around I've done for you in the last couple of days. You've got no heart, that's your trouble, Loretta. If anything happens to me in Berlin, I just hope you'll be sorry."

Loretta sighed. "Don't be such a baby," she said witheringly. "It'll probably be a wild goose chase, just like your trip to Glasgow." Having delivered this Parthian shot, she stalked off to find a taxi home.

* * *

Sunday's papers, including the *Sunday Herald*, reported that an unidentified man was still being questioned in connection with Puddephat's murder. No developments were reported on LBC that morning, and Loretta had to switch the radio off when her friends arrived for lunch. After the meal, someone suggested a walk on Hampstead Heath, and that turned into tea at a small patisserie close to where Loretta had parked her car. It was after six when she got home and started clearing up the detritus of lunch.

When she had finished, she sat down at the kitchen table with the envelope Tracey had given her the night before. Inside, there were four sheets of paper, each of them a photocopy of a newspaper cutting. Three were familiar; she recognized the *Sun* headline, "Warning For Death-case Egghead," and the more subdued headlines from the *Observer* and the *Guardian*. Loretta guessed Tracey had simply copied the entire contents of the file on the dead girl. For a moment, she thought she had wasted his time. Then she saw that the last cutting was new to her. It was a long report of the inquest on Melanie Gandell which had appeared in the *Daily Telegraph*. The story, which mentioned Puddephat by name, should have appeared in his file, but she had been right to doubt the efficiency of the *Herald*'s library staff.

Glancing down the columns, she immediately discovered some new information: Puddephat had been accompanied at the inquest by his wife, she learned with surprise. Surely they had been separated, and on bad terms, by the time of the inquest? But the paragraph that interested her most concerned Melanie Gandell herself. "Formal evidence of identification was given by the dead girl's aunt, Mrs. Lucretia Grant, who travelled to the inquest from her home in Herefordshire," the story said. "Miss Gandell's parents died in an air crash in 1968, when she was five. She was an only child. Her mother was the talented young painter, Livia Gandell." Poor Melanie, Loretta thought to herself. The girl's short life had been dogged by tragedy. She felt a

116

surge of anger towards Hugh Puddephat. How *could* a man in his position take advantage of so vulnerable a creature as Melanie Gandell? She read the paragraph again. She wished she knew more about painting; the name of Melanie's mother meant nothing to her. But at least she now had the name of Melanie's aunt. It was a nuisance that the *Telegraph* was so vague about her address—she wasn't even sure whether Herefordshire still existed as a county—but perhaps Bridget would have more exact details for her next day. And Melanie's aunt might be important if Loretta was going to pursue this line of inquiry: presumably it was she who had brought up the girl after her parents' death in the plane crash. Not that Loretta had yet come up with an excuse to contact Mrs. Grant, even if she acquired a proper address, but that problem could wait until after she spoke to Bridget. With that thought, she returned the cuttings to their envelope and put it away in a drawer of her desk.

There had been no more news about the murder inquiry by the time Loretta arrived at her office on Monday morning. She was tied up until lunch with yet another department meeting but, after a sandwich in the refectory, found herself with a clear afternoon.

Returning to her office, she wondered if she should phone Bridget, but decided to leave it until later in the day: the first-years would be arriving at Bridget's college in the middle of the week, and her friend would be as tied up as Loretta had been the week before. Just before five, it occurred to her that Bridget might have forgotten her promise to check Melanie Gandell's address, and she dialled the number of her college rooms. She found Bridget in a state of great agitation.

"I was just going to ring you," she said. "You were absolutely right. Theo Sykes didn't do it. Geoffrey's just been telling me all about it. The police have made a dreadful mess of it. Poor Theo, he's escaped a murder charge, but his career here is finished."

"What's happened?" asked Loretta impatiently.

"Well," said Bridget, "they held him all weekend, and tried everything they could think of to make him confess. He didn't. But he went on refusing to say anything at all about what he'd been doing in Paris. Then, last night, the master's wife came home after a weekend away. She went on Friday morning, you see, so she'd no idea Sykes had been taken in. As soon as she found out what had happened, she went straight to the police and told them everything. She's been having an affair with Theo Sykes, and it turns out they were in Paris together at the time Puddephat was murdered. She told them this in confidence, because the master didn't know—he suspected, apparently, which explains why he went off Theo, but they'd always denied it. She gave them the name of the hotel where they'd stayed, the lot. Of course, they had to let him go. Then this morning, the police were all over the college again and, by lunchtime, the master knew. Geoffrey says nobody knows whether they let it out accidentally, or were getting their own back on Sykes for wasting a whole weekend. But there was a terrible scene between the master and Theo Sykes. Apparently you could hear them shouting all round the college. And poor old Mary Morris, how must she feel? Geoffrey saw her put a couple of suitcases in her car and drive off. So it looks as if she's left the master, at least for the time being."

"Trust John to be out of the country," Loretta said wistfully. "He was beastly to me on Saturday night, and it would give me great pleasure to tell him I was right all along. Oh, dear," she added, a new thought striking her, "it doesn't give one great confidence in the police, does it?"

"It certainly doesn't," said Bridget. "And, if you want to carry on looking into it yourself, I've got Melanie Gandell's address for you. Have you got a piece of paper?" Loretta had. "It's a village in Somerset. A place called Buckland Dinham." She spelled it out for Loretta. "The actual address is Cherry Cottage. There didn't seem to be a phone number. Our records are not brilliant, I'm afraid."

"That's odd," said Loretta. "I've been looking through the cuttings on the inquest again, and she was identified by an aunt who lived in Herefordshire."

"Perhaps she moved just before Melanie died," Bridget suggested. "As I was saying, the administrative people in the English faculty are not particularly efficient. Didn't the newspaper give the aunt's full address?"

"Unfortunately not," said Loretta. "And her surname is Grant—there must be thousands of people with that name in the county. Perhaps I should concentrate on Somerset first. Assuming Melanie's aunt did move from Cherry Cottage, she may have left a forwarding address with the new owners."

"Let me know if I can help," Bridget offered. "I'm rather busy during the week, but things will calm down by the weekend."

Loretta thanked her. "I'll be in touch," she said. "First of all, I need to sit down and work out a plan of campaign."

8

LORETTA LOOKED AT HER WATCH. IT WAS ten past five. She had agreed to have a drink with the deputy head of the English department after work, which gave her a bit of time. Taking a clean sheet of A4 paper out of a drawer, she divided it into three vertical columns. At the top of the first, she wrote "Melanie Gandell." In the second column, she filled in the address Bridget had just given her—Cherry Cottage, Buckland Dinham, Somerset. The third column she left blank. Underneath Melanie's name in the first column, she wrote "Lucretia Grant." It was an odd combination of names, she reflected; an unhappy juxtaposition of the unusual and the mundane. In the second column, she wrote the word "Herefordshire" with a question mark. She returned to the first column. "Veronica Puddephat," she wrote, and put her pen down. She was horribly short on even the most basic information about the people she wanted to speak to. The third column, which she had reserved for telephone numbers, was so far entirely blank. She wondered how she could fill in some of the gaps.

If Melanie's aunt had moved from Cherry Cottage, the phone number would no longer be listed under Grant. There was no way of knowing who lived there now. But wait a minute . . . what if the cottage had belonged to Melanie herself? Been left to her, perhaps, by her parents? It was perfectly possible that one of Melanie's relatives—a cousin, maybe—had inherited it. She picked up the phone and dialled Directory Enquiries. "Somerset," she told the operator. "It's a village called Buckland Dinham. The name is Gandell. G-A-N-D-E-L-L. No, I'm sorry, I don't know the initial." She drew a blank. There were no Gandells at all in the directory that included the village. As a long shot—just in case Lucretia Grant owned two homes—she also checked the name of Grant. Still no luck. The column for telephone numbers of Melanie's family would have to remain empty for the time being. She moved on to Puddephat's wife. Andrew Walker was bound to have Veronica's address and telephone number but a request for them, so soon after she had been asking questions about the woman's husband, might well arouse his suspicions. There must be another way of finding out.

She thought back to Puddephat's *Who's Who* entry. She was pretty sure the only address listed was that of his college. That was no help. But she had only checked in a very recent volume. What if she were to look in earlier editions? She congratulated herself on her improving powers of deduction. Only a few weeks ago, she would have been stumped by now. If the college library stocked *Who's Who*, her task would be easy. A quick phone call confirmed that it did.

A few minutes later, she was standing in front of a shelf stacked with yearly editions of the book. At random, she lifted down the volume for 1977. She quickly found Puddephat, William Hugh. His address that year was the Red House, Hallborough, Oxon. There was also a telephone number. Loretta noted both in the back of her diary, and put the book back. She checked 1980. The address remained the same. She tried 1981. The only address shown was that of the college. The marriage must have broken up some time in 1980. She hoped Veronica Puddephat had not moved out of the Red House after the separation.

Feeling pleased with herself, Loretta went back to her office. She filled in the columns next to Veronica's name, and stared thoughtfully at the piece of paper. All she needed now was an excuse to contact her. She was disappointed to find that nothing came immediately to mind. How much easier it would be if she were a newspaper reporter, like Tracey, she thought. It was the perfect excuse for ringing up complete strangers and asking all sort of personal questions. But did she dare impersonate a journalist? No, she didn't. It would only take one phone call to blow her cover. She wondered if she could stage an apparently accidental meeting with Veronica. She could not think of any means of doing it without involving Andrew. She was still no further forward. Perhaps the best course was simply to come clean—to explain how she came to be involved in the case, and enlist Veronica's help? Loretta was not enthusiastic. It would mean putting herself in the hands of a complete stranger, a stranger who might even be involved in Puddephat's murder. After all, Veronica's request to use the flat in rue Roland two months before the murder, and the odd business with the keys afterwards, remained unexplained. Now *there* was an idea! Veronica had been to the flat: wasn't it possible she might have left something behind which Loretta could claim to have found? A moment's thought told her it wasn't. Andrew was not even sure that Veronica *had* used the flat. It sounded as if her plans had changed at the last minute and, embarrassed by all the trouble Andrew had gone to on her behalf, she had taken the easy way out by returning the keys without a message.

But what about Puddephat himself? How about telling Veronica she had found something in rue Roland which belonged to her husband, and asking if she could return it? That was a much better plan. She mulled over what the object might be. She remembered the book she had found in the flat, but rejected it. It would have to be something of value to justify her going to all this trouble. A wallet? But a wallet would contain all sorts of personal items which she couldn't get hold of. The same went for a diary, or an address book. Then she saw the major snag with the whole idea. The point was that she—and the killer—were the only people who knew Puddephat had been to the flat at all. If she went to Veronica with this story, she might as well tell her the complete truth.

It was back to square one. She wondered if she should consult Bridget. After all, Bridget had put her in touch with Geoffrey, and Geoffrey had got her into Puddephat's rooms. Loretta pushed her hair back from her face with a cluck of impatience. What an idiot she was! What was wrong with the excuse she had used to Geoffrey: that she was trying to retrieve a set of her own notes from Puddephat. There was no reason why she should know that Veronica was separated from her husband. She could simply ring Veronica—no, it would be better to go and see her—and explain her supposed problem. If she had come all the way from London, the woman was hardly likely to turn her away. It was simple! How soon could she do it?

Loretta took out her diary, and looked at her schedule for the week. She could just about manage Thursday, she thought. But that was no good—what if Veronica worked? It would be safer to try over a weekend. Saturday looked clear. It would also be better from the point of view of traffic—she hadn't yet looked up Hallborough on a map, but she guessed she would need her car to get to it.

It wasn't until Thursday that it occurred to Loretta that if she was going near Oxford, she might as well call in on Bridget. She might even be able to stay at her friend's house on Saturday night.

That evening, she rang Bridget at home, and explained what she was up to. She was very welcome to stay on Saturday night, Bridget said, although she herself was going to the Oxford Playhouse. "Why don't you stay Sunday as well?" Bridget asked. "I'm having a little party for my tutees. Geoffrey will be there as well, and a couple of my postgraduates." Loretta was able to refuse, mindful of a 10 a.m. lecture on Monday, when Bridget added: "I'll tell you who else is going to be there. The mysterious R. At least, it turns out it isn't R."

"I'm sorry," Loretta interrupted. "I'm not following this." Bridget knew how important it was to find the author of the letter. Why hadn't she got in touch with Loretta straight away? It didn't make sense.

"His real name is Jamie Baird," Bridget explained patiently. "He's in his second year, and Puddephat was his tutor last year. Although the second- and third-years don't officially come back until next week, Puddephat's tutees have been called back early so they can be allocated to new people quickly. I've got him. The faculty's worried about the effect on their studies, you see. I've taken three of them, and one of them is this Jamie Baird. The name meant nothing to me, of course, but I recognized him as soon as he walked into my room this morning. I realized then that we'd been barking up the wrong tree." Loretta's baffled silence prompted Bridget to a further attempt at elucidation. "Remember the photo, the one you found in Puddephat's rooms? And we thought the boy in it was R? Well, he isn't. He's called Jamie Baird. Now d'you see?"

"But why didn't you tell me sooner?" Loretta demanded. "Even if this boy, Jamie, didn't write the letter, he might know who did. Who R is, I mean. I *must* talk to him!"

"So come to my party on Sunday," Bridget said. "He'll be there. Though I don't know why you think he's so important, now we've discovered he isn't R. Just because he was Puddephat's tutee, it doesn't mean he knew him terribly well. We all have a couple of dozen tutees—surely you're not planning to interrogate every one of Puddephat's?"

"Of course not," Loretta said impatiently. "You're forgetting where we found the photograph. It was hidden at

124

the bottom of a drawer, remember. You can't tell me there isn't something odd about that. Either Jamie Baird was particularly close to Puddephat, or Puddephat wanted him to be. That's what makes Jamie worth seeing. This is a terrific piece of luck, Bridget."

"I'm not convinced," Bridget said. "There could be other explanations for the photograph. Perhaps Jamie dropped it on a visit to Puddephat's rooms, and Puddephat put it in a drawer until he saw him again. But I'm not trying to dampen your enthusiasm. What time shall I expect you on Saturday?"

Two letters were lying in the hall when Loretta got up on Saturday. She studied the envelopes as she wandered into the kitchen to make breakfast. One contained the proofs of an article she had written for an academic journal; she scanned the contents of the envelope briefly and pinned it to her noticeboard to be dealt with on her return from Oxford. It took her a moment to recognize the handwriting on the second envelope and when she did, she put it down while she plugged in the kettle and took a croissant from the breadbin. She had a good idea of what the envelope would contain, and she was already feeling faintly irritated. She placed the croissant under the grill, and sat down to open the letter.

It was written on House of Commons notepaper, and folded around a duplicated sheet of paper. "Dear Loretta," she read, "I've just come back from an official trip to Italy, and I squeezed in a visit to a peace camp while I was there. I thought the enclosed would interest you." Unfolding the notice, she found it was a call to Italian women to demonstrate at the NATO base where the camp had been set up. She turned back to the letter. The rest of the message consisted of a single word: "Dinner?" She raised her eyebrows. Last weekend Tracey had tried to resurrect his relationship with her, now it was Anthony Swan. You had to give Anthony top marks for persistence, she thought to herself. She had told him in no uncertain terms, on more than one occasion, that she wanted no more to do with him. Yet every six months or so he found another excuse to get in touch with her. She supposed you had to be pretty thick-skinned to be a Member of Parliament. She screwed up the letter and dropped it into the kitchen bin. She had not replied to any of his earlier messages, and she would not respond to this one. She knew that if she kept the note, she might be tempted. She had liked Anthony a great deal and, at this distance in time, the attractions of her affair with him were easier to remember than the drawbacks. The latter had included, she reminded herself sternly, his insistence on secrecy, her guilt at deceiving his wife, and the discovery that he was simultaneously conducting two other clandestine affairs. She was glad she had a busy weekend in front of her, and little time to brood.

An hour later, she climbed into her Panda and set off for Oxford. Hallborough was five miles north-west of the city, and she thought she should be there by noon. It was a beautiful autumn day, clear and cold, and she swept along the M40 listening to a tape of Grace Jones on the cassette player. As she approached the Princes Risborough turn-off, and the section of the road which cuts through high chalk cliffs, she changed the tape for a glorious version of *Tosca*. She was filled with a sense of well-being which augured well, she thought, for the success of her journey.

Hallborough turned out to be a picturesque Cotswold village with one main street. Loretta drove slowly, peering from side to side for a glimpse of the Red House. If it lived up to its name, she thought, it should stick out like a sore thumb among the warm, yellowish stone of the other buildings. She saw three public houses and a shop selling papers, but nothing that looked a likely candidate. The houses began to peter out, and eventually stopped. Loretta decided she had gone far enough, and used the beginning of a farm track to turn the car in. Back in the village, she pulled up outside the paper shop, which turned out to double as a general store, and went in. Her friendly enquiry as to the whereabouts of the Red House was met by a hostile stare from the woman behind the counter. Nonplussed, Loretta explained that she had driven right through the village without finding it. The expression of the shop assistant was making her most uncomfortable. Finally, the woman appeared to relent. The house, she admitted grudgingly, could be found by driving through the village and taking a narrow turning to the left. Loretta would be able to recognize the road by the high hedges which flanked it. She thanked the woman and returned to her car. For a fleeting moment, she wondered if the woman might have given her deliberately wrong directions but, shrugging the thought away, she started the car and turned back in the direction from which she had just come.

About two hundred yards from the village, she spotted the turning. The road was wide enough for only one vehicle at a time, and she hoped she wouldn't meet another car. The tall hedge to her left suddenly gave way to a low brick wall, and she found herself driving past the Red House. Her assumption had been correct: its identity was as apparent from the colour of the bricks as from the nameplate on the gate. She stopped, then reversed back a few feet until she could turn into the open gateway. Her heart leaped into her mouth, and she paused. It was one thing imagining the scene from the comfort of her London flat but quite another to find herself going through with it. It occurred to her that she didn't even know that it was Veronica's house; why on earth hadn't she checked Directory Enquiries to make sure she was still living there? She heard the sound of another car behind her, and saw that she was blocking the narrow road. She turned into the drive of the Red House, and brought the car to a halt close to the front door.

The house was more modern than she had expected—at a guess, she thought it must have been built between the wars. It was large and double-fronted, and conspicuously well kept. The front door was painted a shiny black, and the brass knocker gleamed spotlessly. There was no sign of a bell. Loretta got out of her car, walked up to the door, lifted the knocker and rapped timidly. Disliking the tentative sound she had made, she knocked again more forcefully. She listened intently for signs of life, but heard nothing.

She stepped back and looked over the house. The windows stared blankly back at her. It occurred to her for the first time that there was no sign of a car, apart from her own. It seemed unlikely that anyone would choose to live in this out-of-the-way place without some form of transport—if she hadn't been so nervous, that would have occurred to her earlier, she thought wryly. She concluded that Veronica Puddephat, if this was indeed her house, was out.

She got back into her car, backed carefully out of the drive, and headed for Hallborough again. She spotted a telephone kiosk, and stopped to look in the telephone directory. There wasn't one, and the phone was out of order except for emergency calls. Loretta swore under her breath. After her reception in the village store, she was not keen to go back with further questions to establish that Veronica still lived in the Red House. As she left the phone box, she looked up and down the street for other shops. There were none to be seen. All she was left with were the three pubs.

The nearest, the Queen's Head, was very much a brewery's idea of what a traditional English pub should look like. Its sign consisted of a portrait of a woman's head, styled in what she guessed was intended to be Tudor fashion. It might be any of the wives of Henry VIII, or Elizabeth I, or even Mary I. There were coaching lamps on either side of the main door, and uncomfortable rustic tables in front of the windows. On the other hand, it did have a sign saying "bar-food," and Loretta realized she was quite hungry.

She went inside, and was relieved to discover she was one of the first customers. She never felt entirely at ease on her own in pubs. Restaurants she didn't mind, but in pubs she always felt too much at the mercy of predatory men. Here, however, she was alone apart from a couple of men seated on stools next to the bar, and a yellow Labrador slumbering at their feet. A handwritten menu stood on the bar. She studied it while waiting for someone to appear and serve her. She rejected the beef curry with rice as too much of an unknown quantity—full of apples and curry powder she suspected—and decided on the steak and kidney pie with chips. Nobody could do very much to a steak and kidney pie, she thought. A barmaid appeared, a woman in her mid-twenties with streaked blonde hair and tight jeans. Loretta gave her order, intending to tag her question about Veronica Puddephat on the end, but was baulked by the woman's suggestive banter with the two men seated at the bar. Taking her glass of wine to a table near the fire, she decided the question could wait until her food turned up. The fire, which turned out to be the real thing and not the gas imitation she feared, gave out a welcoming warmth. Loretta took the *Guardian* from her bag and settled down to read it. She paid little attention when the door opened, and two more customers came in. It was only when they reached the bar and addressed the barmaid that Loretta began to take notice.

"Mornin', love. Two pints of your best, and have one yourself," one of them said in a loud voice. As the woman behind the bar began to pull the pints, he went on. "Wonder if you can help us, love. We're looking for a Mrs. Puddephat, lady who lives in the big red house down the road. Seems to have been some sort of mix-up. My mate and I've come all the way from London to see her, and she seems to have gone out."

"Friends of hers, are you?" asked the barmaid.

"That's right," agreed the man in the raincoat. "There's been some sort of misunderstanding, that's all it is. You don't happen to have seen her, do you?"

To his obvious surprise, the barmaid failed to rise to

these friendly overtures. "Some mistake," the woman said, plonking the second pint down on the bar. "Gone to Spain for a couple of weeks, she has. P'raps she forgot you were coming? That'll be one pound sixty-eight." She put the money in the till, walked to the other end of the bar, and began ostentatiously polishing glasses.

The two newcomers exchanged glances, and picked up their beer. After a few half-hearted sips, one of them made a great show of looking at his watch, and put his glass down. "Well, looks like we've had a wasted trip," he said with patently false bonhomie. "Might as well get back on the road. Thanks, miss." The two men left, closing the door noisily behind them.

"Here, Sandra," said one of the regulars sitting at the bar, "first I've heard about Mrs. P. going off to Spain. Seems a bit queer, with the body only just being found, an' all that. You sure that's where she's gone?"

"'Course not," said Sandra, a huge smile on her face. "She hasn't gone anywhere, not to my knowledge, anyway. I saw her in the paper shop this morning. I'm just sick of reporters tramping in and out, wanting to know her business. He must be the tenth this week. You can tell 'em a mile off. They all wear those macs, and flash their money about. Bloody vultures."

Loretta breathed a huge sigh of relief. She had been quite taken in by Sandra's invention. It also explained the hostility her questions about the Red House had aroused. It had not occurred to her that the newspapers might still be on the trail of Puddephat's widow.

Now that she started to think about it, she could guess what they were after. "Murdered Don: Tragic Wife Speaks," perhaps. Or even "My Heartbreak, By Peer's Daughter." She applauded the barmaid's methods of getting rid of them. As a bonus, she had got the information she needed without having to ask for it.

She put down her newspaper as Sandra brought over the

steak and kidney pie. It looked all right, although Loretta thought the china dish it came in was a bit unnecessary. Much cheered, she bit into the first forkful. The crust was piping hot, and the innards lukewarm. A microwave oven, Loretta guessed. She was on the verge of complaining to the barmaid, but decided that she was not all that hungry after all, and at least the chips were hot. They would see her through until the evening.

When she had finished eating, she wondered what to do next. She might as well try Veronica's house again, although she was disturbed to find that she was on the same track as hordes of newspaper reporters. Being pestered by the press was hardly likely to put Veronica in the mood for unexpected visitors. But it could not be helped. She returned to her car, and drove back to the Red House.

As she drew abreast of the drive, she saw that a car was parked next to the front door. Two heads swivelled to peer at her, and she recognized the reporters from the pub. She accelerated hastily, and drove on. She was amazed by the men's persistence. Presumably the house was still empty, and they were staking it out. Loretta decided she would have to abandon her attempt to see Veronica for the rest of the day. As soon as she could find a convenient place to do so, she turned the car and headed back towards Hallborough. As she passed Veronica's house, she noticed that one of the men had got out of the green Maestro and was making his way round the back of the building. Surely they wouldn't go so far as to break in? She spotted the out-of-order phone box and drew up beside it. She had never before contacted any of the emergency services, and she was surprised by how long the operator took to put her through to the police. Without giving her name, she supplied them with Veronica's address, and the information that she had just seen two men acting suspiciously in the garden. A patrol car would be sent to the house immediately, a policeman said. Loretta got back into her car and drove off towards Oxford. She hoped the police would give the two journalists the hard time they deserved.

She was woken the next morning by Bridget, who appeared in her room carrying a cup of tea and a copy of the *Sunday Herald*. "Good play?" Loretta enquired. She had gone to bed by the time Bridget returned from her trip to the theatre the night before.

"So-so," said Bridget. "I had my doubts about the woman who played Ophelia. She was too healthy for my liking. But look at this. Your husband's been having a busy week." She passed Loretta the paper. "I heard him being interviewed on the news a few minutes ago," Bridget added. "Talk about a dog with two tails."

Tracey's picture byline glared at Loretta from the front page; had he really intended to look so fierce, she wondered, or was it an attempt to hide his embarrassment? "Top East German Spy Exposed," the headline read. So that was what he'd been up to in Berlin, Loretta thought. No wonder he hadn't been keen to tell her about it. He was well aware of her view that spy stories were *Boy's Own Paper* stuff, not worthy of a moment's serious attention. "The *Sunday Herald* has obtained evidence that a British diplomat working in our consulate in West Berlin is a spy," the article began. It went on to describe Tracey's confrontation with the unfortunate man, and his subsequent disappearance, presumably over the border into East Germany. "Defence sources in Britain say the man may have done incalculable damage to the NATO alliance before his exposure last week," Loretta read. There was even a blurred picture of the man shutting the door in the face of the *Herald* photographer.

"Why bother?" Loretta asked Bridget, shaking her head. "We do it, they do it, they're just a bunch of public schoolboys playing games. And I'd like to know how John got hold of the story in the first place. Talk about trial by newspaper. I just hope his source is more reliable than the Yard chap who told him confidentially that Theo Sykes killed Puddephat."

"Talking of Puddephat, there's an article about him on page five," Bridget said. "But I don't think there's anything in it that we didn't know already."

Loretta turned the pages. "Nice picture of the college," she remarked. "Oh, so that's what Puddephat looked like." A close-up of Puddephat's head was inset into the main picture. It showed a wide face, the cheeks slightly puffy— from overindulgence of some sort? Loretta wondered. The hair was dark and longish, falling forward over one eye.

"That's a rather flattering picture of him," Bridget said, looking over Loretta's shoulder. "He usually looked a bit seedier than that."

"You're right," said Loretta, a moment later. "There's nothing new here. I'll have to try Veronica again this afternoon. I just hope she's in this time."

Anxious not to interrupt Veronica's Sunday lunch, Loretta waited until three to set off for Hallborough. On the way, she ran through the speech she had prepared in her mind. It wasn't as convincing as she'd like, but it would have to do. Anyway, there was no guarantee that she would find Veronica in. When she arrived at the Red House, a large Citroën was parked at the top of the short drive. It was empty, and there was no other car in sight. Loretta parked neatly behind it, and walked nervously to the front door. She knocked twice. Almost at once, she heard footsteps. The door opened very slightly, and a woman peered out.

"Mrs. Puddephat?" enquired Loretta.

"If you're a reporter, you can just go away!" the woman said peevishly.

Loretta was horrified. "I'm not, really I'm not," she said urgently. "I am sorry to bother you, and I'm honestly

133

not from a newspaper." Was the woman going to shut the door in her face?

"Who are you then?" she asked, opening the door a fraction wider. Her tone had softened slightly.

"My name's Loretta Lawson, and I lecture in English at London University," Loretta explained. "I came to see you about some notes I sent your husband. I know it's a terrible time for me to turn up on your doorstep, but I only want to speak to you for a moment. Please," she added.

The woman looked her over. "You don't look like a reporter," she admitted. "I suppose you'd better come in." She stood back, allowing Loretta to step into a wide hall. "This way." Loretta followed her into a spacious drawing-room, and seated herself in a chair to one side of the tiled fireplace, while Veronica took the chair opposite. "Now, how can I help you?" she asked.

Loretta launched into her story, at the same time covertly taking stock of Hugh Puddephat's widow. Veronica was in her mid-thirties, she guessed, and her clothes were good rather than fashionable. Her dark blonde hair was cut into a short, feathery style, which had been popular a few years ago. All in all, her appearance was what would be described as "classic" by the type of women's magazines read by Loretta's mother. The one exception was her glasses, whose frames were a startling pink—perhaps an attempt to liven up her image? If so, it hadn't quite worked.

When Loretta stopped speaking, Veronica remained silent for a minute. Then she took a deep breath. "How did you get this address?" she asked.

Loretta was prepared. "I rang the college, but they weren't much help. They said everything to do with your husband was in the hands of the police. I'm afraid I persuaded the woman I spoke to to give me this address. Don't blame her, it's my fault for pressing her."

"I see," Veronica said. "You obviously didn't realize I was separated from my husband?"

Loretta had the grace to feel uncomfortable, if not for the right reasons. "I didn't," she mumbled. "I'm very sorry. If I'd known . . ." She let the rest of the sentence trail off.

"I'm afraid you've had a wasted trip," Veronica said. Her tone was surprisingly sympathetic. Loretta wondered what to do next. The only thing she could think of was a request to use the lavatory, but that would tell her little beyond the colour of Veronica's bathroom suite. Unwittingly, Veronica came to the rescue. "The least I can do is offer you some tea before you set off," she said. "Do you prefer China or Indian?"

"Indian please," Loretta said gratefully.

While Veronica was absent, presumably in the kitchen, Loretta looked about her. Most of the furniture was mahogany, and antique. An upright piano stood against one wall, a row of framed photographs on top of it. Loretta didn't dare go over and examine them. The upkeep of such a house would require a substantial income, she thought to herself; she remembered that Veronica came from a wealthy family.

At that moment, Veronica returned, setting a tray on a small table which she moved in front of the fire. She smiled brightly at Loretta and apologized for the lack of food in the house. "All I've got are these," she said, waving one ringed hand towards a plate of Bakewell tarts. "And I can't claim to have made them myself." She spoke as if she were admitting to a considerable lapse of manners on her part. Loretta, who could not remember when she had last baked a cake, was quite taken aback. "You've told me who you are," Veronica continued, "so I ought to introduce myself properly. My name's Veronica. Some people shorten it to Ron, my husband mainly, but I can't say I like it. Ron Puddephat always sounds like the manager of a second-division football club to me."

The cup and saucer rattled in Loretta's hand. She was astonished by her own stupidity. It was hard to see why such an obvious solution to R's identity had never occurred to her. She perched her cup on the edge of the table, thinking hard. What on earth had Hugh Puddephat done to provoke such passionate hatred in this well-mannered woman? That was only one of dozens of questions she wanted to ask Veronica. But she must proceed carefully. Apart from anything else, Veronica—as author of the letter—must now be a prime suspect.

Loretta's attempt to work out her next move was interrupted by Veronica's voice. "What sort of things do you teach?" she queried. "I do envy you. I used to think about an academic career when I was a student. That was before I got married, of course." She spoke as though the two things were entirely incompatible. "I was very fond of Jane Austen and Fanny Burney at one time," she went on. "But then, of course, I met Hugh."

At one of his lectures on Lawrence, Loretta recalled, thinking back to her afternoon in the *Herald* library. She couldn't help thinking that Austen was a lot more up Veronica's street than Lawrence. Perhaps the marriage had been an attraction of opposites. She wondered which parts of her own teaching schedule might interest Veronica. "I'm teaching a course on Virginia Woolf at the moment," she hazarded. "That's with the first-years."

"Oh, *To The Lighthouse*," Veronica said with a marked lack of interest. "I never really got anywhere with her."

"Next term I'm going to be teaching part of a course on the influence of gender on style," Loretta added, again to little response." And I'm writing a book on Edith Wharton," she said desperately, doubting whether Veronica would have heard of her. But she had scored an unexpected success.

"Edith Wharton," Veronica repeated in reverential tones. "Do you know, *The House of Mirth* is my favourite book. Do tell me all about it."

It was a way of gaining Veronica's confidence, Loretta thought, launching into a description of the work she'd done so far. She wondered when it would be safe to steer the conversation back to Veronica. "Did you ever think about doing postgraduate work?" she asked, when there seemed to be a suitable lull.

"Well, no, not after Hugh and I became engaged," Veronica said awkwardly. "And I don't suppose I would have been bright enough."

Oh! thought Loretta. How women lack self-confidence! It was rare to hear a man expressing such views. She was willing to bet Hugh Puddephat had never suffered similar doubts.

Suddenly Veronica's eyes lit up, and she leaned forward. "But I have been thinking about taking a course," she said. "I haven't told anyone else yet, but I'd like to do something practical, like social work." She hesitated, as if expecting Loretta to pour scorn on the suggestion. "I help in a home for handicapped children three days a week," she added. "As a volunteer, of course." So Veronica didn't support herself, Loretta noted. As if reading her thoughts, Veronica hurried on. "I don't . . . didn't, I mean, take anything from my husband," she said defensively. "I absolutely refused to take a penny from him when we split up. I have a trust fund." Loretta waited hopefully, anxious to hear more about Veronica's relationship with Puddephat. But Veronica had stopped short, perhaps embarrassed by making these revelations to a stranger, and Loretta had a distinct feeling that she was expected to go now. "I'm sorry," Veronica said, beginning to get to her feet. "It's very rude of me to burden you with my troubles."

"Not at all," protested Loretta, desperately trying to think of a ploy to delay her departure, and failing.

"I'm afraid I'm feeling rather low," Veronica explained, leading the way to the front door. "I've been pestered by reporters for days, and it really is getting on my nerves."

"I'm not surprised," Loretta said, without thinking. "There were two of them in your garden when I came to see you yesterday. I was so appalled by their behaviour that

I called the police." She stopped suddenly. She hadn't mentioned that she'd paid a previous visit to the house. Wouldn't Veronica think it suspicious that she had gone to the lengths of calling two days running?

"You called the police?" Veronica asked. Her face broke into a smile. "Then I've got a lot to thank you for. They were here when I arrived, and they'd caught one of those chaps taking pictures through the kitchen window. They took him and his friend off to the police station. I'm very grateful. And I haven't even been able to help you regain your notes."

"It doesn't matter," said Loretta, grateful that her un-premeditated action the day before had made a good impression on Veronica. She took her chance. "Look, why don't I give you my phone numbers?" she offered. "You're welcome to give me a ring if you're feeling overwhelmed." She was killing two birds with one stone, she thought cheerfully: she really did feel sorry for Veronica, and keeping in touch was the only way she'd find out more about the woman's relationship with her husband. She handed over the numbers, and said goodbye.

As she got into her car, she pushed away the worrying question of what she would do if she found evidence that implicated Veronica in the murder of Hugh Puddephat.

9

THE WARDROBE IN BRIDGET'S SPARE ROOM had a full-length mirror inside one of its doors. Loretta picked up a straight black skirt from the bed and stepped into it. Peering over her shoulder into the mirror, she adjusted the waistband until the back split was dead centre, and did up the zip. Turning round, she folded up the collar of her black T-shirt experimentally and, liking the effect, fastened a double row of pearls around it. She rummaged in the open jewellery box on the bed, and took out a pair of large drop earrings which she had bought in Liberty's the week before. Each consisted of a green glass stone in an oval setting. As she passed the wires through her pierced ears, she was aware that the earrings were much heavier than she was accustomed to wearing. Glancing at the mirror, she decided the effect was worth it. She would need all her self-confidence tonight. It had been a difficult afternoon, and she was not sure she was up to an evening of trying to extract information from Jamie Baird. Relaxing a little, she told herself that having discovered the identity of R, it was not so essential to grill him after all; but on the other hand, there was still the matter of the concealed photograph to be explained. Well, she would play it by ear. She looked at her watch: half past seven already. The doorbell had sounded several times while she was changing and, as she descended the stairs, a hum of voices was audible from the drawing-room.

She opened the door and hesitated on the threshold, allowing herself time to take in the scene. She never felt comfortable on entering a room full of strangers, and she hoped Bridget would be near at hand. Instead, Geoffrey Simmons surged forward to greet her, enthusiastically planting a kiss on her cheek. "Great to see you!" he exclaimed, taking her arm and propelling her into the room. He stood back and looked at her. "You're looking pretty glamorous, I must say," he said, his voice carrying across the room. "Mind you, we didn't part in very auspicious circumstances, did we? You were looking like a drowned rat after our little foray into Puddephat's rooms. Bloody hell, we didn't know what we were letting ourselves in for. There we were, messing around with his things, and all the time he was dead as a doornail in Paris. I wonder if they're keeping him in the morgue, by the way? I always think there's something sinister about that expression. The Paris Morgue. It sounds like something out of a horror film. You expect the attendants to look like Peter Cushing. Quite appropriate in the circumstances, of course. The rumour going round college is that the body was in a right old mess."

At this point, a young woman who'd been sitting on one of Bridget's sofas jumped angrily to her feet and shouted at Geoffrey. "Stop it! Stop it!" she shrieked. "How can you? Have you no feelings?" She slumped back on to the sofa, burying her face in her hands. Her long blonde hair tumbled artistically about her person.

A figure moved across from the dark corner in which he had been having an earnest conversation with a black boy, and sat down next to her. He rested a hand on her shoulder, and spoke softly, "Come on, Gilly, he wasn't thinking." His hair was darker than it appeared in the picture, and he looked older, but Loretta had no difficulty in recognizing Jamie Baird.

"Well, I certainly seem to have put my foot in it," said Geoffrey, breaking the uncomfortable silence that had fallen on the room.

"Gilly was one of his favourite students," said a small woman with an American accent who was standing in front of the french windows. "She's taken it pretty hard."

"You haven't?" asked Loretta, struck by the woman's offhand tone. She moved across the room, away from Geoffrey Simmons.

"I'm a graduate student," the woman answered. "I've seen his type before." There was a nicely judged degree of contempt in her voice, Loretta thought; it implied that the speaker had quickly got Puddephat's measure, and didn't intend to waste any more of her time on him. "The guy was a schmuck, if you want my opinion," the woman added.

"He has, sorry, had, a considerable reputation," Loretta reminded her, curious to hear more.

The American rose to the bait. "He had a loud voice, a wide vocabulary, and a big line in sarcasm," she said. "Some people, kids particularly, mistake that for originality. What I'm interested in is ideas, and I didn't think much of his, or his opinions. He was the sort of guy who jumped at every opportunity to make you look small." She put on a passable imitation of a BBC accent. "The *English* novel, Miss Chester? You want to talk about the *English* novel? Oh dear, I think you'd be more at home in Dr. Sykes's little classes. In my opinion, the only interesting developments in literature in the last ten years have taken place in East Germany. Of course, one needs German to understand what the author is trying to do."

Loretta laughed. She could imagine Puddephat saying these lines. "The more I hear about him, the less I like him," she admitted. She was about to introduce herself when Bridget made a dramatic entrance into the room, bearing a steaming bowl of punch on a tray. Her arrival, and the exclamations of admiration that greeted her, suc-

141

ceeded in defusing the last of the tension caused by Geoffrey's tactless remarks.

"Can I get you some punch?" Loretta asked her companion. When she accepted, Loretta moved across the room and helped herself to two glasses. "I'm Loretta Lawson," she said, returning and handing one of them to the American woman. "I lecture in English at London. I met Bridget when she was doing her PhD. Are you one of her students?"

"Evelyn Chester," the woman replied. "I'm doing a doctorate and yes, Bridget's my tutor. Loretta Lawson, I know that name. D'you write for *Fem Sap*?"

"That's right," said Loretta, with a little glow of pleasure. "I'm on the editorial collective, as a matter of fact."

"I read your article in the last issue," Evelyn said. "I thought you made some pretty good points. I heard from Bridget there's some kind of row going on about masculine endings. Where d'you stand on that?"

The conversation had taken an unexpected turn, thought Loretta, gathering her thoughts. "I suppose I have to say I'm a conservative," she admitted. "I think language has to evolve slowly. I mean, I don't object to sensible changes —saying chairwoman when it's appropriate, for instance. But I think the problem with French, say, is on a bigger scale. I don't think you can impose wholesale changes overnight."

Evelyn's face became animated, and she shook her short brown hair. Drawing a packet of cigarettes out of her shoulder bag, she lit one and put it to her lips. "But if you're a feminist, the whole idea of masculine verb endings including the feminine is a complete joke," she protested. "It's an insult."

"Oh, I wouldn't argue with that," said Loretta. "Where you and I probably differ is on the question of what to do about it. What some women are suggesting at *Fem Sap*— abolishing masculine endings overnight—just seems to me the wrong way of going about it. All it will do is alienate a lot of women who aren't radical feminists, and open us up to ridicule from our enemies. And we've got plenty of those."

"You're not telling me you're afraid of ridicule, Loretta?" enquired a familiar voice at her elbow.

Loretta turned to find that Geoffrey Simmons had been listening to the conversation. She was far from delighted to see him. It was only thanks to the scene made by Gilly that his admission about their visit to Puddephat's rooms had gone unnoticed. Bridget hadn't been exaggerating when she warned her of his lack of discretion.

"Of course I don't like being ridiculed," she said sharply. "And I think anyone who pretends otherwise is just indulging in macho posturing. The point is that sometimes it can't be avoided—there are some issues which are so important that you have to take a stand and say to hell with how people react. But sometimes it's better to keep a low profile. To make changes slowly, and carry the maximum number of people with you." It really was rather tedious, she thought, having this kind of discussion at a social gathering. Looking round the room, she wondered how to escape from Geoffrey.

He, it seemed, was not in the least put off. "In other words, Loretta," he said, poking her in the ribs with his elbow, "you're a gradualist!"

His tone suggested he'd caught her out in some minor misdemeanour, Loretta thought angrily—putting penny coins in a parking meter, or dodging fares on the underground. She decided to extricate herself with dignity. "A thirsty gradualist," she said firmly, holding up her empty glass. Smiling at Evelyn, and ignoring Geoffrey, she made her way across the room to the punch bowl. It was already empty, apart from the odd slice of orange stuck to its sides, and she decided to try the kitchen. The only occupants of the room were a couple of young men who were sitting at the table, smoking Turkish cigarettes. Loretta guessed that Bridget, a non-smoker like herself, had banished them there. Listening with half an ear as she examined the cluster of bottles on the draining-board, she caught the names of several authors and concluded that they were discussing contemporary novelists.

"My sister gave me a book by this woman Anita something, the one that won the Booker prize," she heard one of them say.

"Brookner," interrupted the other.

"That's it," the first speaker agreed. "She said it was all the rage at her school, and she'd got an A minus for her essay on it. It was all about a woman who goes on holiday to a hotel in Switzerland. I've never read anything so dreary—I gave up half-way."

"I'm surprised you got that far," said the other. "I can't see the point in her books at all. You might as well watch a documentary about depressed women on Channel 4. What about Martin Amis? Have you read him?"

"Oh, yes. I see him as a sort of spiritual descendant of Norman Mailer, just as Mailer took on the mantle of Lawrence—in fact I wrote an essay on that very subject in my last term at school. 'Scuse me, but I think you'll find the wine's run out," the speaker added, having just registered Loretta's presence.

Mumbling a reply, Loretta opened the fridge and peered inside. She remembered that Bridget had put a couple of bottles of white in the freezer compartment at the last minute. She drew one out, grumbling silently to herself. Public school twits, she thought, an old prejudice welling up in her. Their accents alone were enough to drive anyone mad. Thank God her college wasn't yet fashionable enough to attract more than the odd one or two. How on earth did Bridget put up with them? She picked up Bridget's corkscrew and examined it. It was not a design she had encountered before.

"Can I help?" asked a voice just behind her. Turning, she found herself confronting Jamie Baird. Lost in her condemnation of the two young men at the table, she had

144

not heard him come in. "I wasn't implying you couldn't do it yourself," he added hastily, seeing her expression. Realizing she was still frowning, Loretta put on a smile. It was a nuisance, she thought, that Jamie had come upon her unawares. She had not yet decided how to deal with him.

"I'm sorry," she said. "My mind was elsewhere." She handed over the corkscrew.

"Listening to those two?" he asked, nodding towards the table.

Loretta blushed. "I'm afraid so," she said, glancing towards them. They were, she saw with relief, still deep in conversation. By now, they'd moved on to Hemingway.

"Typical pseudo-intellectuals," Jamie said in a low voice. "At heart, they're no different from the other public school type—the rugger-bugger sort, the ones that follow daddy into the services. They both have an unshakeable confidence in the rightness of their own opinions. This lot are the public schools' great concession to modernity. Now we don't need so many generals and governors, they let some of them read a few books. As long as they're the right sort of books, of course. I know what you're thinking," he added. "I sound just like them myself. But I'm not. You shouldn't hold my upbringing against me. I'm doing my best to cast it off." His tone sounded genuine, but Loretta was quick to spot what looked like an inconsistency.

"Then why did you come to Oxford?" she demanded. "Why not break with tradition altogether and go to Leeds, say, or London?"

Jamie hesitated for a moment, leaning forward to fill her glass. "Family reasons," he said shortly, putting the bottle down.

The atmosphere between them had suddenly become frosty. Loretta chided herself for her tactlessness. Although Jamie was no longer as vital an interviewee as she had once thought, it was silly to antagonize him. She could hardly follow up the exchange they had just had with a question about his relationship with Puddephat. Casting around for a safe topic, she remembered that she had not introduced herself. "My name's Loretta Lawson," she said, doing her best to look relaxed. "I'm an old friend of Bridget's."

"Jamie Baird," he replied flatly, his good humour not fully restored. "And you knew Hugh Puddephat too, didn't you?"

Loretta blinked. How did Jamie know? And, more importantly, what did he know? He did not keep her in suspense.

"I heard that chap Simmons say something about you getting into Hugh's rooms," he explained. "You know, the small dark chap who's a don at my college. I didn't really understand what he was on about, to tell you the truth. But it made me think you must have been a friend of Hugh's. He was my tutor, you see, that's why I'm interested."

Loretta silently cursed Geoffrey. His indiscretion had not gone unnoticed, after all. "Oh, that," she said, attempting lightness. There was nothing to worry about, she told herself. Jamie had no idea of her real motive for searching the dead man's rooms. She smiled ruefully. "I'm afraid it's a rather discreditable story," she said. "In my defence, I should say it happened before the body was discovered. I wouldn't have dreamed of doing it if I'd known he was dead." She launched into a brief account of her visit to Puddephat's rooms, leaving vague what she had done there and making much of the fright she had got when the fire bell went off. Just to be on the safe side, she kept Bridget out of it altogether. "So it was all a waste of time," she ended brightly. "No sign of my notes at all."

"I always thought Hugh was very lucky to have those rooms," Jamie said. "You won't have appreciated it at night, but the view over the gardens is breathtaking. Not that I cared much for the way he kept them. That dreadful picture—you must have noticed that? It's an original, you know."

"I guessed it was," Loretta agreed. "Not my taste either, I must admit." She remembered the violent daub over Puddephat's desk.

"And nothing else to look at," Jamie went on. "Not a single photo of his family or friends."

Loretta's ears pricked up. There was something funny about his tone of voice, almost as if he were asking rather than telling her. The photograph, she thought, in a flash of intuition. He knows about the photograph. He's trying to find out if I saw it. Convinced she was on to something, she felt emboldened.

"How did you get on with him?" she asked, taking a sip from her glass to avoid looking directly at his face. She didn't want to give anything away.

Jamie paused. "Gosh," he said at last, "that's a difficult one. To be absolutely honest, I was in a rather awkward position." He stopped, and Loretta looked up. Was she imagining it, or had a look of caution entered his eyes? He glanced towards the two students at the table, and lowered his voice. "I don't know how much you know about Hugh's private life, but the fact is he had rather a crush on me. It really got very difficult. It took me a while to take in what was going on, of course. When I first arrived, and he seemed interested in me, I was rather flattered. I mean, I was just an obscure first-year, and he went out of his way to encourage me. But after a while I began to think there was more to it than that, and I didn't know how to handle it. He was always inviting me to little supper parties and so on, and it became so noticeable that other people began to make snide comments. I wasn't imagining it, honestly. I don't have any delusions about myself. But I didn't know what to do. He was my tutor, after all. I couldn't risk falling out with him completely. So, although I'm sorry he's dead, I'm rather relieved to have Bridget this year."

"I'm sure you are," Loretta said warmly, congratulating herself on her powers of deduction. She had been right in her assumption about the photograph—she was sure now that it had been taken at one of those supper parties, and without prior warning. Even though the episode had nothing to do with Puddephat's death, her intuition had not led her astray. She was so pleased with herself that she had no qualms about adding: "D'you have any theories about his death? Any idea who might have wanted to kill him?" It was worth a try, she thought. It was still possible that Jamie knew something she didn't, without realizing its significance.

But Jamie shrugged. "Your guess is as good as mine," he said. "I'd been trying to see as little as possible of him towards the end of term. My last interview with him was very brief. Do you want some more wine?"

Loretta nodded, only slightly disappointed. Watching him refill her glass, she noticed he had unusually long fingernails for a man. All in all, she thought, flicking her hair back from her face, he was quite an unusual person. His clothes—a Fair Isle pullover and collarless white shirt— were quaintly old-fashioned. His attitude to public schools, on the other hand, was anything but traditional.

"Loretta," he said suddenly. "That's not a name you hear very often. Is it after Loretta Young?"

"No," she admitted, surprised by the abrupt change of subject.

"I thought perhaps your mother had seen *The Call of the Wild* as a child, and liked the name," he explained. "You know—Loretta Young and Clark Gable?" Loretta looked blank. She had never heard of the film. "Loretta Lynn then? No, of course not, she's too young for you to have been named after her. So where did it come from?"

Loretta felt herself blush. "I got it from a novel I read at school," she said, looking down and shuffling her feet. "I can't remember what it was called, or who wrote it. But it stuck in my mind. I was christened Laura, you see," she added, in a rush of confidence, "but I never liked it. And when I left home for the first time, it suddenly occurred to me that there was no reason why I shouldn't change it. So I did." She tailed off, embarrassed. She did not very often tell this particular story. But Jamie's smile was friendly.

"How very enterprising of you," he said. "And it's certainly very memorable. Loretta Lawson. In fact, I'm sure I know it from somewhere. Maybe something you've written?"

Loretta's mind flew back to her conversation with the American postgraduate earlier in the evening. Surely she hadn't found another reader of *Fem Sap*? The journal's subscription list proved its readership to be overwhelmingly female. After an initial flurry of outraged interest from male English dons and undergraduates, it had gone on to be studiously ignored by them. But then Jamie, as she was finding out, was no run-of-the-mill student.

"Yes, that's it," he exclaimed, confirming this view. "You wrote an article about Eliot in a feminist magazine I picked up in Blackwell's. All about how he was a bit of a shit, and you couldn't get it out of your mind while you were reading *The Waste Land*. Very refreshing after listening to two terms of this death-of-the-author stuff."

Loretta glowed with pleasure. The evening was turning out to be much more enjoyable than she'd anticipated. "I've just finished a piece for the January issue," she said. "It's on women characters in books about the Holocaust. I don't know if you've read any of them. Things like *The White Hotel* and *Sophie's Choice*?"

"Oh, those," Jamie said dismissively. "They're just the sort of things your friends over there would like. Absolutely riddled with misogyny."

Loretta opened her eyes wide. This was precisely her own conclusion, but Jamie was the first man she'd met who agreed with her. She was about to pursue his remark when she felt a hand on her arm. Turning, she found Bridget, accompanied by a black student she had noticed earlier.

"There you are," she said to Loretta. "I've been wanting to introduce you to Edward all evening. He's one of my

149

PhD students, and he's writing a thesis on Virginia Woolf."
Jamie waited politely until these introductions were over,
and then excused himself. Trapped, Loretta had no choice
but to give her attention to Bridget and Edward.

"You were deep in conversation," her friend said curiously.

"We were talking about misogyny," Loretta said firmly.
There was a suggestion in Bridget's tone she did not want
to respond to.

"I thought Jamie would be more cut up about Hugh
Puddephat," Edward said idly. "Hugh always had a little
group of favourites, an in-crowd so to speak," he explained
to Loretta, "and Jamie was definitely one of them. He
seems to have got over the shock pretty quickly."

"A remarkable recovery," drawled a young woman who
had just joined the group. "After all, they were very close
friends." Her meaning was unmistakable. Edward recoiled
slightly.

"D'you ever have a good word for anyone, Natasha?"
he enquired coldly. Loretta bit her tongue. It was none of
her business what people thought of Jamie Baird. She
turned to Edward and, ignoring the girl called Natasha,
asked a question about the progress of his thesis.

The first guests began to leave an hour or so later. Loretta
had wandered back into the drawing-room, and was chat-
ting to a classics don who taught at the same college as
Bridget. Out of the corner of her eye, she could see Jamie
in conversation with two people she didn't recognize. She
was trying to engineer her escape from the classics lecturer
when Jamie made his way over. He waited for the other
woman to finish what she was saying, and then smiled
shyly at Loretta.

"I have to leave now," he said, "or I'll miss my lift. But
I enjoyed talking to you. I hope we'll meet again some
time." His tone was a little stiff, and Loretta was not sure

what to read into it. Disconcerted, she said goodbye, and watched him leave the room.

"I suppose I ought to be making tracks as well," said the classics don. "I've got a department meeting at nine o'clock tomorrow morning."

In a very short time, the only relics of Bridget's party were the empty glasses perched on every horizontal surface in the drawing-room, and Geoffrey Simmons, who was displaying not the slightest inclination to leave. Bridget flopped on to a sofa, stretched her legs out, and groaned. "What a mess!" she said, surveying the scene. "Did they really have to trample crisps into the carpet?"

"Why don't you sit there and have a rest, while I clear up?" suggested Loretta.

Bridget sat up straight. "I won't hear of it," she said. "You and Geoffrey are my guests. I've got a very nice bottle of dessert wine I put in the fridge an hour ago—I know you like Muscatel, Loretta. Come and get some clean glasses. You two can have a quiet drink while I sort through the debris." Loretta was about to protest at this arrangement—she had not yet recovered from her irritation with Geoffrey—but decided it would be more diplomatic to follow Bridget into the kitchen. Although Geoffrey appeared to be absorbed in a book he had picked up, she had no doubt that he had at least one ear open to the conversation. As she left the room, it struck Loretta that he was being uncharacteristically quiet; perhaps he had had too much to drink?

Closing the kitchen door, she turned to Bridget. "Look, I know Geoffrey's a friend of yours," she began, "and I admit he's been very helpful, but I'm really quite angry with him. His behaviour earlier on was absolutely awful. I didn't even have time to say hello before he was telling the whole room about us breaking into Puddephat's rooms. And then he made all sorts of tactless remarks about the state of the body. So it would be much better if you left the washing up to me, and went and had a drink with him yourself."

Bridget was looking affronted. "I think you're being a bit harsh," she objected. "I know he's indiscreet, but he doesn't do it out of malice."

"Maybe not," said Loretta. "But that doesn't affect the outcome. There was quite an unpleasant scene before you came in with the punch. You were lucky to be in the kitchen at the time."

"From what I heard afterwards," Bridget said dismissively, "Gilly was behaving like a drama queen. Right over the top. After all, she didn't know Puddephat that well."

"Well, I'm giving her the benefit of the doubt," said Loretta. "If one of my lecturers had been murdered, I wouldn't like to hear someone gloating about the details."

"Now you're overreacting," Bridget said. "I'm sure Geoffrey wasn't gloating. It was just thoughtlessness." She adopted a more conciliatory tone of voice. "You and Geoffrey got on very well last time you met. He can be very amusing, you know. You could do a lot worse."

In a flash, Loretta realized what was going on. "Is this your own idea, or is Geoffrey in on it?" she demanded. "The trouble with you, Bridget, is that you can't help interfering. If I want to start an affair with someone, I'm perfectly capable of doing it without your assistance!" She stopped suddenly, wondering if she was being unfair to Bridget. If it had been Jamie Baird who was waiting for her in the drawing-room, would she have been so angry? She pushed the idea away. It was preposterous. What about the difference in their ages? Geoffrey Simmons was evidently not the only one who had had too much to drink. Irritated with herself, she took her annoyance out on Bridget. "I suppose this is the real reason why you wanted me to come to your party?" she asked.

"Not at all," Bridget said coldly. "If you cast your mind back, you'll remember that it was your idea to come to

Oxford this weekend. I just happened to know that Geoffrey was keen to meet you again, and you do seem to be at a loose end at the moment. I thought I'd kill two birds with one stone."

Loretta saw the justice of what Bridget was saying, but was able to respond only with ill grace. "All right," she muttered. "I dare say you meant well. But I'd rather you didn't try to run my love life." What on earth had got into her, she asked herself? Bridget was one of her closest friends. Leaning forward, she kissed the other woman lightly on the cheek. "It was a nice party," she said, more grudgingly than she intended.

In the hall, she paused at the bottom of the stairs, torn between her desire to escape and good manners. Good manners won. She opened the door to the drawing-room, hoping there was not going to be another scene. Her anxiety was unfounded. Geoffrey was slumped in an armchair, head on chest, a book about to fall from his hands. From the sound of his rhythmic breathing, Loretta could tell he was fast asleep. Her good humour somewhat restored, she stifled a laugh: however much he had wanted to see her again, Geoffrey's enthusiasm had not lasted the course of the evening. Closing the door gently, she went upstairs to bed.

10

THE NEXT MORNING WAS AN ABSOLUTE DIS-
aster. Loretta's hopes of a conciliatory chat with Bridget
over breakfast were dashed by the fact that she had set her
alarm clock for half an hour later than she had intended.
There was time only to grab a piece of burnt toast before
jumping into her car and setting off for London.

As soon as she drew up to the roundabout at the top of
Woodstock Road, she found herself in traffic which
stretched as far as the eye could see, and when she
switched on the car radio, she discovered that the only
sound it would make was an assortment of squeaks and
crackles. Fiddling with the tuning knob made no difference, and a glance to the left told her what had happened:
someone had stolen the aerial. She let out a sigh of impatience. It had not occurred to her that the car would be
vulnerable while parked in Bridget's front garden. It was a
bad start to the morning, and the rest of the day lived up to
its promise.

She arrived in central London so late that she had to
park in the street outside the English department, with not
a free parking meter in sight. By the time she finished her
lecture and came out to move it, one of the wheels had
been clamped. The rest of the morning was wasted on the
business of getting the car released, and paying through the

nose for the privilege. The car spent the afternoon in a car park nowhere near her office, and she arrived home reflecting that her weekend in Oxford had been an expensive one. What she needed, she decided, was a chat with Bridget. She would apologize for her behaviour the previous evening, and ask her advice on what to do next. She had, after all, been successful in making contact with Veronica Puddephat, although the meeting had raised as many questions as it had answered. What had Puddephat done to his wife to provoke the loathing expressed in her letter to him? And when had the letter been written? Loretta was convinced it was recent. Why would anyone keep such a letter unless they were still considering a response to it? And, above all, did it have anything to do with his death? They were not the sort of questions she could ask on so brief an acquaintance, but she was unable at present to think of an excuse that would allow her to get to know Veronica better.

And then there was the business of Jamie Baird—no, she thought, that was something she didn't feel able to talk to Bridget about. He had nothing to do with the case, and in the cold light of day she was rather ashamed of her unexpected fascination with him. She would eat first, she decided, dropping her bags and coat on the sofa, and then ring Bridget at home. She picked up the phone to ring the Chinese takeaway in Caledonian Road, and discovered the line was dead. It seemed a fitting end to the day.

It proved impossible to get British Telecom round to fix the phone until Thursday afternoon. Loretta decided to put off her chat with Bridget until it was mended—it might be a lengthy conversation, and she preferred to have it out of office hours. On Thursday, she left a key with her downstairs neighbour, and arrived home to find the key and a note on her kitchen table. The phone was working again, the engineer had scribbled on the back of an envelope, and he was very sorry he had broken the table lamp standing next to it on the coffee table. Loretta let out a wail, and rushed to the drawing-room. Her favourite lamp, a white Art Deco figure of a woman, had been reduced to a neat heap of pottery shards. She sat down and was about to indulge in a fit of angry tears when the phone rang. "Yes?" she demanded, snatching it up. There was a moment's silence, and then she heard an unfamiliar voice.

"I'm sorry, I think I may have a wrong number," it said. "I wanted to speak to Dr. Lawson, Dr. Loretta Lawson."

"That's me," Loretta said, in a friendlier tone. It wasn't the woman's fault that her lamp had been broken.

"This is Veronica, Veronica Puddephat. You came to see me on Sunday," she added, in case Loretta had forgotten.

"I'm so sorry, Veronica, you caught me at a bad moment," Loretta said apologetically. Her heart was beating fast. She was not going to have to invent an excuse to ring Veronica after all. "The phone's been out of order all week, and the man who came to mend it has broken a lamp I was very fond of."

"Aren't they the giddy limit!" Veronica sympathized. "The trouble I've had with British Telecom . . . but that's not the reason I phoned." She hesitated. "Look, I know this is the most awful cheek, but you did say I could ring you. I do hope you won't mind me asking you."

"Go ahead," Loretta encouraged. Things could not be going better.

"I've got to come up to London to see yet another policeman," Veronica explained. "A French one this time. Some terribly important person from the Sûreté—is that right? I don't understand the French police system. At any rate, it's apparently vital that I see this chap. He did offer to come to Oxford, but I said I'd rather do it in London. It's the thought of going through it all again, you see, it's so upsetting . . . And I wondered if you'd be very kind and have tea with me afterwards. I'm sure you're very busy, and I know I shouldn't really ask you, but we could meet somewhere near your office . . ." She tailed off.

"What a good idea," Loretta said warmly, trying to keep

156

the excitement out of her voice. Here was her chance to find out exactly what the police were up to—it sounded as if they might have a new lead. Why else would a senior French policeman come all the way from Paris to see Puddephat's wife? The Oxford police must have interviewed her several times already. And, she thought with relief, if new evidence had turned up in France, it might mean that Veronica had had nothing to do with her husband's death. The best possible solution, as far as Loretta was concerned, would be for a total stranger to be revealed as the murderer. "When do you have to see him?" she asked.

"I've provisionally arranged it for tomorrow," Veronica answered. "I tried to get hold of you last night, but the phone wasn't working. And I didn't want to trouble you at work. But I can probably change the appointment, if it's inconvenient."

"Not at all," Loretta assured her, running through Friday's timetable in her mind. "I'm free in the late afternoon, if that's any good. Or in the evening."

"Why don't we have tea at the Waldorf?" Veronica suggested. "Would four thirty suit you?" Loretta said that it would, and Veronica rang off.

The Waldorf, Loretta thought to herself. It was a name she associated with 1930s tea-dances. What a strange world Veronica inhabited. And a lonely one, she reflected. How sad that Puddephat's widow should have no one to turn to at a time like this. Surely she must have some friends? Or was a separated woman still an outcast in Veronica's circle? What she needed was the support of close women friends—a women's group, in fact. Perhaps she should buy a copy of *Spare Rib*, and see if it still carried adverts for consciousness-raising groups. She smiled to herself. The idea of Veronica Puddephat joining any sort of feminist group was entirely incongruous. On the other hand, some women were capable of the most startling changes.

Loretta paused. She had been on the verge of persuading herself that her motive for seeing Veronica was simple altruism. It wasn't. Sorry as she might feel for her now, she had contacted Veronica with the aim of finding out more about her husband's killer. And, at this stage, it would be quite wrong to rule her out as a suspect. She sighed, and remembered she had been on the verge of phoning Bridget when Veronica called. It would be good to talk over her feelings about Veronica Puddephat with her friend—and she still hadn't apologized for her bad temper on Sunday night. She dialed Bridget's number, and let the phone ring for ages. There was no reply. She would have to try again later.

Bridget was out all evening, and next morning something happened which drove thoughts of her out of Loretta's head. An envelope, addressed in handwriting she didn't know, arrived in the post: inside, she found a photocopied article from the back number of an American academic journal, and a postcard reproduction of a painting by Klimt. Turning the postcard over, she saw Jamie Baird's name and college address printed in capitals above a short handwritten message. "I came across this today, and thought it would interest you," it said. It was signed simply "Jamie." The article, which she had not seen before, appeared to be an attack on *Fem Sap* and, by extension, most female English dons. It looked, she thought, very much like an excuse to get in touch with her. He must have got her address from Bridget. Perhaps her behaviour on Sunday night had not been so foolish after all. A sensation she had not felt for months—of muted excitement and expectation—went through her. After all, where had caution and convention got her? She had had a husband and lovers older than herself, and each affair had been fraught with problems. Wasn't it possible that a man of Jamie's age might be more able to cope with her feminism, her academic success?

Loretta paused. She was reading an awful lot into one

small postcard. Yes, it did reveal an interest in her, but was she right in thinking it was a sexual one? She ought to proceed with care. She put the card down, and pondered as she made a pot of tea. Perhaps the best way to go about it was to take his message at face value. She could send him a proof of the article on the Holocaust she had written for *Fem Sap*. Then it would be up to him to make the next move. A moment's thought led her to reject this course of action. That was precisely what women had done in the past—sit back and wait for men to make the running. There must be some way she could make an approach without incurring too great a risk of rejection.

She was pouring a cup of tea when the solution came to her. As a member of the editorial collective of *Fem Sap*, it was part of her job to commission occasional articles. She could ring Jamie and suggest that he write something for it. Apart from providing her with an excuse to respond to his card, the idea in itself was a perfectly good one. His attitude to those languid undergraduates at Bridget's party, and to writers, was not a conventionally masculine one. She would do it that very evening.

Loretta arrived first at the Waldorf that afternoon, and was astonished to find a *thé dansant* in full swing to the strains of the Palm Court orchestra. After being shown to a seat on the balcony, she spent a fascinated five minutes watching three couples on the sunken dance floor. She had had no idea that such events still took place. No one else seemed to find the scene incongruous, and Veronica passed no comment on it when she arrived.

"I'm sorry I'm late," she said, taking a seat opposite Loretta. "I've had the most frightful afternoon." She rummaged in a Gucci handbag and took out a small bottle of aspirins. "My head is absolutely pounding. Tea for two, and a glass of water," she commanded, catching the eye of a passing waiter. "You do want something to eat?" she

159

asked, turning to Loretta as if she had just remembered her manners. "They do very good sandwiches."

It was too late to refuse. Loretta watched in awe as the waiter returned with plates of muffins, scones, and cucumber sandwiches with their crusts cut off. It was, she thought, like taking part in a TV adaptation of an early Agatha Christie novel. "How did you get on?" she prompted, when Veronica showed no sign of referring to her visit to Scotland Yard. "Have there been any developments?"

Veronica put down the knife she was using to butter a muffin, and looked at her. "Absolutely none," she said peevishly. "Would you believe it? It was just the same thing all over again, except that this time it took twice as long because of the interpreter. You'd think they'd have the wit to send someone who could speak English. When did you last see your husband, did he have any enemies, who did he know in Paris? I keep telling them I was separated from Hugh, and they just don't seem capable of taking it in. It was frightful. As a matter of fact, one of the men from Scotland Yard, a very nice inspector, told me on the way out that the whole thing was a waste of time as far as he was concerned. A matter of protocol, apparently. The French police don't like co-operating with the Yard, and they insisted on sending this chap over. I wish I'd known in advance. I was quite convinced they'd have something to tell me. What have they been doing all this time?"

Loretta shared Veronica's sense of frustration. So much for her hope that the Sûreté would turn out to have solved the case for her. And, on top of everything else, she had no way of knowing whether Veronica was telling the truth. Had there been other questions Puddephat's widow didn't want to talk about? She wondered whether the detectives on the case had made the link between Veronica and the letter in her husband's sock drawer. She couldn't even be sure they knew of its existence, since the note was still there on the night of her own illicit search. Of course, that

160

had taken place before anyone knew that Puddephat had been murdered. The police must surely have carried out a more thorough examination of the rooms since the discovery of the body. These wretched imponderables, Loretta thought angrily. Every time she seemed to be on the verge of making some sort of breakthrough, new questions came up. She could at least make the best of her meeting with Veronica, though.

"When did you last see your husband?" she asked, picking up one of the queries the police had put to her.

Veronica brushed it aside. "Ages ago," she said vaguely. It was clear that this was not what she had come here to talk about.

Loretta gave in, for fear of antagonizing her. "So you've had a wasted trip," she said sympathetically. She would allow Veronica to direct the conversation for a while, and see where that led her.

"No," Veronica said slowly. "As a matter of fact, they did have some news." She stopped, suddenly sounding tearful. "They said they were finished with Hugh's body— that I was free to arrange the funeral." She paused again. "Oh, God," she muttered, fumbling in her handbag for a handkerchief. Finding one, she dabbed at her eyes. "It's going to be awful," she said wretchedly. "They say the formalities are over, so he can be brought over and buried. But I haven't the faintest idea what to do. I've never had to arrange a funeral before."

"What about your family?" Loretta asked cautiously. Veronica's father was Lord Somebody-or-other, she reminded herself, and didn't the aristocracy go in for rather grand affairs? They must be able to help.

"Daddy's the last person I'd go to for help," Veronica said bitterly. "He was fit to be tied when I separated from Hugh, and he seems to blame me for the whole thing. And Mummy won't do anything that upsets Daddy. I'll just have to get by on my own."

Ignoring her own discomfort at hearing a grown woman

use such childish titles, Loretta detected that Veronica's last statement was not so much an act of defiance as a cry for help. "Why don't we make a list of things that have to be done?" she suggested practically. The task of organizing her grandmother's funeral had fallen to her a couple of years before and, although the present situation was bound to be more complicated, she had a fair idea of the steps Veronica would need to take. She drew a notebook out of her bag, and began to make a list.

By the time they had finished tea, Veronica seemed much more cheerful. She paid the bill, which seemed outrageously large to Loretta, without batting an eyelid. "You've been such a help," she said, brushing aside Loretta's half-hearted attempt to make a contribution. Remembering the other woman's private income, Loretta made only a faint protest. Winning Veronica's confidence to the point where she could ask direct questions about her husband's death looked like being a slow job, and Loretta's bank balance would not stand many trips to establishments like the Waldorf. In fact, it might be as well to be ready in advance with her own suggestion of a rendezvous next time Veronica called. It wasn't just a matter of cost. Loretta, who was ignorant of the etiquette attached to these affairs, had been on tenterhooks throughout tea in case anyone should ask her to dance. Her education had not included much in the way of ballroom-dancing.

At least she had one thing to be thankful for, she consoled herself, seeing Veronica into a taxi in the Aldwych: she was in no doubt at all that Veronica would be in touch again. She would not be forced to invent further spurious reasons for contacting the victim's widow. She just hoped she would be spared a pressing invitation to his obsequies.

Loretta had assumed that she would have to leave a message for Jamie with some college functionary, and wait for him to ring back. To her surprise, the phone was answered by someone who volunteered to go and see if he was in. A couple of minutes later, she heard footsteps approaching at the other end of the line. Her heart beat faster.

"Hello?" said Jamie's voice.

"It's Loretta Lawson," she said lightly, in case the messenger had not passed on her name. There was nothing to worry about, she assured herself. The suggestion she was about to make was entirely reasonable. If he didn't respond, all she had to do was ring off. "Your note arrived this morning," she went on, "and it gave me a rather interesting idea. Remember what you were saying on Sunday evening—about misogyny, and the kind of attitudes instilled in boys at public schools? Why don't you write something about it for *Fem Sap*? It could be about particular authors who've been through the public-school system, or even about the way the system works at close hand. What d'you think?"

There was a pause. "I'm very flattered you should ask me," Jamie said slowly. "But aren't there two rather obvious objections? For one thing, I'm an undergraduate. I haven't produced a single piece of writing of lasting value in my life. And for another, I'm not a woman." His tone was cool. Loretta could not decide whether he was genuinely unenthusiastic about the idea, or whether it was the alienating effect of his upper middle-class accent.

"If that's all you're worried about, there's no problem," she said. "*Fem Sap* has never recognized the sort of hierarchy which says that only published authors, or professors of literature, have something worth saying. I admit that the vast majority of contributors are women, but this is one occasion when the article I'm thinking of could only be written by a man. When women write about misogyny, they do it from the standpoint of victims. You'd be tackling it as someone who was brought up to perpetuate it. On the other hand," she said, careful to allow him a way out, "I quite understand that you might be too busy to take on work that's well outside your syllabus." There, she'd got it all out. What happened now was out of her hands.

"All right, you've convinced me," Jamie said suddenly. "But I think we ought to talk it over first. Just so I know exactly what I'm doing."

"Of course," Loretta said, taken aback by his abrupt acquiescence. "I suppose the difficulty is going to be finding a time in the next couple of weeks when we're both free."

"Why wait?" Jamie asked recklessly. "Are you busy tomorrow? I could come to London in the afternoon."

With a slight sense that things were moving faster than anticipated, Loretta admitted that she had no firm plans for the next day. "Why don't you come to my flat?" she suggested. "Say about three?" Jamie asked whether she could make it slightly later, giving him time to finish an essay that should have been completed during the summer vacation. Loretta agreed, and gave him directions to her flat.

After she had put the phone down, she felt in a daze. She had been convinced at first that it had all been a mistake, that she had indeed misread the unspoken message contained in the postcard. But now Jamie seemed, if anything, even keener than she that they should meet again. Perhaps, she thought, deciding there was no point in worrying about it, he was simply nervous. She went over to her bookshelves, and began to look for books that Jamie might find useful in writing his article.

Saturday morning's mail brought a postcard from Germany. "Too tied up for sight-seeing," Tracey had written, "so can't tell you much about what Berlin is like. Everything is ludicrously expensive—thank God the *Sunday Herald* is paying my expenses. More relevations this weekend. Cheers, John." As an afterthought, he had scribbled another line at the bottom: "Any luck with the Gandell girl?"

Shaking her head over Tracey's capacity for self-absorption, Loretta reflected that she had not yet made any progress in her attempt to track down Melanie Gandell's relatives. To be fair, it was not an easy task; her only clue to date was the address in Somerset. She did not even know whether the occupants of Cherry Cottage had any connection with the dead girl. And if Melanie's family had moved, would the new people be able, or willing, to pass on information about their whereabouts? It was a long way to drive on the off-chance that something would come of it. She could address a letter to "the occupier," but so impersonal a request might well go unheeded. She wondered whether she should ring Bridget—she still hadn't spoken to her since leaving Oxford on Monday morning—but, with Jamie's visit imminent, she shied away from the thought. She did not want to talk to her friend about Jamie, and she did not trust herself to hold a lengthy conversation with Bridget without mentioning his visit. She decided to think about it later.

Turning over Tracey's postcard, she found a striking picture of a bombed church. She propped it up on the mantelpiece, and went to the kitchen. She had been invited to dinner on Sunday evening by another member of her women's group, and she had promised to take a pudding. Taking a bag of soft white ricotta cheese from the fridge, she set about making a *budino Toscano*.

It was just before five when the buzz of the entryphone announced Jamie's arrival.

"Come up," Loretta called gaily, pressing the button to release the street door. Now he was here, she felt unexpectedly at ease; maybe it was because she was on home territory. She opened the door, and found him huddled in an overcoat, hands deep in pockets, a red scarf thrown carelessly around his neck. "You look frozen," she exclaimed, stepping back to let him into the hall. "Come in and get warm."

"The train had no heating," he said, blowing on his gloveless hands. "I'm sorry I'm late. We stopped for half an hour in Reading to wait for a connection." He took off his coat, and handed it to Loretta. "I was going to bring you some flowers," he said awkwardly, "but the flower stall was closed at the station."

"Never mind," she said, charmed by the thought. She led the way into the drawing-room, and pointed to a pile of books and journals on the floor. "I've found mounds of stuff for you," she said.

His attention was elsewhere. "A real fire," he said admiringly, going straight to it. "Do you have them often?"

"It's the first one this autumn," Loretta admitted, "but I usually have them at weekends in the winter." Switching on her surviving table lamp, she knelt on the sofa and closed the curtains. "What would you like to drink?" she asked, turning back to Jamie. "I can offer you tea, coffee, or whisky if you'd rather."

"Whisky," he said. "It's one of the many things I acquired a taste for at school. Illicitly, of course."

Loretta smiled. Watching Jamie out of the corner of her eye while she poured whisky for both of them, she reflected that it was all going very well. He was sitting in the armchair to one side of the fire, still warming his hands. The Fair Isle pullover had given way to another in pale blue and the firelight struck almost red notes from his hair. Handing him his drink, she sat down on the sofa. "Now, about this article—" she began.

Jamie interrupted her. "I hope you don't think this is rude, but there's something I want to ask you," he said. Surprised, Loretta waited. "It's about those notes you sent Hugh. It's just something I don't understand," he added, his earlier awkwardness returning. "The thing is, what made you ask his advice? Hugh was scathing about any form of non-structuralist criticism, particularly if it came from a feminist—I should have thought you and he would have had absolutely nothing in common. So why did you do it?" His brown eyes slid away from Loretta's.

She was not as disconcerted as she had expected to be. For an awful moment, she thought that Jamie had found out something about her real connection with Puddephat. But this was a question she could handle. She managed a rueful laugh. "I can see why you're puzzled," she said. "So was Bridget when I first told her about it. I'm afraid it's another story which doesn't reflect much credit on me—I seem doomed to show you the worst side of my character. Anyway, it's all a matter of department politics. There are two professors in the English department where I work, and in the last twelve months, one of them has got very keen on structuralism. I know he's a late convert, but he's not the only one. He's put a lot of pressure on people like me to take it seriously. It means I'm in a rather difficult position—the department's under pressure to make cuts, and I haven't got tenure. You know what that means?"

"That you can be sacked," Jamie nodded.

"More or less," said Loretta. "There is a possibility that this chap will move to another university next year, but for the time being I've had to look for a way to take the heat off. I decided to draw up a proposal for a book which would attempt a synthesis of structuralist and feminist ideas—not with any enthusiasm, and with the hope that it would never actually get done. But to show how willing I was, I sent the outline to Hugh Puddephat. I thought it would sound good at department meetings to say I'd consulted him. I was so uninterested in the damn thing that I didn't bother to keep a copy. That's why I panicked when I heard he was missing. The last thing I wanted was to have to write the outline again. But now it looks as though I'll have to." She stopped. Was Jamie convinced? As far as she could tell, he wasn't looking suspicious.

"Poor old you," he said sympathetically. "Another victim of Thatcherism. I had no idea university politics were so cut-throat until I came to Oxford. I suppose there must have been a time when it wasn't like this?"

Loretta agreed. The part of her story about the pressure of Government cuts was true, and it seemed a long time since she'd existed in a world that wasn't penny-pinching.

"I take it you're not a Tory?" she asked, deftly moving the conversation to safer territory.

Jamie laughed. "Certainly not," he said. "I'm proud to say I'm the first member of my family to join the Labour Party. My mother's in despair—says she can't look her MP in the face when she meets him at Church. She's your archetypal Tory lady, always holding jumble sales to raise funds, all that sort of thing."

Loretta smiled, picturing the consternation in the Baird household at the prospect of a Socialist in the family. Reluctantly, she put the image aside. "We really should talk about your article," she said. "Shall I tell you my thoughts about it?"

Jamie was in the middle of a story about a disagreement he'd had with a master at his school over the A-level English syllabus when the phone rang. It was Judy, the woman who had invited Loretta to dinner the following evening. "Could you arrive a bit later than planned?" she asked. "I've promised to take Elinor and one of her schoolfriends to the zoo, and I'm worried about getting back in time."

"Of course," said Loretta. "Shall I leave it till after eight to be on the safe side?"

"As long as it won't ruin your pudding," Judy said gratefully. "It's not something dramatic like a soufflé, I hope?"

Loretta laughed. "Far from it. It's something cold, and it's already sitting in the fridge. See you about eight-thirty." She put down the phone and turned back to Jamie.

He was looking slightly alarmed. "Gosh, I'm terribly sorry," he said. "I didn't realize you were going out to dinner. I'm holding you up. Look, I'll go at once." He was already gathering together various pieces of paper.

"Wait a minute," cried Loretta. "You've got it all wrong. It was tomorrow night I was talking about. I'm quite free this evening."

Jamie brightened up. "In that case," he said, "how about having dinner with me? I'm absolutely ravenous—I missed lunch, and there was no buffet car on the train, as well as no heating. Are there any reasonable places to eat near here?"

"There's a very good pasta restaurant at the bottom of the road," Loretta admitted, trying to conceal her enthusiasm. "Shall I ring and see if they've got a table in half an hour or so?"

They arrived early enough to consume a vast *spaghetti carbonara* and a litre of house wine before the little Italian place became crowded. "Shall we get some more wine?" Jamie shouted above the noise, holding up the empty carafe, but before Loretta could answer, a waiter showed two more people to their table.

"Do you mind sharing?" asked one of the new arrivals, a woman in her thirties.

Loretta looked at Jamie. "Let's go back to the flat," she suggested. "There's plenty to drink there."

They left the table to the newcomers, and got their coats. As they opened the street door, a blast of cold air hit them.

"I think we'd better run," said Jamie, taking her arm. Heads down, they set off at a fast trot which lasted until Loretta twisted her ankle.

"These shoes aren't made for running," she laughed, checking her high heel to make sure she hadn't broken it.

"I could carry you," Jamie offered, half seriously. Loretta refused with a laugh, and they continued at a more sedate pace.

As she led the way upstairs to her flat, it occurred to Loretta that she was feeling slightly light-headed. "More wine?" she asked, throwing her coat carelessly on to a sofa in the drawing-room. "Or do you want to go back to whisky?" She noticed that Tracey's postcard had fallen off the mantelpiece, and put it back. "From my ex-husband,"

169

she explained. "He's in Berlin at the moment."

"Whisky would be very nice," said Jamie, taking off his overcoat. "Shall I put some music on?" He knelt down in front of her stereo system. "*Traviata*," he exclaimed, picking up a cassette. "My favourite opera."

As Loretta handed him his drink, the room filled with the sound of high violins. She leaned forward to turn the volume down, muttering something over her shoulder about the neighbours. She felt his arms around her waist, and turned to face him. "Do you want to stay?" she asked, still sober enough to be anxious that there should be no misunderstandings. Jamie smiled, and kissed her.

Daylight breaking through the hastily closed curtains at her bedroom window woke Loretta next morning. Surfacing from sleep, she blinked as she noticed Jamie's head on the pillow next to her. He was still asleep, and she lay in pleased contemplation of his face for several minutes. Then, sliding carefully out from under his outstretched arm, she slipped out of bed. Wrapping herself in the pink kimono hanging on the back of the bedroom door, she went softly down the stairs to the kitchen. She filled the kettle and leaned back against the sink, waiting for it to boil. She realized she was humming a pop song to herself, and blushed. The kettle switched itself off, and she peered in a cupboard for a rarely used teatray.

When she returned to the bedroom, Jamie was awake. Neither of them spoke. She put the tray down beside the bed, and sat down with her back to him to pour the tea. His hand caressed her shoulder, and she smiled.

"Are you interested in breakfast?" she asked, handing him a cup of tea. "There isn't much food in the flat, but I can go to the Asian shop round the corner. They have things like sausages and bacon."

"Sounds wonderful," he said. "But why don't you let me cook it? Tell me where the shop is, and I'll go." After an amicable wrangle, they agreed that they would get dressed and go shopping together.

"We can have showers later," Loretta promised. Jamie was already pulling on his trousers; Loretta rummaged in her dressing-table drawer for clean socks to wear with an old pair of trousers.

"I'll meet you in the hall," Jamie said. "My coat's still in the drawing-room."

Loretta finished dressing and was about to leave the room when she caught sight of the unmade bed. Force of habit compelled her to stop and straighten the quilt.

As she got to the bottom of the stairs, Jamie emerged from the drawing-room. The smile froze on Loretta's face as she caught sight of his expression: his eyes were wide and staring, like those of a cornered animal.

"I've got to go," he blurted out, skirting past her to the front door. "I've just remembered . . . something's come up . . ." His look was almost one of revulsion. He wrenched open the front door, and was out of the flat before Loretta could speak.

"Jamie, wait—" she began, but he was already slamming the door behind him. For a moment, she was rooted to the spot. What had come over him? Everything had been going swimmingly only a moment before. Fighting back shocked tears, she ran to the front door. She was just in time to hear the street door slam, two floors below. She ran down the first flight of stairs, and then turned and dragged herself back to the flat. Feeling as though she had been punched in the stomach, she staggered into the drawing-room and sank on to the sofa. Their empty glasses were still on the coffee-table, reminding her of the night before. Why had he looked at her like that? She hadn't coerced him in any way. He had been as eager as she. A thought struck her, and she leapt up to peer into the mirror over the mantelpiece. Had he changed his mind about her in the cold light of morning? She looked tired, she thought, pushing her hair back from her face, but not markedly different

171

from the previous evening. Not enough to make him suddenly aware of the difference in their ages. Her eyes stared back at her from the mirror, aghast. She was behaving like a reader of *Woman's Own*. If Jamie was the sort of man who cared that much for looks, he wasn't worth having. She sat down again, hugging herself with both arms. A second explanation occurred to her, one she liked no better than the first. "After all, they were very close friends," a voice repeated in her head. She recognized it as that of the girl Natasha at Bridget's party. She had believed Jamie when he told her that Puddephat's passion for him was not reciprocated. Had she been right to do so? Wasn't it possible that his sexuality was much more ambivalent than he had let on? He wouldn't be the first homosexual man to go to bed with a woman in the hope of proving he wasn't gay. The thought made her shudder. Huddled on the edge of the sofa, she stared sadly into space. Her right hand crept up to cover the lower half of her face, as if to protect it.

11

LORETTA WAS LYING MISERABLY ON THE bed, in an unsuccessful attempt to catch up on her sleep, when the phone rang an hour later. She sprang up to answer it: perhaps Jamie was ringing to explain his abrupt departure.

"Good morning, it's me," said a hearty voice. "I'm back in London."

"Oh, it's you," Loretta said grumpily. Tracey was the last person she felt like speaking to.

"Got out of bed the wrong side?" he asked teasingly. "Or are you having a late lie-in?"

"Neither," said Loretta shortly. "I just thought you were someone else."

"Thanks very much," Tracey said sarcastically. "I take it you haven't seen the *Herald* yet?"

Loretta admitted she hadn't. She remembered picking it up when she went downstairs to make tea, but she'd put it on the kitchen table without looking at it. "I suppose you've been doing your John Le Carré stuff again?"

"Len Deighton, more like," Tracey reproved her. "D'you remember *Funeral in Berlin*? I actually rang to tell you there was an attempt on my life yesterday morning. As you're still technically my next-of-kin, I thought you ought to know."

In spite of her misery, this news startled Loretta. "What?" she gasped.

Her reaction seemed to gratify Tracey. "Don't worry, I'm all right," he said graciously. "But I have to admit I was shit scared at the time."

It must have been a pretty alarming experience, Loretta thought, to have wrung this admission out of Tracey. "What happened?" she demanded.

"I got a lead on two more spies this week," he began, "working for the Government in Bonn. I was rushing round double-checking the details all week, and the plan was that Bill and I would confront them yesterday morning. Bill's my photographer, by the way. So we left Bonn in a hire car, on the way to the house of the first one. Then this car tried to force us off the road into a ditch. It was a big black Merc, tinted windows, the lot. I thought we'd had it, quite frankly."

"What did you do?" asked Loretta, unconsciously holding her breath.

"It wasn't me who got us out of it, it was Bill," Tracey admitted. "He turned on all the lights, hazard warning ones as well, and kept his hand on the horn. You should have seen us—we were careering along like a fire engine. By chance—at least, they said it was by chance—a cop car came up from behind and the Merc took off. But it was a pretty close-run thing."

"Did you get its number?" enquired Loretta.

"False plates," Tracey said succinctly.

"And what about your spies? Did you get to see them?"

"Oh yes, and we got great pictures," Tracey enthused. "You should have a look at the paper. It's all over the front page."

"But what happens now?" Loretta asked anxiously. "Have you asked for police protection?"

"'Course not," Tracey said scornfully. "They won't try anything now we're back in England. No point. But I must say it's nice to get some sympathy from you for a change.

How are you, by the way? What news on the dismembered don?"

"He wasn't dismembered," Loretta objected. "Not unless you've been keeping something back from me."

"'Fraid not, I just liked the alliteration," Tracey said cheerfully.

"Well, I have managed to get to know Puddephat's wife," Loretta said warily. Talking about Puddephat reminded her uncomfortably of Jamie. "And it turns out that she's R—she wrote the letter I found in his rooms. Puddephat used to call her Ron, short for Veronica. But I still don't know what he did to make her write it. Or whether it was bad enough to make her kill him."

"Most murders turn out to be domestic affairs," Tracey said cheerfully. "The husband commits some sin like not helping with the washing-up, and the wife sticks a knife in his back. You'd be surprised at what a dull business murder really is. Your cunning killer with a cool head and a phial of untraceable poison is heavily outnumbered by the ranks of disgruntled wives and husbands. I'd say Veronica is suspect *numero uno*, no doubt about it."

Loretta suddenly recalled that she hadn't spoken to Tracey since the release by the police of Puddephat's unfortunate academic rival. "I seem to remember you thought much the same thing about Theo Sykes, and he had nothing at all to do with it," she pointed out.

"So I gather," Tracey said breezily. "But then I always had my doubts about that one."

Loretta decided she hadn't the energy to respond to this provocation. Instead, she changed the subject. "What are you doing now you're back in England?" she asked. "Won't life be a bit quiet after all this excitement?"

"As a matter of fact, I'm having a few days off," Tracey said. "I thought I'd head off to Bath. D'you remember Eddie Russell, used to be a feature writer on the *Herald*?" Loretta did. Russell had left the paper two or three years before to start a news agency in the West Country. "I'm going down to stay with him and his wife," Tracey went on. "It's a nice part of the country, and I could do with a few long walks and a change of scenery."

As he spoke, an idea came to Loretta. Tracey's remarks about Veronica, flippant though they were, had succeeded in making her very uncomfortable. The more she got to know Puddephat's widow, the less Loretta liked the idea that Veronica was the killer. But wasn't there an area of Puddephat's life which remained to be investigated? Who was to say what suspects might not turn up if someone did some serious digging into the Melanie Gandell business? It was just as well she had resisted the temptation to antagonize Tracey by poking fun at his obsession with espionage.

"Are you driving down to Bath?" she asked. Tracey said that he was. "Could you do me a favour?" she continued. "It wouldn't take you much out of your way. Only about twenty miles or so."

"Depends on what it is," Tracey said cautiously.

"I've got the address of the house where Melanie Gandell lived," Loretta explained. "I've been thinking of going down there myself, but it's difficult for me to get time off near the start of term. In any case, the whole thing would be easier for you than for me. You could say you were looking into Puddephat's death for the *Herald*, and you were trying to contact her relatives for a feature on the case. It would be much more plausible than if I turned up on the doorstep with some cock-and-bull story."

"There's no guarantee they'd talk to me," Tracey objected half-heartedly. She could tell from his voice that he was not averse to the idea. Perhaps he'd be glad of something to do while he was in Bath. Whatever he said about wanting a few days in the country, she knew from experience that he was easily bored.

"They may not even live there any longer," she pointed out. "In which case, all you have to do is get their new address for me. I'll do the rest. Please, John," she coaxed.

"All right," he agreed. "Give me the address you've

got. I'm driving down tomorrow, but I can't promise I'll have time to do it on the way. It might have to wait until Tuesday or Wednesday."

"That's quite all right," Loretta assured him. It would be a relief to know that something was being done, and that she could sit back and wait for results for a day or two. "Ring me when you've got something." She put the phone down, and went to the kitchen to look at the *Sunday Herald*. It had really gone to town on the spy story, she discovered. The main headline asserted that the paper had broken up a spy ring. Another, in smaller type, sent a shiver down her spine: "'Herald' Men Pulled Out After Murder Attempt," she read. She sincerely hoped that Tracey would take care of himself over the next few days.

The temptation to ring Jamie was, Loretta found, hard to resist. Surely, she kept saying to herself, there must have been some sort of misunderstanding, something that could be sorted out if they had a rational discussion? Her hand hovered over the phone, and each time drew back. She could not bear to have either of the explanations she feared put into words. On Tuesday morning, she received a letter which reminded her that she had not yet heard from Tracey.

It was from the convener of the *Fem Sap* collective, and its purpose was to summon her to another meeting in Paris —an emergency one this time. Far from approaching settlement, the row over masculine endings was now threatening the very existence of *Fem Sap*. The members of the collective in favour of the radical position had collected sufficient signatures to force a meeting this very weekend, and they had issued an ultimatum: either their position should be accepted, or they would leave. They had even drafted a manifesto, a copy of which the convener enclosed with the notice of meeting. It denounced everyone who opposed the change, including Loretta, as "wishy-washy reformists" and "linguistic fascists"; it ended by announcing their intention, if the collective did split, of

177

setting up a rival journal under the title *Mother Tongue*. The convener apologized for the short notice at which the meeting had been called but pointed out that, under the rules, her hands were tied. Loretta sighed: she could raise little enthusiasm for what was clearly going to be another acrimonious session. It looked as though a split was now inevitable; the only question left to be resolved by Saturday afternoon would be whether or not to persevere with *Fem Sap* after its desertion by half the collective. But if she was going to Paris, shouldn't she make another visit to rue Roland to look for clues? The thought of returning to the flat made her shudder. In any case, what was the point? She knew from Andrew that someone had done a very thorough cleaning job on it.

She had almost decided to send her apologies when two more thoughts occurred to her. As a founder member of the *Fem Sap* collective, could she really abandon the journal to its fate without a fight? The second was less altruistic; if she travelled both ways by air, she would be able to treat herself to a free day in Paris on Sunday. She deserved it after the blow her self-esteem had just suffered at the hands of Jamie Baird. She looked out the previous week's copy of *Time Out*, and circled a couple of adverts for cheap air fares. She also opened her desk drawer, and wrote a postcard to Bridget. She was feeling guilty about not getting in touch with her friend, but feared that the subject of Jamie might come up if she spoke to her direct. "Very many thanks for the party, and apologies for not writing earlier," she scribbled shamefacedly. "Off to Paris for another meeting this weekend. Will ring when I get back. In haste, Loretta." She found a stamp in her purse, and posted it on the way to work.

The phone was ringing as she came up the stairs to her flat that evening. On picking it up, she heard Tracey's voice, and felt a little surge of excitement: was he about to give her a completely new lead, one that would take her well away from Veronica Puddephat? Her hopes were immediately dashed.

"Not much to report, I'm afraid," Tracey admitted. "I drove over to Buckland Dinham this afternoon—it's a pretty place, by the way—but I didn't get very far."

"Couldn't you find the cottage?" Loretta asked with a heavy heart.

"Oh, I found it all right," said Tracey. "It's a big house, as a matter of fact, I don't know why it's called Cherry Cottage. I suppose it may have started as a farm cottage, but it's been extended and modernized out of all recognition. It's right at the end of the village, more or less on its own. The road goes across a bridge, and it's on the other side of the stream, on the left. I parked the car in the drive and knocked, but no one was in. I had a pretty thorough look round, but it was definitely deserted. So I drove back into the main part of the village, and went into the village shop. It's one of those places that sells everything you can think of—free-range eggs, newspapers, vegetables, the lot. I told the woman behind the counter that I'd stopped off on my way to Bath to visit some friends I hadn't seen for ages. I said they didn't seem to be in, and I was beginning to think they might have moved away from the village. She was very helpful, asked me their name—I gave her both to be on the safe side, Grant and Gandell—but they didn't ring a bell. She couldn't remember what they were called, the people in Cherry Cottage, but she thought it was a name beginning with B. Apparently they don't have their papers delivered, and don't do much shopping in the village—I could see why, from the prices she was charging—so she doesn't really come into contact with them. Mind you, she's only been at the shop a twelve-month. So it could be that this Grant woman lived there before her time. But that doesn't help you very much, does it?"

Loretta agreed that it didn't. "But thanks for trying," she said, remembering her manners.

Tracey heard the despondency in her voice, and tried to cheer her up. "Look, I'll be back in London on Friday," he said. "Why don't we meet for dinner and talk it over? If we both put our minds to it, we may be able to come up with another way of tracking down the girl's relatives."

"I can't," Loretta explained. "I've got to go to Paris for another *Fem Sap* meeting."

"Good God," exclaimed Tracey. "You're a glutton for punishment. Haven't you had enough of Paris? We're still trying to solve the last murder you got involved in there!"

"Thanks, John," Loretta said bitterly. "That's just the kind of helpful comment I can do without. I'll phone you when I get back." She rang off, and stared moodily into space. What was she going to do? She was left with nothing but her suspicions about Veronica Puddephat. Did she really want to press on with a course that might implicate the woman in her husband's murder? On the other hand, hadn't she some sort of duty to bring the killer, whoever it might turn out to be, to justice? She was still wrestling with this dilemma when the phone rang again. Of all people it had to be Veronica herself.

"Oh, Loretta, thank God you're in!" she cried, breaking into sobs. "It's on Thursday, and I don't know how I'm going to bear it."

Loretta guessed at once that Veronica was talking about the funeral. Uncomfortable though she felt at talking to the object of her suspicions, she couldn't just put the phone down. Calming Veronica down, she managed to elicit that the ceremony was to take place at the little church in Hallborough which Puddephat had attended when he lived in the Red House. There was to be a considerable group of mourners—the dead man's colleagues, his widowed mother, several members of Veronica's family, and anyone in the village who had known him by sight and could find an excuse to take the afternoon off. "Not to mention the press!" Veronica added, threatening to break into further sobs.

"The press?" queried Loretta. "Are you sure?" The story had dropped out of the papers in the last week or so, presumably for lack of developments; it also seemed in bad taste for reporters to turn up at somebody's funeral.

"Oh, yes," Veronica assured her. "They've been ringing me, and Daddy, and the vicar." Loretta was appalled. She could quite see why Veronica was distressed. At the same time, she was becoming more and more nervous; any minute now, she thought, she's going to ask if I can come to the funeral. How on earth could she get out of it? But Veronica took her by surprise. "It's not so much the funeral I'm afraid of," she said, a note of desperation creeping into her voice. "It's afterwards. When everyone goes away. I'll be all alone. I'm frightened, Loretta! I don't know what I'll do." The drift of what she was saying was unmistakable: Loretta felt a trap closing in on her.

"Can't you ask your mother to stay with you?" she asked weakly.

"Mummy would just make things worse," Veronica protested. "In her eyes, a broken marriage is the worst sin a woman can commit. She'd just go on about what a fool I was ever to split up with Hugh. She doesn't understand—not like you do, Loretta."

Loretta shifted uncomfortably. Veronica was appealing to her as a sister. How could she possibly turn her down? If she did, and Veronica made an attempt on her own life, she wouldn't be able to live with herself. "All right," Loretta said, resigning herself to her fate, "what do you want me to do?"

"Could you possibly spend the evening with me?" Veronica asked, her voice as insubstantial as a small child's. "I mean, you don't have to stay the night. Just the first two or three hours after everyone leaves?"

Loretta agreed that she would. But it would be the last time, she promised herself. She would take with her a copy of *Spare Rib* and, incongruous or not, suggest that Veronica use it to find some sort of women's group. "What time

181

will it be over?" she asked, anxious to arrive after the mourners had dispersed. It had crossed her mind that Andrew Walker might be among them, and she did not want to be forced into explaining how she came to know the dead man's widow.

A handful of people would be coming back to the house, Veronica told her, but she expected them to be gone by five. Loretta promised to arrive an hour or so later, and consoled herself with the thought of her weekend in Paris. She was going to need it.

Expecting heavy traffic on the M40, Loretta set off from London much earlier than she needed to on Thursday afternoon. She arrived at the Oxford ring road just after five, and decided to head into town to kill time. Her route took her past Puddephat's cottage, and reminded her forcefully of her encounter the previous weekend with Jamie Baird. She was suddenly filled with rage: how dare he treat her like that, rushing out of her flat without a word of explanation? With little thought for the vehicle behind her, which had to brake to avoid a collision, Loretta pulled into a space between two cars and parked the Panda on double yellow lines. She would go and remonstrate with him.

She got out of the car and locked the door. Then she paused. Was she not on the verge of making an even greater fool of herself? After all, what would be left for her to say if Jamie simply insisted that he had changed his mind? She was about to get back into the car when she began to berate herself for her cowardice. Why shouldn't she go to his room as if nothing had happened and ask what he intended to do about his article for *Fem Sap*? That would at least demonstrate that, far from suffering agonies as a result of his rejection of her, she had put the entire episode behind her.

Looking quickly to left and right, she threaded her way through the traffic to the other side of the road. Her resolve faltered momentarily when she spotted the florid countenance of Des Koogan peering from the college gateway, but he stepped back to let her pass with an unusual degree of civility. He even volunteered directions to Jamie's room, as well as its number. Perhaps, Loretta speculated, he was a decent enough sort when he wasn't being pestered by reporters. Following his directions, she climbed the stairs to the first floor of a modern annexe behind the great hall. Stopping outside the door which bore Jamie's name, she knocked before she could get cold feet.

"Just a minute," his voice called, and then the door opened. Jamie paused on the threshold, a smile fading from his face. He fell back into the room, the utmost consternation apparent on his face. Irritated by this reception, Loretta followed him into the room. She was already regretting that she had embarked upon this adventure, but now she was here, she was determined to go through with it. She waited for him to invite her to sit down. When he didn't, she began to speak with forced brightness.

"You've got a nice view," she said, walking to the window and looked out at the great hall. It was an inane remark, but she could not bear the silence any longer. She turned to face him. He had always been pale, she thought, but now he was looking absolutely deathly. What did he think she was about to do? Rape him? She concealed her anger. "I can't stay," she assured him. "I just happened to be in Oxford, and I thought I might as well drop in to ask about your article."

"Article?" he repeated blankly. She began to wonder whether he was mentally retarded, or taking drugs. He was standing in front of a cork noticeboard, and she caught sight of a photograph over his left shoulder. It showed a girl with freckles and reddish hair, standing outside what looked like another Oxford college. A new explanation of his odd behaviour occurred to her. Maybe he had been telling the truth about his relationship with Puddephat, and this young woman was his girlfriend. Was it guilt about her that had prompted his precipitate disappearance from her flat on Sunday? It even crossed her mind that the girl might be due to arrive at Jamie's room at any moment—which would explain why he was so nervous. As if reading her thoughts, he moved to one side and blocked her view of the picture. "I hadn't given it any thought," he said wildly, running his hand abstractedly through his hair. "I've been very busy. I didn't think there was any hurry."

"Oh, there isn't," Loretta said. "It's just that I'm off to Paris this weekend for a meeting of the collective. I wanted to let them know when to expect it." Jamie was not to know that *Fem Sap* might well cease to exist in two days' time. When he didn't respond, she decided she had tortured herself long enough. "Well, it sounds to me as though I'd better leave it for the time being," she said sternly. "You can get in touch when you've done it." And pigs might fly, she thought silently. She walked past him to the door, and let herself out.

In the corridor, she gave a deep sigh. She must have been mad to come here, she told herself. As she went down the stairs, she looked at her watch. It was just after five thirty. It should be safe now to set off for the Red House. The idea filled her with relief. Whatever the evening held in store, it couldn't be worse than the scene she'd just been through with Jamie. When she got back to the car, she discovered she'd been given a parking ticket.

She had timed her arrival perfectly; there was only one car parked in the drive of the Red House, and that was the Citroën belonging to Veronica. Loretta parked behind it, wondering how Puddephat's widow had stood up to the afternoon's ordeal. Funerals tended to liberate all sorts of emotions at the best of times, and that of a murder victim had every reason to be even more fraught than most.

She knocked at the front door, and it opened immediately. Loretta had the impression Veronica had been waiting behind it—at least someone was glad to see her. The first thing she noticed was that the other woman was wearing an extraordinary combination of sober clothes and bright pink jewellery. Her black jacket and pleated skirt were very much what Loretta had expected, but a shocking pink enamel rose nestled in the tie neck of her grey silk blouse. Her earrings were smaller versions of the same design, and had been chosen to match the colour of her spectacles. Didn't she own another pair? Loretta wondered. The effect was disconcerting, as though Veronica had not been able to decide whether the day's events were a matter for joy or sorrow, and had hedged her bets.

"Loretta, so good of you to come," Veronica was saying, stepping back to allow her into the hall. "And absolutely on time. Did you have a good journey?"

She might have been welcoming a guest to a small dinner party, but Loretta guessed that she was seeing the role Veronica had chosen to get her through the afternoon, and hoped she did not intend to keep it up all evening. The kind of small talk demanded by so polished a display of manners had never come easily to her. On the other hand, if Veronica has suddenly developed this degree of self-control, it might allow her to get back to London relatively early in the evening. She followed the other woman into the drawing-room, taking the seat she had occupied on her last visit to the house.

"Sherry?" Veronica offered, pointing to the decanter already waiting with two glasses on a side table. Loretta accepted, and waited for Veronica to take a seat opposite her.

"How did it go?" she asked nervously when the silence between them had stretched to uncomfortable proportions. The question sounded all wrong, as if she were enquiring about the success of a job interview, but she could not think of any other.

The effect of her words was dramatic. Veronica put her glass down abruptly, removed her spectacles, and gave way to a prolonged bout of weeping. Black streaks appeared on her cheeks as her mascara ran, and she made the mess worse by dabbing ineffectually at her eyes with her fingers. Loretta spotted an open packet of paper handkerchiefs on the sideboard, and brought them over to her. Veronica took them, and blew her nose.

After a while, her sobs subsided. She sat forward, twisting a crumpled tissue in her hands. "I didn't cry all afternoon," she said apologetically. "I suppose it had to come out sooner or later."

"Of course," Loretta soothed her. She found tears easier to cope with than the brittle politeness with which Veronica had greeted her.

"It went very well, in the circumstances," Veronica went on. "The vicar had a word with the photographers, and most of them did keep well back from the grave. He gave a marvellous oration. Very moving."

Loretta said nothing. She was not a Christian, and she doubted whether the vicar's words would have consoled her in the way they had Veronica. "Have you eaten anything?" she asked, seeing her lean over to refill her sherry glass.

"I had a sandwich," Veronica said vaguely. "And a scone. I may have had more than that. I'm not sure."

There were no signs of food in the room, and Loretta marvelled at how quickly the debris had been cleared away. Then she realized her mistake. Veronica would undoubtedly have employed caterers for the afternoon. And the event had probably taken place in the village hall, not in the house. "Can I make you some tea?" she asked, anxious that Veronica should not consume too much alcohol on an empty stomach. Veronica nodded, and led the way to the kitchen.

It was a large room with pine cupboards and a split-level cooker. Veronica waited passively by the door, wiping away occasional tears, while Loretta filled the kettle and emptied the teapot. Half a dozen empty glasses on the draining-board revealed that a small group of mourners had come back to the house after the wake. Loretta wondered how many glasses of sherry Veronica had got through before her arrival. She had to ask where the tea caddy and cups were kept, and each time she spoke she had the impression that she was interrupting a lengthy internal dialogue on the part of the other woman. She found a tin containing biscuits, home-made by the look of them, and added it to the other things she had assembled on a tray. Veronica allowed herself to be shepherded back to the drawing-room, and resumed her seat. She accepted a cup and saucer from Loretta, but stared blindly into the cup instead of drinking from it.

"I feel empty," she said as Loretta sat down. "I don't think I really believed he was dead until this afternoon."

Loretta was unsurprised. She had encountered this reaction before in the recently bereaved. She waited for Veronica to go on, thinking it would do her good to talk about her feelings.

"In the church this afternoon, it suddenly hit me that he was gone. He's never going to come to this house again. It seems . . . incredible." She paused.

Loretta wondered whether Veronica had given any thought to her own plans. At their first meeting, she had spoken wistfully of taking a course—some sort of social work, Loretta thought she had mentioned. Now might be the time to encourage her. She was about to raise the subject when Veronica spoke again.

"Did you know my husband was a homosexual?" she demanded suddenly. Loretta was taken aback. She had not expected the conversation to take this turn, and it made her very uncomfortable. Given Veronica's background, her attitude to homosexuality was unlikely to be an enlightened one; the break-up of her marriage, presumably as a result of Puddephat's tortured sexuality, was certain to have strengthened her initial prejudice. It was a subject on which it was impossible for them to agree. At the same time, Loretta feared that in her present emotional state, Veronica would interpret anything less than total support as a declaration of hostility. While she struggled to devise a reply which would divert Veronica's attention to safer channels, the other woman spoke again. "That's why I threw him out," she said abruptly. "I found out he had been seeing . . . a boy. I found out because he came here," she added, refuting the unspoken implication that she had been spying on her husband. "Can you imagine how I felt? He was sixteen or seventeen, this person. He worked in a local garage. At first, I didn't know what he was talking about, what his connection was with Hugh. After he left, Hugh . . . told me. He wasn't the only one, apparently. There had been several of them. It had been going on for years. Behind my back. Oh, Hugh said he still loved me. He was desperate to go on living with me." She laughed bitterly. "Discreet homosexual dons who stick to their own kind are one thing. It's quite another if they happen to be interested in . . . boys. He was terrified people would find out. It suited him to have a nice respectable wife who was too naïve to ask questions. He went berserk when I told him to go."

For the first time, Loretta felt a pang of sympathy for Hugh Puddephat. She had always thought the age of consent for gay men a ridiculous anomaly, and he had been a classic victim of it.

"I blame myself for what happened next," Veronica continued. "I behaved very badly. I wanted to hurt Hugh as much as he'd hurt me, and I didn't care how I did it. I wasn't very discreet when people rang here for Hugh, people who didn't know I'd thrown him out. And of course they began to talk. Hugh was at his wit's end. And he used one of his students as a smokescreen. She had a crush on him, you see. Melanie Gandell, her name was, I could never forget it. Hugh was so worried about the rumours I'd caused that he went out of his way to encourage her. She took it seriously—Hugh could be very charming, he could make you feel really special." There was a faraway look in Veronica's eyes, and Loretta guessed she was remembering her own courtship. "In the end, she became rather a nuisance. Hugh had to tell her...what he'd told me. She killed herself."

Loretta's brief sympathy for the dead man evaporated. He was extremely lucky that none of this had come out at the inquest, she thought. Deliberately using an impressionable girl in such a way was unforgivable.

"Hugh was devastated by her death," Veronica went on. "He came here and told me all about it as soon as it happened. He blamed himself dreadfully. He really did," she added, sensing Loretta's scepticism. So that was how he got Veronica to accompany him to the inquest, Loretta was thinking. Hugh Puddephat had certainly known how to look after number one. "We were on better terms afterwards," Veronica said. "We used to go to the theatre together in London. I even thought he might have...got over it."

Loretta shifted uneasily. As she had suspected, Veronica regarded homosexuality as an illness, something that could be shaken off. She said nothing.

"Some time this year, it was in June, he even suggested that we spend a weekend together in Paris," Veronica said dreamily. "He wanted to stay in the flat where we spent our honeymoon—it belongs to an old friend of ours, someone who was at college with Hugh." Loretta's ears pricked up: was she about to discover the truth about Veronica's trip to Paris? "I borrowed the keys from Andrew," Veronica said. "Hugh hadn't spoken to him for ages, and said it would sound better if I asked for them. He came here to collect them—he was going out a day earlier than me, you see. And then, about ten days before we were due to go, he cancelled the whole thing. He never explained why. I thought he'd got cold feet."

Went to Paris with someone else, more like, Loretta thought cynically. It sounded to her as if the entire business had been a deliberate ruse to get hold of the keys on Puddephat's part. He had almost certainly copied them, and

189

sent the originals anonymously to Andrew. But why go to all that trouble? Something disreputable, she was sure. She felt a surge of sympathy for Veronica.

"I didn't hear from him for a while," the other woman went on. "I thought I'd leave him to sort himself out." Hope certainly does spring eternal in the human breast, Loretta thought wonderingly. Had it never occurred to Veronica that her husband really was a lost cause? "He rang up again some time in August," Veronica added. "He said he had to talk to me and I thought . . ." She tailed off. What she had thought was all too painfully clear. "Anyway, when he got here he was very excited. I've never seen him so agitated. He told me he'd fallen in love. Yes, with a man," she added. "Or at least, a young man. He didn't tell me anything about him, except to say he wanted to live with him as soon as he was old enough. He said it was what he'd always wanted, but he'd been afraid to face it. He even apologized for marrying me, said it has been a terrible mistake. He seemed to think living with this man would make everything all right. And then he . . ." She stopped, and Loretta wondered what was coming next. "He said he wanted to have a baby, and he wanted me to be the mother." Seeing the amazement on Loretta's face, she spelled it out more exactly. "The idea was that they'd both come here, and we'd all drink champagne, and then . . . That way, you see, they wouldn't know which one of them was the father. Hugh would move in while I had it—he said he was fonder of me than any other woman, so he'd like me to be its mother—and eventually he'd go off to live with his lover, baby and all. I would be able to visit it, of course. He wanted me to agree before he mentioned it to his lover. It was going to be a surprise for him."

Loretta sat in appalled silence. Of all the things she had ever heard about Hugh Puddephat, this was unquestionably the worst. She had never encountered selfishness on such a grand scale. He must have been mad, she thought. And what about the lover, what would he have thought about it? Puddephat had apparently taken his acquiescence just as much for granted as Veronica's. She spoke her thoughts aloud: "He must have been mad. There's no other explanation."

"If he was mad, I was demented," Veronica said. "I started screaming at him, I used words I didn't know I knew. He didn't seem to understand why. He got angry himself after a while, he said I'd ruined his only chance of happiness. That was the last time I saw him."

Loretta waited for Veronica to mention the letter, whose contents were now explained. But she appeared to have come to the end of her narrative. "You didn't know he was going to Paris?" she asked.

"No, why should I?" Veronica demanded sharply. "Can't you understand how much I hated him? It wasn't until after he was dead that I . . ." She stopped. "I didn't invite you here to tell you all this," she said, suddenly defensive. "I've never breathed a word of it to anyone before now. I kept it all inside me. It's been going round and round in my head ever since they found Hugh's body. I suppose it had to come out some time."

Loretta regarded her bleakly. She was not at all sure that Veronica was telling the truth. It seemed much more likely that she had been carefully selected as a suitable confidante. After all, if Veronica had a burning desire to entrust her terrible story to someone, who better than Loretta? She was not a member of the family, someone Veronica would have to meet on a regular basis. As far as Veronica was aware, Loretta didn't even have any connection with her husband, apart from the slightest professional acquaintances. As a feminist, she would have a ready sympathy for another woman. And, on top of everything else, Loretta did not, as far as Veronica was aware, know any details of the murder. And wasn't that significant? Loretta asked herself. For what Hugh Puddephat's wife had just told her amounted to an excellent motive for murder. Plenty of murders were committed out of simple jealousy, and Puddephat's behaviour had been far, far worse than abandoning his wife for another woman. And it wasn't just a question of motive. Loretta suspected that Veronica had also had the opportunity. According to her version of events, she had rejected her husband's proposal out of hand. That much was borne out by the existence of the letter, which counted as independent evidence of her story. But what had happened afterwards? Wasn't it possible that Veronica had sought revenge? Had she feigned a change of heart to lure Puddephat to his death? "I've had time to think about it, and I've changed my mind," Veronica's voice was saying in her head. "Why don't we meet in Paris, at Andrew's flat. We spent our honeymoon there, and this will be a sort of honeymoon. But don't let's tell your friend I'm coming. You and I will arrive first, and make all the arrangements. There's money to consider, and my access to the child. I'll want to see it, of course. Your friend can join us a day later. As you said, it'll be a surprise for him." Loretta shook her head, and the picture faded. She had allowed her imagination to run away with her. She did not believe Veronica capable of such cold-blooded calculation. Besides, there were practical objections. Even if Puddephat had copied the keys to rue Roland in June, Veronica had no way of knowing that he had done so. Yet neither she nor Puddephat had approached Andrew for a further loan of the originals. Perhaps she had taken copies as well, a little voice persisted. Loretta refused to listen to it. If she was right, why hadn't Puddephat's lover reported the discovery of the body to the police? The whole thing was preposterous. Far from being evidence of her guilt, Veronica's candour spoke eloquently of her innocence. The subject of these thoughts, who had been sitting silently in her chair, looked up suddenly. "I feel so much better for getting it off my chest," she said with an embar-

192

rassed laugh. "It's been such a weight on me." Loretta was suffused with guilt. Veronica had trusted her, and she had responded by constructing a dangerous fantasy about her. "Are you hungry?" Veronica was saying. "The least I can do is buy you dinner."

Loretta thought that after what she had been through, food would taste like ashes in her mouth, but she pulled herself together. "That would be very nice," she said lamely. Veronica suggested that they eat at a hotel in Woodstock, and went to phone for a reservation. When she came back, her face had been scrubbed and freshly made up. The subject of her marriage, Loretta thought with relief, seemed to be closed. They agreed to take both cars, and Loretta followed Veronica's Citroën to the restaurant.

During dinner, Veronica talked cheerfully about her plans for the future, which included selling the Red House and applying for a place on a social-work course. At ten, Loretta decided it was safe to take her leave. "I must get back to London," she said, putting on her jacket. "I'm off to Paris tomorrow." She told Veronica about the *Fem Sap* conference, and reached in her bag. "Have a look at this," she said, producing a copy of *Spare Rib*. Veronica took it politely, but with barely concealed distaste.

They walked out to the cars together, and Veronica waited while Loretta fastened her seat belt. She did not suggest meeting again, an omission for which Loretta was profoundly grateful. Veronica would only be embarrassed by the memory of her revelations, and Loretta could see no point now that Puddephat's wife was no longer a suspect. Pulling out of the car park, she slipped a tape of *Don Giovanni* into the cassette player. It seemed an appropriate choice, even if Puddephat's inclination had been towards men rather than women. It was in his sexuality, she was now convinced, that the clue to his death lay. The most likely explanation was that he had picked up some stranger on the streets of Paris and fallen victim to him at the flat.

The chances of the killer being apprehended, even if she were to supply the police with her meagre stock of information, seemed remote. With a lighter heart than she had experienced since her return from Paris, Loretta turned up the Mozart until it drowned out her thoughts.

12

THE RESTAURANT WAS A LITTLE NORTH AF-
rican place near Les Halles. It took Loretta some time to
find it, as it was tucked away in a back street. Inside the
door, she paused and took stock.

She was standing at the end of a long, narrow room with
tables down each side. A variety of Moroccan cooking
utensils and striped blankets hung on the walls. The room
was dark, but not unpleasantly so. She could not see her
friends—two women from the *Fem Sap* collective with
whom she had arranged to have dinner—so she asked for a
table for three, explaining that the others would be along in
a moment. She sat down at one of the tables with her back
to the wall, giving her a good view of the door. Years
before, while she herself was a student, she had spent a
holiday in Morocco, and she was pleased to see a number
of tagines on the menu as well as the predictable couscous.
The street door opened and she looked up for long enough
to register that her friends had not arrived, then returned to
her perusal of the wines offered by the establishment.

Suddenly her left hand was seized and raised to the lips
of the complete stranger whose arrival she had noted a
minute before. Before she could protest, he had presented
her with a single red rose and taken a seat opposite her. His
French was, initially, too fast for her to understand, and

she peered anxiously round the room to see if there was any obvious explanation for his unaccountable behaviour. The mild curiosity on the faces of two waiters dispelled the notion that the stranger was employed by the restaurant to provide an eccentric greeting service for its guests. Waiting until he paused for breath, she began to speak. "*Excusez-moi, Monsieur, je ne comprends pas*," she said, referring both to his rapid French and the situation in general. The stranger appeared to be slightly disconcerted, but then shrugged it off. Leaning across the table, he confided that she was much more beautiful than her photograph. Loretta's astonishment increased. When and how had this unknown man seen her photograph? She started speaking again in careful French, assuring the stranger that she did not know him, and that there must be some mistake. As her English accent became apparent, a look of horror appeared on the man's face. He stopped her, and enquired whether she was not Mademoiselle Françoise Sauzède, aged twenty-eight, dental nurse just arrived in Paris from Rouen? When Loretta confirmed that she wasn't, he clapped his hand to his forehead in a theatrical gesture of remorse. He was so sorry to have intruded upon her, he said, it was the most terrible mistake. He had come to the restaurant to meet Mademoiselle Sauzède, whom he had contacted through a computer dating agency. He had never seen her, but was in possession of a photograph in which she bore a striking resemblance to Loretta. Her suspicion that this was a novel method of picking up women proved to be unfounded when he reached into his inside pocket and produced a picture of a woman who really did look a little like her. Still apologizing, he stood up, bowed several times, and scampered off to a table as far away from her as he could get. Loretta was just reaching into her bag for a book when he materialized in front of her again. Without saying a word, he retrieved the rose, which was still lying on the table, and scuttled back to his seat. Loretta smiled to herself; if her restaurant jinx had come back, it was taking a less threatening form than had her last run of bad luck.

A few minutes later, the door opened and she was able to watch in silent amusement as her erstwhile suitor went through his paces again. In the flesh, Mademoiselle Sauzède did not have much in common with Loretta apart from the style and colour of her hair. Her make-up was much heavier than Loretta was accustomed to wearing, and her heels a great deal higher. From the furtive glance the small man cast Loretta a few seconds after the arrival of his date, she got the clear impression that he felt he had got a better bargain second time round. She pretended to search in her bag to hide the broad smile which had spread across her face, and thought to herself that the dental nurse was welcome to him. Just then, her friends arrived, apologizing for being late, and she was able to regale them with the story in a low voice.

After ordering, they turned to a more serious subject. The other women, a lecturer in English from Reading University and a French novelist, were on the same side as Loretta on the grammar question but, she soon discovered, were even more pessimistic than she about the outcome of the next morning's meeting. Simone, who had spoken to the convener of the *Fem Sap* collective earlier in the day, thought that the whole thing would be over by midmorning; she had heard that the radicals intended to cut short discussion and force a vote as quickly as possible.

"What we have to decide," said Mary, the woman from Reading, "is whether we soldier on with *Fem Sap* in the hope of hanging on to most of our contributors, or whether we start afresh with a new journal of our own."

"Or abandon the whole thing for the time being," Simone added glumly.

Loretta understood her pessimism; either of Mary's suggestions would involve a daunting amount of work and a battle with the radicals' proposed new journal, *Mother Tongue*. Nevertheless, having given the matter some thought on the way to Paris, she was now convinced that

197

Fem Sap, or something very like it, should carry on. "We can't give up now," she urged. "We've built *Fem Sap* from nothing. Most of the things in it wouldn't get into print if it didn't exist. *Mother Tongue* isn't going to accept anything like our range of contributions. I agree with Mary. The question is whether we keep the title, or start something new ourselves."

They agreed to talk again next day after the vote had been taken. Although the room at the Sorbonne had been booked for Saturday only, Mary suggested they should try and reserve it again for Sunday morning. There would be a great deal to discuss, she pointed out. Bang goes my day of sightseeing, Loretta thought sadly. Still, it couldn't be helped.

The next morning's meeting of the collective was as tiresome as Loretta had anticipated. The discussion that preceded the vote confirmed her suspicion that the radicals were using the issue of masculine endings to force a split to allow them to set up an entirely separatist journal. The vote itself was held up by procedural wrangles until just before one, and the radicals lost narrowly. One of their number, an Associate Professor of Women-Authored Fiction from Ohio, immediately stood up and announced their withdrawal from the *Fem Sap* collective. The inaugural meeting of the *Mother Tongue* editorial board would take place in the room in which they were sitting at two-thirty that afternoon, she said.

"They're wasting no time," Mary whispered indignantly to Loretta. "I wonder if I should point out that this room was booked by the *Fem Sap* collective, and they've just left it?"

"Why bother?" asked Loretta. "I think we all need a break. We were planning to have our meeting tomorrow morning anyway. Let's collect together a few people who are on our side and go to a café."

As Mary drifted off to speak with Simone, the door

198

opened and the porter peered into the room. Making no secret of his reluctance to enter it, he attracted the attention of the woman nearest him and passed her an envelope. The woman, one of the separatists, gave it a cursory glance and silently handed it to Loretta. Her name was clearly typed on the front of it, Loretta saw, examining it with a puzzled expression. Who could be sending her a note? Everyone she knew in Paris was at the meeting with her.

Opening it, she found a single sheet of paper bearing a typed message. When she read it, she was so shocked that she sat down abruptly. Gathering her thoughts, she peered round the room for Mary. "I'll be downstairs, by the porter's desk," she said urgently, rushing from the room.

She found the porter in his cabin, a makeshift affair constructed of plywood, by the front door. She rapped on one of the windows to attract his attention. "Who delivered this?" she demanded curtly in French.

The man lumbered to his feet. "A young lady," he replied.

"When?" Loretta pressed him. He shrugged his shoulders. Half an hour, maybe three-quarters of an hour ago, he said. He had thought it better to wait until the meeting ended before bringing it up.

"What did she look like?" Loretta insisted. The porter shrugged again, and said she was just a young lady. Then he smiled slyly. She had red hair, the young lady, he did remember that, he said.

Deciding she would get no more out of him, Loretta walked slowly to a bench which ran the length of one side of the entrance hall. She sat down, and read the note again. It was just as perplexing on the second reading, and Loretta realized it had also induced in her a twinge of fear. "Meet me at the Café Costes at three o'clock this afternoon," it said simply. The sting was in the tail. The note was signed "Melanie Gandell" and, leaving no room for ambiguities, the sender had typed the name below the signature to make sure she got the point.

It can't be, Loretta told herself unbelievingly. There was no doubt at all that the girl was dead. She had been identified by a member of her own family. The inquest into her death had made no mention of any confusion. The signature could only be interpreted as bait to lure her... to what? Who would be waiting for her at the Café Costes, wherever that was?

Then she remembered what the porter had said. The note had been delivered by a girl with red hair. Melanie Gandell had red hair, but Melanie Gandell was dead. Someone wearing a wig? Whoever it was had gone to a lot of trouble to get the details right. Or a relative of Melanie Gandell, a member of that elusive family she had been unable to track down? Not a sister, since Melanie had been an only child. And an aunt was hardly likely to qualify for the porter's description of the messenger as a young lady.

"There you are," said Mary, interrupting her thoughts. "Are you all right?"

Loretta fleetingly wondered whether she should tell Mary what had happened, but decided it would take too long. "I'm fine," she said brightly, putting the note into her bag.

She joined Mary, Simone and three other women in their search for somewhere to have coffee. The weather was not particularly cold for October, inclining instead to an intermittent drizzle. As the rain was threatening to start again, they made for the nearest bar. An animated discussion about the future of *Fem Sap* immediately sprang up, but failed to hold Loretta's attention. Looking at her watch, she calculated that she had just over an hour until the rendezvous. She tried to approach the puzzle logically, compiling a list of people who knew she was in Paris, and precisely where she could be found. It was quite long, but did not include anyone who seemed a likely suspect in the matter of sending the note. Tracey knew, of course, but his tastes did not include spiteful practical jokes. The same went for her mother. She had mentioned the trip to several people at work, including the department secretary, but that didn't get her any further. She also remembered speaking to Veronica Puddephat about it, but that made no sense either. Even if Veronica wanted to confess to murdering her husband, which Loretta didn't believe for a moment, there were simpler ways of bringing about another meeting. She supposed someone could have phoned the department and discovered she was going to Paris but, far from narrowing the field, that thought opened it up impossibly wide.

She returned to the porter's description of the girl. Relegating theories about the substitution of bodies to the realms of fantasy, she was left only with the fact that the girl was not Melanie Gandell. A new thought occurred to her: perhaps the girl had nothing to do with the case, but had been bribed to deliver the note on account of her red hair? That was the most likely explanation. So it was the identity of the author of the note she must concentrate on. First and foremost, it was someone who knew that the dead girl's name would mean something to her. Therefore, it must be someone with a good idea of the extent of her knowledge of the case. She panicked for a moment, wondering if the killer had, without her knowledge, observed her in rue Roland and again, by chance, in the course of her investigation. Fear for her own safety, which had gripped her at the scene of the murder, suddenly returned in full force for the first time since she fled the flat in rue Roland. But surely that was what the note had been meant to do? she asked herself. As well as playing on her curiosity, wasn't there something sinister about sending a note in the name of a dead woman? After all, if the writer simply wanted to meet her for a chat, why not ring her up and say so? She did not like it one little bit and yet, she realized, it hadn't crossed her mind not to keep the appointment. She waited for a break in the conversation, and asked Simone if she had heard of the Café Costes. She discovered that it was a very fashionable place on the fringes of Les Halles, famous for its splendid Art Deco interior. At least her unknown correspondent had taste, she thought wryly.

Loretta decided that, rain or not, she could do with some fresh air. Apologizing to her companions, who were clearly surprised by her lack of interest in their discussion, she said she had a headache and needed a walk. She arranged to ring Mary's hotel that evening for details of the time and place of the next day's *Fem Sap* meeting, and left the bar.

Outside, the drizzle had started again, leaving the pavements wet and dirty. She wished she had brought an umbrella; her dark pink quilted jacket, with its bright pink silk lining, was warm but hardly waterproof. Nor was her straight black skirt likely to be improved by the addition of muddy splashes. However, now was not the time to worry about her appearance, and she was at least glad to be out of the stuffy bar. She stopped at the next corner to consult her map, and headed towards the river.

Loretta asked for directions to the Café Costes on her arrival at Les Halles, and found it with ease. It was only twenty to three, and she decided to kill time by having a look at the Pompidou Centre. It always struck her as more like an oversized model for a central heating system than an exhibition centre, and she was not sure how much she liked it. Irritatingly, she could not recall the name of the architect; it floated just out of reach in the recesses of her brain as she rode the escalators to the top of the building, it remained elusive as she looked down on the rainwashed slate roofs of the city, her obsession with unimportant detail a measure of how tense she was feeling. Deciding it was time to go back to the café, she returned to the top of the first escalator.

As she reached it, she was jostled by several youths who overtook her and chased each other down the moving staircase. She grabbed the handrail, and breathed deeply. She had flinched as though she were about to be attacked. What was she expecting? she asked herself. A Hitchcock-style attempt to throw her from the top of the city's most famous twentieth-century landmark? She must get a grip on herself.

A couple of minutes later, she was pushing open the door into the Café Costes. Even in her highly charged state, she had to admire the stunning decorations. The café was on two levels, the upper floor forming a balcony overlooking the ground. In front of her was a flight of stairs to the upper floor, surmounted by a luminous clock face, its second hand at least four feet long. The staircase was pale green, fanning out to double width at the top, flanked by magnificent pink pillars at the bottom. There were mirrors everywhere, concealed lights, a pink ceiling; it was like stepping into a 1930s film set, although Simone had told her the work was recent. Looking round, she saw that most of the tables on the ground floor were occupied. She did not recognize any of the drinkers, nor did they seem to recognize her.

She ascended to the balcony floor, turning left at the top and doubling back on herself. She was standing at the end of a double row of tables, half of them set back against the wall to her right, the rest overlooking the floor below. Two or three tables along, his arm outstretched along the balcony rail, she saw Jamie Baird. She walked slowly towards him, taking in his unusually seedy appearance. He hadn't shaved, and he was wearing an old green jumper. The words which came into her head seemed unduly melodramatic, so she said nothing, simply pulling out a chair and joining him.

"You came," Jamie said unnecessarily. She guessed he was as nervous as she was. Down below, she watched a waiter collect coffee cups and a Ricard water bottle from an empty table. "I took the liberty of ordering you a drink," he said, pushing a glass towards her. "I hope you like *kir*." She had never drunk it before, but thought vaguely that it had something to do with blackcurrants.

"Thanks," she said, speaking for the first time. She took

a sip, liked it, and drank more. Ideas were jostling for place in her mind and yet, amid the confusion, one stood out with absolute clarity.

"You killed him," she said matter-of-factly. Jamie nodded. They sat in silence, for all the world like a pair of lovers whiling away a damp afternoon. Loretta was sorting through the gaps in her knowledge, wondering what to ask first. As the shock receded, her nervousness came back in full force, and she remembered that she was not merely enjoying a drink with a friend. She realized that one question was more urgent than any of the others.

"Why did you want me here?" she asked baldly.

Jamie gave her a measuring look. "Haven't you guessed?" he countered.

"You're hardly likely to throttle me in front of all these people," she replied lightly, aware that her heart was pounding. Unconsciously, she moved her chair back slightly, poised for flight.

"Of course not," he replied with equal lightness. "But what d'you think you've been drinking?"

Loretta opened her mouth and glanced round wildly. She started to rise from her seat, looking for signs to the lavatories. If she could get there in time and put her fingers down her throat . . . She saw how clever he had been. If she was too late, he'd be gone by the time her body was found. She was about to run when he placed a hand on her chest and pushed her back into the chair. "How does it feel?" he snarled, his voice contorted by anger.

As she sprang to her feet again, he caught her arm and spoke more calmly. "Relax," he said, "I didn't put anything in your drink. Look, it really is OK." He lifted her glass and drained the remains of the *kir*. Loretta fell back into her seat, fighting off the urge to vomit. "Here, drink some water," he said, pouring it into her glass from a bottle on the table. "I haven't poisoned this, either," he added in a tired voice, demonstrating the truth of what he was saying by taking a sip from the glass.

Loretta took a mouthful and looked at him wonderingly. "Why did you do that to me?" she asked at last. She was astonished that he was capable of such cruelty.

"I couldn't resist giving you a taste of your own medicine," Jamie said, pulling a face. "Not very polite of me, was it? Not a *gentlemanly* thing to do. But you put me through hell in the last couple of weeks, teasing me with what you knew. I didn't plan it this way, if that's what you're thinking."

"Teasing you?" Loretta repeated blankly. "I don't know what you're talking about."

"Come on, you were putting the frighteners on me," Jamie sneered. "Leaving the postcard from your husband where you knew I'd find it."

Loretta gasped. So that was why Jamie had fled from her flat. The thought had never entered her head. "And coming to Oxford to make sure I knew you were on your way to Paris. I suppose you were hoping I'd break down and confess, and save you the trouble. It would have added no end to the value of your story, wouldn't it? Dead don, murderer tells all. What would you have got for it? Ten thousand, twenty? No doubt you were leaving that side of it to your husband. Did you get the evidence, by the way? I presume that's what you're really here for. Have you found anyone near the church who recognized your description of me? Just as a matter of interest." He stopped, breathing heavily. He had worked himself into a passion of fury. Loretta was staring at him in amazement.

"Jamie," she pleaded, leaning across the table and putting a hand on his arm. He shook it off. "Jamie," she repeated urgently. "This is madness. Until I walked up those stairs and saw you sitting there, I hadn't the slightest idea you had anything to do with the murder. Really I hadn't. I was astonished when you rushed out of my flat on Sunday. I thought . . ." She tailed off. There was no point now in telling him what had gone through her mind. She fell back in her seat.

Jamie's eyes were fixed on her face. "You mean all this—" he swept his arm in an arc round the room "—all this was for nothing? You had no idea?"

She shook her head. "None at all." Silence fell. Suddenly, Loretta felt her cheeks burn. "Is that why you were keen to see me again after Bridget's party?" she demanded. "Because you thought I suspected?"

Jamie lowered his eyes. "It wasn't just that," he said defensively. "I was puzzled about why you had consulted Hugh, but that's not the only reason I came to your flat. I could have left much earlier in the evening if that had been the case, as soon as you'd put my mind at rest. You didn't force me to stay the night."

Loretta closed her eyes and forced back tears. Was he telling the truth? Perhaps it didn't matter. "Are you related to Melanie?" she asked in a sudden flash of inspiration.

"Cousins," Jamie said briefly. "But more like brother and sister. We were brought up together after her parents died."

"And your parents have a house in Buckland Dinham," Loretta said, working it out piece by piece.

"So you did know?" Jamie challenged her, suspicious again.

"No, I hadn't even made the connection until now," Loretta said sadly. "I found out Melanie's address, Cherry Cottage that is, and my ex-husband went down there. But your parents weren't in. The woman in the village shop couldn't remember their name, except that it started with a B. I was expecting Gandell, of course, or Grant. I'd got as far as discovering that was the name of the aunt who identified Melanie's body."

Jamie nodded. "She lives near Leominster, actually. My parents were in Italy when Mel died."

A waiter appeared, and Loretta asked for some tea. She needed it. Jamie said he'd have black coffee. "What I don't understand," he went on, "is why you were interested in

206

Hugh's death in the first place. I assume I'm right in thinking your notes were an invention?"

"Yes," Loretta agreed. "I was there, you see. At the flat in rue Roland. I was supposed to be spending the weekend there, the weekend you . . . killed him. I arrived very late on the Friday night, and saw him in bed. I thought he was asleep. I'd no idea who he was. Or that he was dead. I went to a conference next morning, and when I got back he was gone. All I found were the sheets. He left a book there, by the way, in the bookcase in the living-room. That's how I was able to find out who he was."

"God, you must have just missed me," Jamie said, appalled. "What time did you get to the flat, that first evening?"

"I'm not certain," Loretta admitted. "Some time after midnight. What time did it . . . happen?"

"Around eleven," Jamie said curtly. "But you really didn't know?" he asked again, changing the subject. "D'you know, I even thought you'd spotted the picture of Mel when you came to my room. I was sure you knew who she was."

So that explained the identity of the girl in the photograph, Loretta thought. She hadn't been a girlfriend, after all. She was oddly comforted. The waiter returned, and she sipped her tea. It was very hot. "You killed him to revenge her?" she asked, putting the cup down.

Jamie looked up from stirring his coffee, surprised. "Good God, no," he said. "It was an accident. Self-defence, even. The idea of murdering him never entered my head. I just wanted to make him suffer . . . like Mel did." Loretta recalled the look in his eyes a few moments before when he was pretending to have poisoned her. She felt uncomfortable. "He led her on, you know," Jamie blurted out, suddenly emotional. The old-fashioned phrase sounded oddly on his lips. "He made her think he was in love with her. He denied it afterwards, when he wanted to get rid of her, but she told me all about it in her letters. We

207

were very close, you see, and she wrote to me a lot in her first couple of terms. Whatever he said later, at first it suited him to have her around. But when she became a nuisance, and wanted some commitment from him, he gave her the brush-off. He was quite brutal about it. He told her exactly why he wasn't interested in her. Mel was . . . distraught. She went back to her room and swallowed a whole bottle of pills. She should have got in touch with me," he said fiercely. "If only I hadn't been away at that damn school . . . She tried to protect Hugh, even at the end," he said. "She left a note for my mother, saying she'd fallen in love with him and it was all her own fault. That was the note the coroner saw, and very convenient it was for Hugh. But she posted a letter to me as well. I got it at school. She was dead then, of course. She told me what had really happened. I think she didn't want to die without anyone knowing her side of the story. And I got the idea I was going to avenge her. I know how foolish it must seem. It does to me, now. But I was much younger then. I'd led a sheltered life, you see, we both had. All my experience came from books. I saw her as Dido, calling for revenge after being betrayed by Aeneas."

Loretta's knowledge of Virgil was limited; she knew just enough of the *Aeneid* to understand the reference. What an unworldly pair they had been, she reflected.

"I got to Oxford quite easily," Jamie said, continuing his story. "Everyone in the family always expected I would, so there was nothing odd about that. I knew from school that I had the sort of looks some men find attractive, and I thought I'd use that to make Hugh suffer. Though I'm pretty sure I'm heterosexual," he added, blushing slightly. "It seemed the perfect way to get revenge, you see—to make him fall for me, and then reject him. Everything was on my side. He'd have to be very careful—I was under age, as well as one of his students. It would be easy to string him along until he was really obsessed, and then turn him down as unpleasantly as he'd done to Melanie. I think it started off as a fantasy, but it worked better than I ever dreamed. He really did get a crush on me, and at the same time he was terrified of the slightest breath of scandal. So he suggested a romantic little trip to Paris at the end of the summer term. He said he had the use of a flat over there, and we wouldn't even have to risk staying in a hotel. Then I got cold feet, and said I couldn't go. He bombarded me with letters and phone calls at my parents' house when the long vac. started, and in the end I decided I'd have to go through with it to get him off my back. I was afraid he'd turn up in Buckland Dinham, or something like that.

"We arranged to travel separately to Paris—as I said, he was very nervous—and meet at rue Roland. He was already there when I arrived, and we went straight out to dinner. We got back to the flat—Hugh was expecting the big consummation scene, of course, and I'd no idea how much he'd had to drink. When I told him I didn't want him, and tried to leave, he went mad. I don't know whether it was rage or lust—probably a combination of the two. He wouldn't let me get to the door. He grabbed me, and starting shouting. I don't think he even took in what I was trying to say about Mel. I was struggling, trying to get away from him, and he hung on to me like a limpet. The next thing I knew, we were fighting. I felt blood on my face, from where he'd punched me. I couldn't believe it was happening." He stopped, shuddering at the memory.

It was clear that Puddephat had never mentioned his crazy scheme to live with Jamie, Loretta thought grimly. If he had, things might never have got this far. She waited for Jamie to continue.

"I suppose I just panicked," he said eventually. "I wanted him to stop hitting me, and I grabbed the nearest thing to hand, which happened to be the bread knife. Even then, he didn't stop straight away." He paused again.

A frenzied attack, Loretta remembered. That was how someone from Scotland Yard had described it to Tracey. She shivered.

"Why did I ever go through with it?" Jamie blurted out. They sat in silence for a moment. "I wrapped him in a sheet and got him on to the big bed," Jamie continued. "I covered him up to make it look like he was sleeping. I couldn't believe it had happened, I wanted to look into the room and find he was just asleep. I stuffed all his things into his suitcase, he didn't have much, and put it under the bed. Then I cleaned up the blood—I knew if I didn't do it there and then, I'd run out of the flat and never come back. It made me so sick I left as soon as I'd finished. I went straight to a bar, and had so much to drink I ended up being arrested. I spent the night in a police cell. Can you imagine how I felt when I woke up? Thank God I didn't talk in my sleep. Or if I did, it was in English and they didn't understand. They didn't let me go until the shift changed at 10 a.m. By then, I'd sobered up enough to know that I had to do something about the body. I went back to rue Roland, and on the way to the flat I passed a church. There was scaffolding on the outside and it looked as if a lot of work was being done on it. The workmen had left the door unlocked, and there was a wheelbarrow just inside. I went and bought some overalls, two sets, and took them to the flat. I dressed Hugh in them—" he made a *moue* of distaste,—"and put the other set on myself. Then I got the body into a large sack I'd found in the church, and dragged it to the service lift. It was a struggle to get him in, but I managed it. At the bottom of the stairs, I heaved him on to the wheelbarrow. Then I set off for the church. If anyone stopped me, I was going to pretend to be delivering something that the workmen needed on Monday morning. I wasn't thinking straight, or I'd have seen how suspicious that would have seemed—an Englishman in brand-new workmen's overalls trundling a heavy object along the street on a Saturday afternoon. But I was lucky. I only passed one person, an old man, and he didn't look twice at me. Perhaps he thought I was putting in a bit of overtime.

"After I'd hidden the body in the church, I went back to

the flat. I collected together all my stuff, and Hugh's, and checked into a hotel about five minutes' walk away. Then I slept for the next eighteen hours. When I woke up, I made little parcels out of Hugh's clothes, and spent the day dumping them all over Paris. I burned his passport—that took some doing, I can tell you."

"And then you went back and cleaned the flat again," Loretta said.

"That's right, on Sunday evening," Jamie said, surprised. "How did you know that?"

Loretta explained about Andrew, and Jamie sat back in his chair, absent-mindedly sipping his coffee.

Another question occurred to Loretta. "Who was the girl, the one with the red hair who brought the note?" she asked. Jamie looked up with the ghost of a smile.

"Oh, that," he said. "I'm afraid I played on the porter's misogynist sentiments to get him to lie about that. I told him my girlfriend had left me because she'd fallen in with the bunch of women's libbers and lesbians meeting upstairs, and I was desperate to see her on my own. I said I'd signed the note in my sister's name, and it was vital that she didn't know I had anything to do with it."

Loretta frowned, remembering the porter's sly smile when she pressed him for details of the messenger. It was a shabby trick, she thought angrily. She was about to tell Jamie so, when she checked herself. She was getting more upset at the thought of this small deception than she had during his account of the murder. Where was her sense of proportion? She must be suffering from shock, she supposed. "I still don't understand why you wanted me to come here," she said.

Jamie laughed. "Believe it or not, I was going to throw myself on your mercy," he said. "Though I did rather fuck it up with my little performance when you arrived. I really didn't plan that scene, by the way. I just lost my temper when I saw you coming up the stairs. Not that it hadn't occurred to me to kill you," he said evenly. "When you

211

stood in my room at college, bragging about going to Paris
—well, that's what I thought you were doing," he added,
seeing the pain on her face, "I thought I'd follow you and
kill you. From my limited experience of the deed, I
thought I'd have more chance of getting away with it in a
foreign city. But then I realized there was no point. I remembered your husband, you see. I was convinced you
were in it together, and he'd know why you were in Paris.
If you disappeared over the weekend, my name would be
all over the front pages in no time at all. So I dreamed up a
new plan. I decided to get you here and plead with you.
Not that I thought that would be enough on its own. I was
going to find out what you expected to get for your story
—my night of passion with a killer, and all that—and offer
you more. I come into a lot of money from my grandmother next year, when I'm twenty-one, and I was going to
try and buy you off with a share. God, I'd have offered you
the lot if you'd agreed not to turn me in." Loretta stared at
him, bereft of speech. How could he have so misjudged
her? She was about to voice this thought when Jamie held
up his hand. "It's all right, you don't have to convince
me," he said wearily. "I got it all wrong, I see that now. It's
not money you're after, it's justice, isn't it? Too bad for me
you turn out to be a nice, decent person instead of the bitch
I thought you were."

Loretta said nothing. She didn't feel particularly nice or
decent. And why had she set out to find the murderer? She
had never really examined her motives. She supposed it
had come about almost by accident, like the murder. In the
first place, she hadn't been sure enough to go to the police
—and she had had a pressing reason for going back to
England in the shape of her mother's hysterectomy. Then
the evidence had disappeared. By the time the body was
discovered, she had been too afraid for her own skin to go
to the police. It wasn't a sense of justice that had involved

212

her in the investigation, it was straightforward guilt. Her gaze slipped away from Jamie.

Downstairs, a young woman entered the café, a black leather folder under one arm. She peered round, and then spotted two friends at a table. Joining them, she barely paused before unzipping the folder, which Loretta now saw to be a portfolio of paintings. The girl was an art student, Loretta guessed. She handed a sheaf of paintings to her two companions, and waited anxiously while they examined them. One of the men finally began to speak, and the girl's face broke into smiles. Whoever the men were—friends, teachers, art dealers?—the verdict was evidently favourable.

Loretta turned back to Jamie, who was staring unseeingly into space. He had become impenetrable to her, and she had no idea what he was thinking. She supposed she ought to stop a waiter and ask him to call the police. There was some tea left in her cup, and she drank it, making a face at its lukewarm temperature. She leaned down beside her chair, and picked up her bag. "Excuse me," she said, "I'll be back in a minute."

She walked down the pale green stairs to the ground floor, and saw the sign to the lavatories, down more steps in the basement. She descended the stairs and went in. The lavatories were in a row to her right; to her left, a series of floor-length mirrors had been placed at angles to each other. In each V, a washbasin had been formed by the skilful insertion of a piece of glass. She took a couple of tissues from her bag, and put it on the floor. Trickling a few drops of water on to the tissues, she used them to wipe her cheeks and forehead. She bent down and rummaged in the bag, taking out her mascara and lipstick. Carefully reapplying both, she blotted her lips on a fresh tissue. She put the cosmetics away, and took out a comb. She ran it through her hair, observing with mild disapproval how the drizzle had made it curl. Putting the comb away, she slung her bag over her shoulder and went back up the stairs to the ground floor. She stood back to let a waiter pass, and walked to the street door. A glance upwards and to her right told her that Jamie was gone. It was raining outside, and for the second time that day she wished she had brought an umbrella.

About the Author

JOAN SMITH was born in London in 1953. She studied Latin at Reading University and then trained as a journalist on the Blackpool *Evening Gazette*. She joined the London *Sunday Times* in 1979 and has been a free-lance journalist since 1984. Her work has appeared in numerous leading publications. Ms. Smith currently writes theater criticism for *Today* and is at work on a new Loretta Lawson mystery.

Regency presents the popular and prolific...
JOAN SMITH

Available at your bookstore or use this coupon.

____AURORA	21533	$2.95
____DRURY LANE DARLING	21506	$2.95
____HERMIT'S DAUGHTER	21588	$2.95
____IMPRUDENT LADY	23663	$2.95
____LARCENOUS LADY	21261	$2.50
____LOVE'S HARBINGER	20955	$2.50
____MEMOIRS OF A HOYDEN	21329	$2.50
____ROYAL SCAMP	21610	$2.95
____SILKEN SECRETS	21372	$2.95

FAWCETT MAIL SALES
Dept. TAF, 201 E. 50th St., New York, N.Y. 10022

Please send me the FAWCETT BOOKS I have checked above. I am en-
closing $_____ (add 50¢ per copy to cover postage and handling).
Send check or money order—no cash or C.O.D.'s please. Prices and
numbers are subject to change without notice. Valid in U.S. only. All
orders are subject to availability of books.

Name_____

Address_____

City_____ State_____ Zip Code_____

14   Allow at least 4 weeks for delivery.   TAF-67